Dowry's Meadow
Book one of the Dowry series

C.C. González

ISBN: 9798626028911
Imprint: Independently published

Cover design by: Nalia Rolón
Art by: Nicole Subong
Printed in the United States of America

The only difference between the saint and the sinner is that the saint has a past, and every sinner has a future

- Oscar Wilde

ACKNOWLEDGMENTS

Back in 2001, you gave me an old laptop and said, "write whatever you feel like," then left me alone to my thoughts. I was just twelve years old and I haven't stopped writing ever since.
Thank you, Mom.

PROLOGUE

As long as she was alive, she would never forget the smell of blood, gun powder, or the sound of agonizing screams. It was engraved in her mind like the memory of a first kiss.

Such a young child shouldn't be able to withstand the sight of violence the way she did. Yet, Alexandra Victoria Dowry stared in pure horror, burning the sound, the smell, the Dantesque imagery before her into her memory. Her instincts bellowed for her to run, yet the small eight-year-old trembled behind the large doors, looking through the crevice into the dining room. Sucking in her breath and covering her mouth, she realized that she was too loud at being quiet.

The act that the men were performing on her mother was nothing that she had ever seen before. She never thought that she would be able to understand the horrifying act that they were perpetrating upon her mother in her lifetime. She wondered, what could a mere little girl do to stop three men who laughed and pulled up their pants with demon-like grins on their faces? Where was her father when she needed him the most? If she walked in, what would they do to her?

Upon the men's exit through the kitchen door in the far-right corner of the room, Alexandra stepped in, hands trembling, lower lip quivering, dumbfounded and afraid. Her breathing was ragged, short, and desperate as her eyes looked upon her bleeding and deadly wounded mother. Her knees gave out, and she fell beside the woman with a loud thud, which probably called the attention of the men that had left just seconds ago.

Biting her lower lip to stop a loud, nervous whimper from escaping from deep within her chest, Alexandra pulled her mother as hard as she could, which resulted in the body rolling towards her.

Alexandra's small fingers combed the black hairs away from her mother's face as she looked at what the men had done. Her face was painted in red,

1

black, and blue colors. A tearing sob slipped out, enough to make her cover her mouth again. She needed to be quiet. She needed to survive. And she needed to get her mother out of here, but how?

The loud bang of a slamming door made her jump in her skin. She looked to the door, then back at her mom who she shook softly. "Momma," she called out in a loud whisper.

A second door slammed, making her stomach lurch in jitteriness, and she found new strength to pull on the dress harder. "Get up! Momma, get up!"

Her pleas weren't answered.

The sound that came from outside the closed door was enough for fresh tears to pour out of her eyes. Laughter. The crevice allowed a thin ray of candlelight to illuminate the dining room. Alexandra stared at the light and witnessed how the laughter boomed and filtered. It got louder and louder; one voice, then a second one, then a third one that asked the words Alexandra dreaded. "Where is the child?"

"Momma, please." She sobbed in desperation. She cupped her mother's face as tears fell upon her face and cleaned the blood that had dried on her cheeks.

A hand fell on her waist, and a loud shriek escaped her before she realized that the hand that held on, was her mother's. Her eyes were open, searching for her daughter. Alexandra didn't waste a second, she moved closer. A smile came to her face at the realization that her mother was still alive.

"Run…"

Alexandra's smile disappeared. She shook her head, no.

"Run, Alex, please." The words came out in a gurgle of blood, which made Alexandra move her hands away.

The doors burst open with mighty force, breaking the hinges off. Alexandra fell on her bottom, scared, and frozen in place. The demons were back, looking down at her, two with incredulity, another with a sided grin. Her mind went blank as one took the first lunge, followed by the rest.

And that's when Alexandra heard it, her mother's last words. "Run!" She was quickly silenced by the blast of a gunshot.

She had become momentarily deaf. She turned on her heels and escaped through the kitchen door. She ignored the fast-approaching steps as she jumped over tables, sofas, and finally out a hidden window at the back of one of the maid's quarters.

After slipping not only once, but twice, she managed to fall outside onto the wet grassy ground next to the mansion. It was pouring, resembling the emotions that were growing inside of her small mind. Coldness, anger, violence.

She made it to the small stable outside where she pushed the door open with all her might. The animals inside neighed, stomping their hooves on the ground, showing their distress for the weather and the strangers that had made it to their master's home.

Alexandra's heart was racing as her chest heaved. Her long blonde hair was sticking to her forehead and cheeks as her dress was covered in grass stain, blood, and dirt. Her mother would've thrown a fit, her father would ground her.

Alexandra sobbed as she sat down on a corner, protected by one of the horses her father owned. She whimpered, closed her eyes tighter, and covered her ears with her small hands. She could still hear the scream and the ringing it caused deep within her ears, mind, and heart.

What she didn't know was by doing so she was cultivating a wave of anger that would consume her.

She gritted her teeth yet again in anger, frustration, and fear. It all spiraled down to her stomach. She wanted to go back to the house, carry her mother out, but with what strength? It was ludicrous...

"Papa," she started, trying to force out other words as she struggled to breathe through her tears. Something told her that she was doing the right thing. That she should hide it out in the stables and wait for her father. He would be home soon, like a knight in shining armor, ready to beat the bad guys into a bloody pulp.

***

A man jumped off his horse and looked over the mansion with a stagger expression on his face. Patting his horse, he waited for his men to follow close behind him. Wordless, he commanded two of them to go to the stables and the remaining to go with him to the mansion. Apprehension fell on him like a cold blanket, scared of what he would find the moment he walked into his mansion. He really hoped that what he read in that lost note was not right.

The door was jammed. A chair had been placed underneath the doorknob. He had to kick it open with the help of his companions in a heave of slurs and curses. When they were finally inside, the tallest man, a blond, walked across the large living area. He pushed the dining-room door open, and his blank expression was wiped away.

"Vivian!" he cried, ignoring the fact that he was not alone. He stumbled hard, his knees hitting the wooden floor as his hands fell in a puddle of wet blood. He picked up the broken body of a woman and settled her into his strong arms, so she faced him and him alone.

"Vivian!"

The dress he had bought for her as an anniversary gift was tainted with blood. Her slim body felt broken in his strong arms, and her face was painted with different shades of blue and purple. His trembling hand came to touch her neck and he felt what he was afraid of; nothing.

"Vivian..." he whispered as he hugged the corpse closer to his broad chest. "Who did this?"

His companions didn't know how to react or what to say. They looked at each other before one of the other helpers burst into the dining room. "Master Alexander! We found her! She is at the stable! Larkin is with her!"

He shuddered. *What now?* "Please, make the proper arrangements to take the body with us."

"Yes, sir," one said and quickly stepped up beside him before grabbing hold of the corpse.

He stood up, dusted his pants, wiped one sneaky tear away from his eyes, and ran to the stables. He ran just like his daughter had.

"Alexandra!" he yelled before pulling the youngest helper out of his way. He looked at the bundle of blonde hair in front of him and let out a sigh of relief. "Alex…"

She opened her green eyes, jerked her way to the direction the voice was coming from, and just stared. "Papa."

Once again, he fell to his knees, opened his arms, and tried to smile. "Let us go home, Alex."

***

For seven years, a lengthy investigation ensued after the rape and murder of Vivian Dowry-Thompson, wife of Alexander Dowry II. Police investigated the crime scene and found signs of forced entry at the back door. They interviewed Alexander, and he explained that he was on a business trip when a messenger gave him an anonymous note, warning him of his wife's fate. He showed the letter to the police officers and they quickly discarded him as a suspect.

Yet, Alexander Dowry II wasn't completely innocent.

For the next seven years, Alexander, a wealthy horse merchant, moved back to his country mansion with his son.

Alexander paid a lot of money to keep his daughter's identity in the grave. He was fueled by the need to give everything he owned to his only daughter. He and his wife had always intended to do so. He bribed the country priest and a couple of police officers to create a false death certificate that stated Alexandra Victoria Dowry died the same day as her mother, Vivian. He paid the priest to give a sermon for both and a certified doctor to create a birth certificate, which indicated that Alexander Dowry III was born on the same day as Alexandra.

Alexander was a smart man. He knew how the government and the law of the small town that his family and himself had called home worked. He made sure to get rid of the existing evidence as time passed.

The doctor got sick and died at a young age. Everyone cried about his death.

Such an excellent doctor.

Such a terrible loss for the townspeople.

A police officer was killed in a house robbery.

A true hero he was…

Did you hear that Father Barnaby died?

The Lord had called upon him.

Reason? Heart Attack. He was an old man…

Alexander smiled, rubbed his hands together, and nodded at the news his right hand, Larkin, gave him. The young man had proved himself to be useful and trustworthy.

Seven years was enough time to erase any track of lies that he had created.

He made sure to transform his daughter into Alexander Dowry III. Only a few people knew the truth. Alexander made sure to keep his circle close. Close enough for him to suffocate with the daunting reality that maybe, just maybe, one day someone would turn his daughter in, and he would receive the ultimate punishment, death.

Now Alexandra was a teenager. Rebellious, angry, and frustrated. Hormones were kicking in, and the suppressed memory of the person she loved more than life itself was coming back at full force. What was she to do but to act out against the person that changed her into someone she wasn't?

CHAPTER ONE

The swift movements of her sword didn't quite act as an output for her rage. Even though her father taught her well, she still found it hard to beat him in his favorite sport, and therefore, her favorite pastime as well, fencing. Yet, several years of continuous training did turn her into a lethal weapon when it came to sword fighting. She moved back, blocked the sword coming right at her and thrust hers forward, hitting the chest of her opponent.

One of the servants of the house shouted out a command that made both people move and take back their original positions. With a second command, both parties moved forward and launched at each other. Alex's opponent let out an angered growl, stepped forward, and hit her chest with his sword strong enough to make her fall backward.

Once again, the servant called out and decided to step forward and stop Alexandra from jumping and attacking her opponent, but this time with her bare hands.

Alexandra growled, pulled her fencing mask off, and looked up at the man standing right in front of her. "You take everything so seriously…"

The man merely chuckled and took off his mask. He placed it under his arm and smiled down. "Of course, I do. If I did not, you would not be alive," he commented as he grabbed her hand and pulled her up to her feet. "If you want to play the act of a man, you have to take hits like a man." He turned around and ran his fingers through his short hair. "We will train tomorrow if you want."

Alexandra looked at the servant then jerked her head at him, asking him to leave her and her father alone. "If I was born a man…"

"Then everything would've been so easy," he admitted, then rubbed his mouth and turned to look at her before unzipping his fencing uniform.

"Excuse me for not having an appendage dangling between my legs, father."

"You are excused since it was your mother who could not give me a son."

She stopped dead in her tracks and turned around. Her facial expression was the epitome of rage. "Do not talk about Mother like that!"

"I haven't said anything insulting. It happened. There was nothing you could have done. You should be happy. When I die, everything will be yours just like your mother intended." The middle-aged man sighed and cracked his neck. "How about something to eat? I bet you're starving."

Her father was a well-known, rich man with properties all over the state. The Dowry family was highly respected all-around town. Yet, it was also one of the families everyone talked about after the incident. Many knew about the marriage between Alexander Dowry II and Vivian Thompson. A lot of people in town were aware that the couple had children, but they were almost sure it was only a daughter, but then again, a whole city could have been wrong, right?

Alexandra frowned, sat down next to her father, and stared at the empty plate in front of her while her father went through some letters he had just received. "Your sixteenth birthday will be coming soon," he prodded as he tore his eyes from his paperwork and took a quick glance at her. "What do you want as a present?"

"What do I want?" She looked at the plate again. "I do not think you can give me such a present. You are not God."

Alexander slammed his hand against the desk, making the teenage girl jump. "You think you are the only one that misses her? You think you are the only one that loved her? Now, here is some news for you, Alex! I miss her too, and I still love her!"

"You were not there to protect her!" she shrieked in refutation.

"I know, and I am sorry!" The older man shook his head. "I am trying my best to fix everything."

"Fix everything? What in the world are you talking about! She is dead! How?"

Her father didn't let her finish. He stood up from his seat, leaned over, and slapped her with the back of his hand as hard as he could. Silence fell upon the large dining room. "I could have just left you in those stables to die. Then, I could have started a new life by marrying someone else and having a son, but I didn't."

"Should I bow down and kiss your feet?"

"Shut up! What I did instead was that I broke the law!" Alexander stared at his daughter, amazed somehow at how the resemblance between the two was so uncanny. "How am I fixing your mother's death? I am fixing it by making her happy after she died by giving you, her only daughter, our only daughter, the opportunity of having a life that is denied to most women!"

"Master Dowry?

"What?"

"A letter from your brother…"

He turned to look at a middle-aged woman. "Nana." He let out a relieved sigh when he saw it was her. She was one of the few people that knew the truth since she was also the one that had taken care of Alexandra ever since she came to the mansion seven years ago. She had taken the dirty long-haired girl in her arms and proceeded to do as he ordered those many years ago. *"Cut her hair and try to make her look like a boy."*

"I just got it from one of the guards outside the mansion," Nana said before placing the letter on the edge of the table. She smiled at Alexandra and patted the teenager's head before walking away.

He cleared his throat and grabbed hold of the letter before opening it. He took out the sheet of paper, read it over, and then twitched.

"What does Uncle William want?" Alexandra asked out of curiosity. Her father's expressions intrigued her.

"Nothing important. Just letting us know how he is doing," Alexander lied before moving the letter over one of the many lit candles on the table.

"What are you doing?" Alexandra yelled, standing up from her chair and grabbing the candle. She moved it away from the now burning paper and watched how her father moved it away so she wouldn't be able to reach it.

"You should cut strings with your uncle."

Alexandra gasped and frowned. "Why!"

"Listen, Alex. If I die, you will get everything I own. Because you are my son, and that is what the paper says," he said. "If you were my daughter, everything I own would not belong to you at all. It would belong to your uncle. He is a greedy man. I do not want him around us. Please, Alex. I am doing this for you and you alone. You have to understand."

"I do not want to understand. I do not care about your money! I do not care for anything at all. Do you understand? What can money possibly give me?"

"Alex." Her father sighed and moved his hand to touch her red cheek.

"No, please…no." She defensively raised her hands. "Maybe I do not understand this now. Maybe I will understand when I am older. Maybe I will thank you for everything, but today, I just…" She looked around the fancy and large dining room. "I do not see how all of this is going to help me." And with   that,   she   left   the   room.

CHAPTER TWO

A whole month has passed since her sixteenth birthday, and yet, she was still mad at her father. They rarely spoke to each other. It was the usual, "Good Morning" and "Good Night," and even though Nana kept asking her to talk to her father, Alexandra simply refused.

She knew that people tended to forget horrible things. One of her father's guards had spoken to her of how he remembered little about his parents. They left him when he was the same age as she was when her mother was murdered.

Alexandra sighed, ran her hands through her hair, and patted the horse she was on.

"It is wonderful to stretch your legs every once in a while," Larkin, her father's firsthand, told her, smiling his usual polite grin. The handsome young man had been working for her father since he was a young boy. The only known fact about him was that his parents died when he was a kid and Alexandra's father took him in as a servant.

"Yes, I guess," she answered as she kept her face low. "Thank you for coming with me, Larkin."

"No problem." The young man smiled at her. He was one of the few people that knew. He had sworn to protect her and her father, therefore, he had to know.

"It is hunting season. If my father is not up for it next week, would you like to come with me?"

"It would be an honor."

She let out a soft chuckle. "I need to get out and kill something before I go mad."

"Yes," he asserted, kicking his horse as they walked around the forest right behind the large mansion. "Your father mentioned that he was going to get you more involved in the family business," Larkin revealed as he got his horse closer to Alexandra's. "That includes the lands. What would you do with them if your father asked you?"

Alexandra shrugged. "I like it this way. It is nice just as it is."

"What about the meadow right behind the forest?"

"There is a meadow here?"

"You didn't know? There has always been one. Your mother loved to go there. It was her favorite part of the country mansion," Larkin said, patting his horse. "Your father used to take her there almost every day when she wanted to stay here."

Alexandra blinked. She didn't really remember her mother ever taking her to the meadow when they were at the country mansion. There were so many things that she was starting to forget about her mother. Yet, she remembered everything about that night. She frowned. "Maybe I should go and just see how it is. Who knows what I might turn it into?"

"I understand."

"Larkin…" Alexandra began apprehensively. "You are my best friend, my only friend. Not only that, but you also know everything about me, and I trust you. What do you think is going to happen to me in the future?"

"What do you mean?"

Alexandra looked at her white stallion and patted his neck. "Nothing."

"You know what?" He moved close to her horse. "Let me take you to the meadow. If your mother liked it, you are going to love it. I bet that will cheer you up." Before she could say no, Larkin slapped Alexandra's horse, making the stallion lose control and ran after him. Just as planned.

"You bastard! Now, he will not stop at all."

"Good!" Larkin exclaimed as he kicked his horse. The tree branches were hitting the horses, and not to mention, Alexandra.

She was about to curse at him again or at least try to stop the horse, but suddenly she felt no branches hitting her chest or face. She blocked the sun's rays with her hand as she stared at the beautiful field of flowers before her. "What in the world?"

"This is the reason why your father bought the country mansion in the first place," Larkin commented as he jumped off the horse and walked around the large field. "Your mother fell in love with this place, and your father just could not say no to her."

Alexandra also jumped off her horse and looked around the meadow. It was surrounded by trees which indicated the beginning of the thick forest right behind the mansion. "Larkin, this place is enormous!"

"This place is more colossal than it looks, Alexandra." Larkin watched his horse eating the grass. "Well? Do you like it?"

"I love it," Alexandra said, smiling at the taller and older man. "It is hidden right in the middle of the forest. Does this prove that after the meadow, there is more land?"

"Yes. There is more land. I know where it ends. If you continue on your horse, you will reach the end of your father's land in half an hour or so."

"My God… This is like a piece of heaven on Earth," Alexandra whispered as she held the reins of her horse and stared at the massive flower-covered field.

Larkin chuckled and walked over to Alexandra. He opened his mouth to say something, but the sound of horses running to them made him take out his gun and turn to see who it was.

"Young Master!" one servant yelled at the top of his lungs. "Young Master! We need you back at the mansion!"

Alexandra frowned, confused. "What is going on?"

"It is your father! He is not well! Please, hurry!"

Her face turned pale, and without a second thought, she jumped on her horse and raced towards the mansion.

***

"A heart attack? I am still young! I cannot be having heart attacks, goodness gracious."

"Sorry to hear that, Master Dowry, but that's what it is," the doctor muttered as he closed his suitcase. "I need you to stay in bed for a couple of weeks. Rest, and please, do try to stay calm."

Alexander snorted. "Calm? Not when Alex is around."

"Father!" Alexandra marched into her father's chamber right on cue. "Are you okay? What happened? Did someone hurt you?"

"It was a heart attack."

Alexandra blinked and looked at the doctor in disbelief. "A heart attack?" She sighed and stared at Alexander before patting his hand. "Do you need anything? Do you want to eat? Drink something?"

"No. I want to go to sleep."

Alexandra took a deep breath. "Fine."

"Keep him in bed, son," the doctor ordered before grabbing his suitcase and taking his glasses off.

"Oh, I will." She gave her father a menacing glare.

"Please, come to me if anything happens."

"We will. Thank you," Alexandra exclaimed and watched how the doctor left the chamber, guided by Nana.

"A heart attack. This is ridiculous."

"Shh." She kneeled and grabbed hold of her father's hand. "You heard him. Try to relax and not fight." She swallowed hard and pressed her warm lips against her father's cold hand. "I do not want anything to happen to you, even if I cannot stand your guts half of the time."

Alexander twitched. "You just want to get me started, do you not?"

"No." She smiled and rubbed his arm. "I will be in my chamber if you need me. Alright?"

"Yes…" her father answered and watched her walk out of the chamber. He threw his head back on his pillow and looked up at the ceiling as he absentmindedly rubbed his chest. He hissed and swallowed hard, trying his best to repress the pain surging through him.

Alexandra pushed the large door of her chamber open. She was immediately greeted by Nana, who waddled her way to her, cupped her face, and kissed her cheeks before wrapping her arms around Alexandra. The teenager sighed in comfort and reciprocated the signs of motherly affection that Nana emanated every time they were alone.

"Do you want me to prepare a bath for you?"

Alexandra nodded into the hug.

"Alright, give me a couple of minutes."

Alexandra did just that. She sat down on the edge of the bed, not before staring at her reflection in the mirror. She could see the dark circles under her eyes due to the nightmares that crept in at night. She also noticed that her baby fat was leaving her once chubby and adorable cheeks. Her factions weren't of a child any longer, they were blossoming into a young adult woman. Curiosity slithered itself in her consciousness, as she stood from the bed and walked to the mirror, angling it with her callused and rough hands. She wanted to look at her body. She wanted to see the changes of puberty upon herself, and sadly she could see them all being covered up by the male clothes that she wore.

What bothered her the most was the fact that her chest binds were becoming tighter. Her pants were looser to try and hide the curves that slowly revealed themselves. Yet, her face was a duplicate of her father, who Alexandra secretly thanked for being handsome.

Nana saw her when she walked back into her room. She chuckled silently and stood behind Alexandra; her arms akimbo. "You are a gorgeous child. Never doubt that."

"You see me with the eyes of a mother, Nana," Alexandra answered, her voice different from when she spoke outside her room. It was soft, delicate, unlike the deep fake one she used around the mansion.

"I was young once. I know a pretty person when I see one." She giggled yet stopped when she saw Alexandra's pained expression. "What's wrong, dear?"

Alexandra swallowed hard and shook her head.

"Something's wrong. You know you cannot hide it from me."

"I am terrified," Alexandra whispered as she tiredly sat on the ground, walls undone, only for Nana and sometimes Larkin, but no one else.

Nana dropped the towel she had been using to dry her hands and ran to her side. Clumsily, she sat down next to her and pulled her in for another tight hug. "We all are."

"What would happen to me if he…"

"Larkin and I are here, Alex," Nana pulled back and pressed her forehead with Alexandra's smooth one. "We will not let anything happen to you. I promise."

Days after the incident, things were somewhat going back to normal. Alexander was up and about. He was working in his study for a couple of hours, and then he would go back to bed. He would sometimes eat in his room, and sometimes he would head to the dining room.

Alexandra kept her mind busy working around the house. Today, she was outside with Larkin tending to the horses. She had taken a couple of them out of their stables and had given them a bath.

She was used to doing some labor work around the house. It gave her a sense of belonging rather than merely walking around and telling people what to do. Also, her father has always insisted that she should do some work around the mansion to see what their servants went through and, thus, never ask them to do something they wouldn't do.

"Is your father doing better?"

Alexandra looked up from the horse to Larkin and shrugged. "Well, he is up from the bed." She moved her wet hair away from her face as she grabbed hold of the soapy brush. She clicked her tongue and walked over to her horse and began to softly scrub the animal's fur. "He is eating, last thing I heard."

Larkin laughed a bit and patted Alexandra's horse. "Poor old man!"

"Shh! If he hears you saying that he will snap your neck!" she whispered before moving away from her horse and throwing the brush into the bucket of water. "Let us just leave him alone for a while until he gets his heart back on track." She ran her hands through her hair and then sat down on the floor.

Larkin grabbed the brush and continued Alexandra's unfinished job. "Are you two still mad at each other?"

"To be honest, I am not sure. We have not spoken much since he got sick. I guess we just left it as it is."

"Well, if he is up and about, you should take advantage of that and go talk to him. Mend things."

Alexandra shook her head and looked away. "I know."

"Go talk to him."

"Now?"

"Yes! Now! You got nothing to do for the whole afternoon. Get your lazy bum up and go talk to him!"

Alexandra let out a frustrated growl and pushed herself from the floor. She dusted her pants and looked over at Larkin. "Pray for me."

***

It felt like he had woken up with death's wings over his head. His chest felt heavy, his breathing was hard and labored, and his eyelids were lazy. As Alexander read his mail, he felt his body coming down on him. He sighed, stopped for a moment, and rubbed his face tiredly.

"Morning," Alexandra announced as she walked inside the dining room, rolling her sleeves up to her elbows. "How are you feeling?"

Alexander raised his eyes to look at her. He let out a small smile and nodded his head as he answered her question. "I've been better. How about you? How are you? What were you doing?"

"I was outside washing Snow with Larkin," she answered, referring to her white stallion.

"Good." He groaned as he stood up. "Your uncle sent another letter," he announced, moving the closed letter to Alexandra. "It is for you."

Alexandra stared at the envelope in her father's hand before grabbing it and opening it. "He is persistent, is he not?"

"He wants his money…" He growled before sitting back on his chair with a pained grunt.

"Then give it to him." Alexandra went on before reading the letter over. "He speaks of a son. I didn't know Uncle William had a son."

Alexander nodded and rubbed his left collar bone. "Yes. Your cousin, Cassius. He is no older than you if I am not mistaken. Another reason to have our guard up. As part of the Dowry family, I am sure he is looking after his own, especially Cassius." He sighed and ignored Alexandra's frowns thrown at him. "If things weren't the way they are now when I die, everything will go to Cassius." He hissed and touched his chest.

"Are you alright?"

Alexander ignored her question and just looked up at her. "Do you know how much I have worked for my family, Alex?"

"Father, please. The doctor said you needed to be calm."

"No, listen. You think I did all of this just to make your life a living hell? I did this for you."

"We already went through this!" Alexandra yelled right back at him while tearing her uncle's letter. "I did not choose this. You chose it for me!"

"I did this because you are the only thing that reminds me of her! I did this because I lo…" His words were cut off. He felt a sudden pain that went through his entire body, yet it stopped directly on the left side of his chest. His arm became useless, and as he stood up from his chair, he felt like he was beginning to drown with his own breath.

"Father?" She uncrossed her arms and stood in silence. Alexandra watched as he became pale and his eyes searched for an explanation. Her heart sank. "Papa!" she screamed with her real voice.

She ran to his side just in time to catch him before he fell over the table. She pulled his back to her chest and touched the left side of his torso as his breathing became out of control.

"Papa! Papa, relax! Please! Try to stay calm!" She undid his shirt and pressed her hand over his heart as she tried to calm it somehow. "Larkin! Nana!" Alexandra watched around the dining room for anyone to come out and help her, but no one seemed to hear them at all.

He grabbed hold of the hand that was pressed against his chest. He looked up at Alexandra's equally green eyes. He opened his mouth to say something, but nothing seemed to come out. So many things were racing through his head that he couldn't put it into words. He just held on to her. He inhaled deep breaths and became tense as he looked past her shoulder. He shuddered and moved his legs as if pushing himself away from something and cuddled closer to his daughter's arms.

His mouth, absentmindedly, whispered her real name, as if a secret had been shattered into the suffocating air. "Alexandra…"

By the way he looked at her, and by the way his face changed into a scared and then terrified gaze, Alexandra knew what was coming. She had seen those eyes, and she had prayed to God that she would never have to see those eyes again. "Papa…" She sobbed and stared at him. He was gazing into death's eyes, his screams were swallowed by silence, and he didn't react to anything at all. His eyes lost their shine, and his firm grip on his daughter's hand became loose as he suddenly stopped breathing.

Alexandra had to look away. She stared at the wall in front of her as she held her father in her arms. She gulped down her tears and looked up at the ceiling, wishing to be able to look up at the sky. Her gaze was almost demanding. She trembled with anger. Her hand tightened over her father's shirt and pulled his body to her as she hugged it tightly. She had heard once that God didn't punish people. She understood that He only tested, and everything He did was part of a higher plan. She also heard that God only sent tests that mortals could handle.

This was too much for a sixteen-year-old. Seeing both her parents die, seeing the despair in their eyes was something way too grueling for a sixteen-year-old girl.

Suddenly, the sound of boots touching the marbled floor echoed through the dining room. Alexandra didn't care who it was. She just held her father's body.

"Alex, Snow is as clean as a—" Larkin's face grew pale when he saw Alexandra holding her father. "Young master! Master Alexander!" Larkin ran over to her and tried to move her away as if by some sort of miracle, he was able to undo this horrible fate.

Alexandra pushed him away, shoving him to the floor and staring at him angrily. Larkin thought she had gone mad. He stared at her, lying on the floor. "Alex!"

She looked at her father again, touched his cheek, and with that same hand, she wiped her tears and sobbed. "Papa…" she whispered like that night he found her, dirty and confused in that dark stable. "Papa." She grabbed his shirt again and hugged him. God couldn't be this cruel.

***

Alexandra bit her thumb's nail as she stared at the view of her lands. She was sitting on the cliff she had found weeks after she was brought to the mansion. It was her own spot where Alexandra could just go and vent everything inside of her. But today, she couldn't scream like she used to. Alexandra couldn't wail. She needed to step up and become what her father wanted her to grow into ever since she placed a foot on his land. A man. She needed to become a man.

Her tears were freely falling down her cheeks. She had left the body at the mansion and ran out of the place like she did that night seven years ago. She ran until her legs gave out. She was so deep in the forest that she almost got lost, but soon found the cliff and sat down to let her wrath go. She pulled her suit tighter to her body and sighed as she looked at the view.

"A sixteen-year-old should not go through all of this," she whispered as she grabbed a stick from the ground and threw it. "To see your mother get beat up, raped, and then killed right in front of you! Having your father die in your arms… I—" She hid her face between her knees and closed her eyes tightly. "Are these your tests? Is this your idea of a test? Or is this just a big joke for you?" She looked up to the skies and shook her head. "Thank you for nothing!" And then, she stood up and walked away from the cliff.

That's when she heard something. A growl, followed by a whimper. It was clearly an animal, but what exactly? Alexandra looked over her shoulder. She stopped walking altogether as she waited for that sound again. When Alexandra heard it, she turned around and went back to search for the animal that was making the sound. She was about to give up after ten minutes of searching until she heard the noise intensify. Alexandra stared at the ground as she made her way through the woods until she saw a small and hairy gray ball moving on the dirty ground. She raised her eyebrows and moved slowly; the whimpers intensified with every step she took. She kneeled in front of the noisemaker and studied what it was.

The animal shuddered. Alexandra moved her hands and picked it up slowly, and it only wailed and whimpered louder. Alexandra hushed it, scared that it might call its mother. Upon further inspection, she realized that she was holding a wolf pup.

"Well, hello there, little one…" she said as she stared at its tiny head. The animal was so nubile it didn't even have its eyes open. Alexandra decided that it was probably a week old. She was about to stand up and go back to the mansion when she heard a second whimper. Alexandra looked over to the ground and saw another pup. She frowned and placed the first one on the ground before she removed her coat. She placed it beside the puppies and slowly she managed to put them both on top of it. "Where is your mother?"

The answer was two strained whimpers coming from the bundle in her coat. The two pups were covered in ants and dirt. Clearly, they had been abandoned by their mother. Alexandra frowned and decided that it would be wise to take them back to the mansion and take care of both herself. What an unusual way to keep her mind busy.

CHAPTER THREE

Eleanor closed the book, and her eyes sparkled with the illusion brought to her mind and to her heart. Her blue eyes went to look at her father who was writing something on his large desk. "All done!"

The old man turned to look at his daughter and let out a heartfelt laugh. "Already?"

She nodded, jumped out of the chair, and almost stumbled with her dress, but she managed to move to her father's side. "It was good! One of the best I've read."

"I am so happy you enjoyed it, Eleanor." Her father smiled and picked her up to sit her on his lap. "I might have to buy you some new books. I think you just finished every single one in my library," he said as he scratched his bearded face and looked around his small library.

"Do you think that I will find my own prince charming one day, papa?"

"A girl as beautiful as you? Of course!"

"When you married mama, did you love her just like in the stories?" Eleanor asked as she looked up at her father with curious eyes.

He blinked and looked at the desk as he thought about his answer. He could say yes just to see her light up but, he would've been lying. He met his wife on their wedding day at the altar of the church. "Uh. Yes. I did." There, he lied, yet it was all worth it. Eleanor's beautiful blue eyes lit up with the innocence she carried inside of her.

Eleanor smiled and snuggled close to her father. "I want to marry someone I love with all my heart. I have heard that some of my friend's parents met on their wedding day. Now, that is kind of sad, do you think not?"

Her father twitched. For a nine-year-old, Eleanor was quite smart. He wiggled his nose and nodded. "Yes, very sad."

"I am also going to choose who I am going to marry, right?"

18

"As long as I am alive, yes you will." He smiled and patted her cheek with his thumb. "Listen, Eleanor, go and check on your mama for me, alright?"

"If you want to be left alone, I understand," she said, pulling a strand of brown hair away from her face and tucking it behind her ear.

He sighed and let out a nervous chuckle. "That will work."

"I will see you at dinner, then." Eleanor smiled, kissed her father's cheek, and ran out of her father's study.

The old man rolled his eyes and scratched the back of his neck. "I only wish it was that easy, Eleanor." Theo Stownar, a tired businessman, drowned in the paperwork on his desk. As his daughter Eleanor read her fiction books, he looked for ways to get out of debt. His gambling addiction was getting worse, and if he didn't put a stop to it, he would have to face his wife Eliza and tell her that he didn't have a single dime to take care of her and Eleanor.

He leaned on the desk and rubbed his temples to relieve the stress that accumulated in the form of an intense headache. "Lord help me…" He sighed as he muttered another short prayer before falling asleep on his sea of papers.

CHAPTER FOUR

Her green eyes stared at the figure of a man nailed to a cross in front of her. She frowned, kneeled on one knee as she touched her forehead with her index and middle fingers, "In the name of the Father...", and then toned stomach, "the Son," and finally her left shoulder and her right shoulder, "and the Holy Ghost," she made a small cross using her index and thumb, brought it to her lips, and kissed it. "Amen..."

She went back to stand on her own two feet.

"As I promised, I am here for the tenth consecutive year to bring my respects to my parents," she whispered only to herself, but at the same time to someone else. "It is kind of ironic that I am the one standing before you every year, asking for the redemption of my parents' souls," she frowned at the man on the cross. "I am the one living a sin and a lie, and yet I simply do not care for my own soul."

She licked her lower lip before she continued. "I guess I will say the same thing I do every year." She closed her eyes as she thought the prayer over. "God, forgive my father. He did not know what he was getting himself into. Forgive my mother for whatever she did wrong when she was alive. Help my father find my mother in the afterlife and unite them together forever. Tell them that I love them and that I miss them more than anything. Give them wings to come to my aid whenever I need them and please..." She looked at the marbled floor of the church. "Protect me from those who wish to harm me."

After she was done, she did the cross sign over her torso again and turned around to leave the grand church.

"Dowry?"

Alexandra stopped moving. To think that someone might have heard her made her nervous, but at the same time, she didn't say anything that would put her in jeopardy. As soon as she recognized the voice, she felt her blood run through her veins once again. "Father Neil." Alexandra turned to look at the older man. "How are you doing today?"

"It is a surprise to see you here."

"I was paying my respects. A day like today, my father died. I just wanted to talk to your boss about some things," Alexandra said as she tucked her hat under her arm securely. "I was just on my way back home."

"I see," the priest noted, rubbing his wrinkly hands together.

"Did you just give mass?" Alexandra asked as she stared at the priest's clothing.

"Oh, yes. Someone dear to the town died last night. You might have heard about it." He looked to see some reaction from Alexandra. "Theo Stownar died last night."

"Theo Stownar? Never heard of him. Then again, I am always locked up in my mansion. I never really come out," she mentioned, rubbing her chin.

"He was just another rich man gone poor. His wife was devastated, not to mention their daughter, Eleanor."

"Hmm. Well, I would like to stay and talk to you, but I already did what I needed to do here."

"You have lost your faith, have you?"

Alexandra stopped once again. She closed her eyes and nodded. "More or less."

"Children tend to lose faith when something terrible happens, Dowry. Just look at poor Eleanor. She is merely nineteen, and now, she must do something so she does not get thrown to the streets. Her father did not leave her anything to defend herself and her mother."

Alexandra pouted her lips to the side. "Women in this town are so oppressed they cannot even work. They cannot even go to the streets without a maid or a man by her side. What can she do?"

"She could get married to someone rich…" the priest insinuated while he looked at Alexandra, raising his eyebrow. "Dowry, you are a rich and handsome young man. When are you planning to settle down already?"

Alexandra placed her hat on and tugged her coat. "Not any day soon. Have a good day, Father Neil." She turned her face away from him before he could notice that she had actually never grown facial hair in her life. She walked outside the church, jumped on her horse, and clicked her tongue. The animal let out an angered neigh before turning around and heading back to the isolated mansion, which was four hours away from the city.

***

"I heard that they were trying to come inside the mansion last night. We are not sure who, Larkin, sir. We do know that the dogs came in handy.

21

Whoever tried to get in, got quite a bite on his leg or arm." The guard chuckled and quickly closed his eyes as he tried his best to control his amusement. "I went to the back of the mansion and saw the bitch with her snout covered in blood! It was hilarious."

Larkin stared at the front side of the mansion, biting onto one of the many herbs he finds around the forest. "We need to put more guards on at nighttime then," he warned before spitting out the green grass. "We do not want to put Alexander in danger."

"You are right. I will adjust the schedule with the other guards and make sure that the area is secured at all hours."

Larkin smiled and patted the guard's back. "Thank you. You can leave now."

"Of course." The guard bowed and left.

Larkin sat down at the entrance stairs that led to the massive doors of the mansion and scratched his now bearded face. "Someone trying to get in?" he whispered to himself. Then, Larkin jumped as he suddenly heard two loud howls right behind him. He let out a frustrated groan and covered his ears. "Shut up! You two!"

The two beasts didn't listen. Instead, they threw their heads back and howled even louder as they heard the gallops of a well-known horse coming towards the mansion gates.

The large gates were opened and inside came Alexandra. She pulled on her horse's reins and stopped the animal from continuing. Alexandra jumped off, patted its stiff neck, and fixed her coat before walking towards the grand stairs. She could hear her pets' howls, and she just smiled at it. She watched how Larkin tried to silence them both but, to no avail.

"Stick! Pebbles! Come!" she commanded and snapped her fingers twice. Off they went, running at the speed of light, racing with each other. Who was going to be the first to receive a warm pat on the head by their owner? "No! No, no! Down!" Alexandra jumped up a bit as she tried to stop them from licking her face. "Down!" As soon as she yelled that, both wolves sat down and stared up at her, wagging their tails as if they hadn't seen her in years. "Jesus Christ," she gagged as she wiped her lower lip. "I said no tongue."

"Alex!"

She raised her green eyes up to Larkin. Now the thirty-something-year-old man was waving his arms, standing on the grand stairs. She proceeded to walk over to him, ignoring the fact that both beasts were running behind her and licking the palm of her hands. A clear sign of affection.

"Alex," Larkin began, ignoring the animals and their disgusting tactics. "We need to talk."

Alexandra nodded and opened the grand doors allowing both Stick and Pebble to run inside. As she made her way to the living room, she removed her overcoat and let it fall on one of the chairs. Alexandra automatically moved to a small table with a couple of large bottles in it. "It has been a long day, Larkin," she began, pouring some liquor on a crystal glass. "What is it?"

Larkin watched her with a saddened expression on his face as he saw Alexandra quickly drink a glass full of whiskey.

"They are snooping around the mansion." Larkin nodded at his own words "It could be your cousin," Larkin said as he rubbed his hands together.

"What do you mean?" Alexandra asked as she poured herself another drink.

Larkin sighed and slapped her hand, making her face him. "Your uncle died some months ago, and Cassius has his eyes on your father's money."

"I want to see him take it away from me." Alexandra spat as she moved to grab the small glass.

"Will you listen to me? Your uncle spoke to his son about the suspicious circumstances of your appearance. William saw your mother pregnant, Alex. He knew she was not pregnant with twins, and he was damn well sure that she gave birth to a little girl. If he finds out about all of this, you could be sent to prison and sentenced to death."

"What do you want me to do? Prove that I am a man?" She waved her hands as she posed for Larkin. "What more do I need to do?"

"Well…" he stammered before looking at the floor.

"It is not like I can get married to a woman," Alexandra whispered as she stared at the small glass in her hand until something hit the back of her head.

Both Larkin and Alexandra suddenly looked at each other. "Hold it!" they yelled at the same time.

"No! Larkin! I will not pull an innocent woman into all of this… this crap!"

"You can marry an old woman! Hell, she will die fast, yet you prove to everyone that you are a man!"

"What about intimacy! At some point, she will grow suspicious of the lack of intimacy! She can even go to church and ask for an annulment due to the lack of sex!"

"Get her drunk!"

Alexandra shook her head in disbelief. "I cannot believe you just said that. Besides! I am not having sex with an old woman! You might like the extra skin, but I do not!"

Larkin ran his fingers throughout his black hair. "Alexander Dowry III," he began.

"No."

"You want to marry a young woman? Then do so! Just get married! A twenty-six-year-old rich man that is not married surely raises some questions in town. Especially this town that is so old-fashioned. You do not have to be intimate with her. You just give her the title of wife."

Alexandra rubbed her face and quickly drank her alcohol once again before answering, "Why is this getting so complicated? Does my birth certificate say that I am a man or not?"

"It does! To anyone that does not know the Dowry family, they just need to take a good look at you and say, 'Oh dear me, Alexander Dowry II really did have a son.' But to the family! You need to protect what is yours just like your mother and your father intended it to be." Larkin sighed when he noticed that Alexandra was acting as if she was ignoring him. "Yes, yes, your father would have loved to have a son instead of a daughter, but you were everything he had left. And damn it all, he was going to protect what he loved even after his death. Do not let your father's work be in vain."

Alexandra's fingers stroked over the small table. She tapped it for a few seconds as if thinking before turning to look at Larkin. "Eleanor Stownar."

"What?" Larkin frowned.

"Theo Stownar. Do you know him?"

Larkin shrugged and rubbed his chin as he recapped all the town gossip he had heard during the last time he went to visit. "He lost all of his money to gambles and such. Yes, I know who he is."

"He died last night. His wife and daughter are going to be thrown out to the streets. Maybe because they need to pay Theo's debts?" She saw Larkin shrug. "His daughter, Eleanor Stownar, is nineteen years old, and she is single," she continued, crossing her arms over her chest. "Do you think that you can arrange something? I can send you to town, and you can talk your way through anything. I am bad at asking for hands in marriage," Alexandra blurted the last sentence in a sarcastic tone and while rubbing her neck.

Larkin swallowed hard and rubbed his hands together. Alexandra's expression, even though it was shadowed with worry, it was serious and somewhat determined. He sighed and patted her back soundly before letting out his trademark smirk. "I will see what I can do."

***

"Lady Eleanor…"

She was sitting in that same chair she had sat in so many times, in front of the grand desk that somehow seemed to be average sized now. She had her delicate hands folded neatly on her lap as she stared at the now-empty chair her father used to sit down and work in. When she heard her name being called, she turned her head slightly to the side, just to let the other person know that she had heard them.

"I will be leaving now."

The young woman closed her eyes and sighed. She licked the inside of her cheek and wiped her tears away before standing up. "Now?"

The old woman nodded her head and raised it afterward to take one last look at the gorgeous woman. "I hope we will see each other again soon."

She tried to smile but only managed to let out an awkward expression. "I hope so too, Polly."

"It was a pleasure working for you and your mother."

Eleanor closed her eyes tightly and wrapped her slender arms around the old woman's shoulders and hugged her. "It was a pleasure having you in my life. Please, never forget me."

"How could I do such a thing, Lady Eleanor?" Polly asked, hurt by the comment. The older woman pulled away and made Eleanor lean forward until they were at eye level. She raised her trembling hands and made a small cross sign over Eleanor's forehead and then kissed her cheek. "May God bless you."

As soon as the old woman left, another woman came inside but, by the way she was dressed, she was clearly not another maid that had to be sent to the street due to a lack of money to pay for their salary.

"That's the last one of them. The house feels really empty without them all," Eliza Stownar sighed as she pulled a long strand of brunette hair behind her ear.

Eleanor didn't quite listen to her. She walked back to her chair and sat down. "It is quite empty without his jokes."

Eliza shook her head. "Your father did not care for us at all. If he did, he would have left some money for us."

"Money is not everything," Eleanor whispered while stroking a wrinkle on her dress.

"But it is everything we need right now!"

Eleanor was about to answer her when a loud knock was heard. Eliza almost called for one of the maids to open the house before she remembered that there was no one else inside the mansion but Eleanor and herself. She sighed and walked to answer the door. Eleanor stood up from her chair. She took a deep breath and walked toward the study's door. She stroked the expensive wood and closed the doors behind her.

"Alexander Dowry III? The son of the horse merchant?"

Larkin grinned and nodded. How nice was it that Alexandra was known as 'the son of the horse merchant?' "That is him! My name is Larkin Ward. I am his personal assistant and his right hand. I have come on his behalf to talk to you about a marriage between your daughter and him, my lady."

Eliza placed her hand on her chest and held the door tightly. "Alexander Dowry III wants to marry my daughter?"

"If you agree." Larkin smiled. Eliza didn't know what to say. Everything was happening so fast that she didn't want to rush anything on Eleanor.

"Is he rich?"

Larkin looked past Eliza's shoulder to see the person who had just spoken. His jaw fell open when he saw the young woman walk towards them. His eyes grew huge. "Eleanor Stownar?"

"At your service," Eleanor answered, giving her mother an angered gaze. "You left my question unanswered. Is he rich or not?"

"Alexander is one of the richest young men in town, my lady."

"How old is he?"

Larkin moved, feeling a bit uncomfortable by the sudden interrogation. He was the one in charge of asking the questions, not Eleanor. "He is twenty-six."

"He is too old for me," Eleanor snapped, crossing her slender arms under her ample chest, and raising her chin up a bit.

"He is merely seven years older than you. Your father was way older than me and look at how it ended up." Eliza gave Larkin a glare. He was staring at her daughter with lustful eyes and she wasn't going to have that in her house.

"How does he know about me?" Eleanor suddenly asked.

Larkin's brain went blank. How did Alexandra know about Eleanor? "He has heard about your beauty every time he comes to visit the town," he stammered as he blatantly lied. "He always heard wonderful things about Theo Stownar's daughter."

"I am sure he heard about our economic problem. Does he want to be a hero and save me from poverty?"

"Eleanor, that is enough!"

"No, my lady. Let her speak. I do not mind at all," Larkin cooed before facing Eleanor again. "Maybe he did hear about your economic problems. Maybe he just heard about your beauty. Whichever case it may be, he wants to marry you. Now…" He turned to look at Eliza with a serious expression on his face. "Lady Stownar, do you offer your daughter's hand in marriage?"

"He can have her on one condition."

Eleanor was about to strangle her mother. She wanted to shut her mouth and pull her inside the mansion and close the door in that man's face.

"I am not able to give him any money for taking my daughter. Maybe…"

"He will pay whatever debt your husband left behind and he will pass you a monthly pension," Larkin interrupted her as he showed off Alexandra's wealth.

"Very well! Let us set the date!"

Eleanor stared at them both. She looked up to the sky and closed her eyes angrily. God couldn't be this cruel.

CHAPTER FIVE

"This better be worth it, Larkin," Alexandra said as she stared out the window.

"It is. Eleanor is a little feisty, but I think that is just because her father died recently. It has been over a month. Maybe she is calmer now?"

Alexandra rested her chin on her knuckles. "Was I calm a month after Father's death?"

Larkin, who was sitting across from her, stared at her before deciding not to answer.

"It has been ten years, and I am still mad," she muttered, looking at her outfit and groaning. She hated dressing up. She had to bind her chest extra tight, so there was no doubt in anyone's mind that she was a man. The suit she was wearing hid every single feminine curve she had. She turned her eyes at Larkin and saw him sticking his finger between his collar and neck, trying to ease the tightness of the suit. "You look sharp. You can even find a wife there."

"Oh, no. No. I am not the husband type."

"And what makes you think that I am the husband type, Larkin?" Alexandra had to laugh. "This is crazy. I have just condemned my soul to the fiery pits of hell."

"Probably but try not to worry about that. Wait until you see your bride," Larkin said, slapping her knee and winking at her.

***

"He is late."

"From the town to his mansion, it takes about four hours by horse. By

27

carriage, I assume it will take a bit longer. Be patient, Eleanor. If he said he was going to be here, he will be here," Eliza stated as she looked outside her mansion's windows. "That man, Ward, was it?"

"Larkin Ward…"

"Yes! Him. He said he will take Alexander to the church and then come for us. After all, you are going to be handed in by him."

"How pathetic," Eleanor muttered as she smoothed her expensive wedding dress, courtesy of Alexander Dowry III just like every other wedding expense. "What will you do, mother?"

"I will stay here. Bore myself to death like every widow does. Maybe I will take on a new hobby. Knitting sounds fun."

Eleanor frowned at her mother and turned to look at the small table beside the large sofa. "Do you think father would have approved of him?"

"I do not know, and I do not care. I approve and that is what matters right now," Eliza said, rubbing her elbows slowly as she kept her eyes on the outside of the mansion. She turned to look at the grandfather clock in the living room and sighed. "Perhaps, Larkin Ward is running a bit late."

As soon as she said that she saw a luxurious carriage pulled by two white horses stopping right in front of the mansion. Eliza jumped with excitement and clapped her hands together.

"There he is! Up, up, Eleanor! Smile! You are going to get married to the richest man in town!"

Eleanor rubbed her hands together and stood up from her seat. She looked at her excited mother and noticed the door opened by a strapping and handsome Larkin. She had to take a second look at him. He had shaved, so he really did look different from the first day she saw him. Eleanor took a deep breath and tried to smile at him. He had nothing to do with this. He was just a messenger.

"You look gorgeous, Lady Stownar," Larkin whispered, offering his arm to her. "Are you ready to head out to the church?"

She wanted to say no, push Larkin away, run to her room, and lock herself inside, forever. She wasn't ready to get married. Not to a stranger, not to a person she knew nothing about! She cursed in her head and wondered if this was all part of some higher plan.

"Yes," she lied. "I am ready."

***

Father Neil was smirking like a mad man. He patted the Bible in his hand and looked at Alexandra over before shaking his head and chuckling. "What happened, Dowry? I thought you said you were not going to settle down any time soon."

"Silence, old man," Alexandra spat as she fixed her sleeves and ran her fingers through her hair. "I am doing this to help the girl out of her problems," Alexandra went on, giving the priest a dirty glare. "I want to earn a ticket to heaven after all."

Father Neil closed his eyes and chuckled before standing up straight. "It takes more than helping people around you to win a ticket to heaven."

"Sure…" she whispered and placed her callused hand over her chest. She took a deep breath and looked at the altar and then at the people that were facing the platform. As she took a glimpse at every single one of them, she noticed that she didn't know anyone inside that church. "Who are these people?"

"Supposedly, they knew Theo Stownar. They wanted to give Eleanor some support."

Alexandra rolled her eyes. She knew damn well they were there just to witness who Eleanor was getting married to.

An altar boy ran over to the priest, pulled on his white robe, and whispered something to his ears. "Very well," Father Neil said and nodded to the boy before he ran off. "Your bride is here," he announced to Alexandra before patting her back.

Alexandra raised one eyebrow at the priest and then turned to look at the church's door. Everyone grew silent when the antique organ was heard throughout the old building, playing that annoying wedding song. Alexandra stood up straight and placed both of her hands in front of her. She frowned and raised her head up high as she waited.

The church's doors were opened slowly. The sun's rays shone inside of the church, making Alexandra close her eyes a bit. She saw a tall man and quickly assumed that it was Larkin and beside him was the bride. Alexandra let out a loud sigh and wondered why she was starting to panic. She licked her lower lip and rubbed her chin. Everyone inside the church stood up and turned to look at the bride as she walked down the aisle with the unknown man.

Eleanor's grip on Larkin became tense. She clutched onto his sleeve and held the flower bouquet even tighter. She looked up to the altar and saw Father Neil smiling at her. She knew who was standing beside him and decided not to look at the groom in the eyes before standing beside him. She gulped and took a deep breath. "Oh, God…"

Larkin kept his gaze on Alexandra, yet he moved his free hand to pat Eleanor's cold hand. Of course, that didn't help at all. She jumped at the sudden touch, and in his head, he felt like throwing her to Alexandra instead of walking her down the aisle.

Eleanor felt like someone made the church's aisle longer on purpose. She just didn't see the end of it, and when she did, she wanted to turn around and run! "Oh, God," she whispered to herself before looking at Larkin. "Please…"

Larkin smiled and winked at her trying to give her some reassurance. He turned to the priest and bowed his head. "I, Larkin Ward, in the absence of Theo Stownar, hand Eleanor Stownar to Alexander Dowry III in marriage," he said as he grabbed hold of Eleanor's cold hand tightly and pulled her over to Alexandra's side.

Eleanor gasped when she felt someone else grab her hand. She stared at the hand. It was tanned, strong, warm, and she could already feel the callus on them. She thought that maybe the owner of that hand worked outside the house or practiced fencing or held guns too much. She gulped and slowly started to trail her eyes over the long arm, then the shoulder, and finally the owner's face. Eleanor's mouth opened slightly. She stared at the most bottomless green eyes she had seen in her life. She felt something run down her spine when she finally took the person in. Whoever he was…he was gorgeous.

"Hello," Eleanor croaked.

Alexandra was in awe, but she wasn't going to let it show. She looked at Eleanor with inquiring eyes while tilting her head to the side and examining Eleanor's face. Her eyes trailed over Eleanor's full lips and then her blue eyes. Instinctively, Alexandra's thumb rubbed against the backside of Eleanor's hand.

"Hi," Alexandra whispered back to her with a soft smile on her lips. She grabbed hold of the bouquet of flowers Eleanor was holding and gave it to Larkin.

Larkin frowned and looked at the bouquet. He was about to say something but, by the look Alexandra gave him, he decided it was better if he stayed with the bouquet.

"Shall we begin?" Father Neil asked the couple.

"Yes," Alexandra answered for them both and turned to look at the priest and let go of Eleanor's hand.

Eleanor was in shock. No one told her Alexander Dowry III was like the prince she had read about when she was a little girl! As soon as she let go of the groom's hand, she felt like holding it again. That simple caress had made her feel so secure. She wanted to feel like that for the rest of her life. She looked at Alexandra with the corner of her eyes and tried to take in everything. The stern expression this person carried made it hard to wonder how the merchant was around people. Yet, Eleanor couldn't have enough of that face. She had to get to know this person before deciding if she was going to learn to love him or simply hate for the rest of her life.

"Dearly beloved, we are gathered here today to join in holy matrimony the lives of Alexander Dowry III and Eleanor Stownar."

Eleanor felt like she was about to faint. Her stomach was in knots and she could feel her palms begin to sweat. Her breath was caught in her throat as she heard the priest talk. She was trying so hard to stand her ground and hold on to every emotion. She was fidgety and moved from side to side until she turned and saw that the person beside her was staring at her with a scolding dark gaze. She swallowed hard and took a deep breath before focusing on the man with white clothes.

Alexandra had mixed emotions. She wanted to calm the young woman, but at the same time, she had her own inner fight. She was bringing an innocent soul into this amalgamation of problems that she had been dragged through herself since her mother's death, but as she saw the woman next to her, for a moment, the screaming and judging voices inside of her, that kept repeating that all of this was a mistake were silent. All she could hear was a faint whisper of hope amidst all the chaos inside her mind.

"Alexander Dowry III, do you take Eleanor Stownar to be your lawful wedded wife? Do you swear to honor her, love her and respect her in sickness and in health, in richness and poor until death do you part?"

Alexandra looked at the top of the altar where a statue of a man in a cross looked upon her. Her green eyes darted back to Father Neil, and without thinking it over twice, she said, "Yes, I do."

"And do you, Eleanor Stownar, take Alexander Dowry III to be your lawful wedded husband? Do you swear to honor him, love him and respect him in sickness and in health, in richness and poor until death do you part?"

Eleanor felt like she was about to have a heart attack. She looked at the floor and searched for something to say or do other than, "I do." This wasn't how it was supposed to be. She could still remember the conversation she had with her father one night when she was a little girl. She was supposed to fall in love first, to adore everything about the person she would promise to spend the rest of her days with. She wasn't supposed to meet her husband on the same day of the wedding!

"Lady Stownar?"

Eleanor was pulled back to her reality. She was there, at the altar. Eliza was somewhere lost between the many unknown faces of the town people that have decided to join in the "celebration." She was completely and utterly alone. She turned her head to the side, and through the corner of her eyes she looked at the person standing beside her. She thought about what his reaction would be if she denied herself to him.

And so, she took a deep breath as if she were going to jump into the deepest part of the ocean. She closed her eyes and she drowned.

"I do."

Alexandra exhaled the breath she was holding. She wouldn't have been surprised if she decided to say no, make a scene, and leave. If Alexandra was in the younger woman's shoes, she would've done just that. Yet, something was sparked deep inside of her. She felt like she was alive again.

"The rings?" Father Neil gave Alexandra a look.

Alexandra turned to look at Larkin. They understood each other enough to the point that no words were necessary for him to understand what she wanted. He placed his hand inside his pocket and pulled out a small black box which he handed to Alexandra.

Alexandra opened the box and showed the three wedding rings to Eleanor. Alexandra couldn't understand her expression. Was she unimpressed by the rings, or was she in a state of emotional trance, and therefore, she couldn't understand what was going on around her? Either way, Alexandra grabbed the rings from the box, gently held Eleanor's hand, and slipped the ring on Eleanor's finger. Finally, she placed the golden ring on Eleanor's palm, letting her know that it was her turn to do the same.

Eleanor stared at the golden band in her hands. She looked at the large diamond on her finger and then turned to Alexandra. The blonde was glaring at her thoughtfully. She gulped, grabbed the much larger hand, and slipped the band. She had just branded the richest man in town, Alexander Dowry III, as her own.

"Well!" Father Neil smiled and clapped his hands together just once. "With the power vested in me, by God, I now pronounce you husband and wife. You may kiss the bride!"

Alexandra looked down at Eleanor and quickly grabbed hold of her arms. Eleanor let out a soft yelp and closed her eyes tightly. "My lady," Alexandra spoke to her. "I will never, in my life, do something that you do not wish to do. But I must kiss you so God can understand that I plan to make you mine one day," Alexandra said as if it was secret. "Forgive me," she whispered, moving forward and softly kissing the corner of Eleanor's lips.

And her whole world went white. That soft, petal-like touch sent her head spinning, and she had to hold onto the sleeve covered arms of Alexandra. She closed her eyes and took a deep breath. "I thought you were going to—"

"I cannot do that when clearly, you are uncomfortable with the whole situation."

"Alexander, Eleanor, please step right up to the altar," Father Neil whispered to the couple. The old man took hold of Eleanor's hand and helped her up the small stairs to the middle of the altar where a paper, a feather pen, and ink awaited her and Alexandra.

Alexandra helped Eleanor as well, taking hold of the long white dress. The last thing that she needed was having her new wife fall and hit her head at the altar. Now that would indeed be a sign from God letting her know that what she was doing was terribly wrong. Father Neil instructed Eleanor to take the pen and sign her name. She did so, and Alexandra didn't waste any time either. Alexandra quickly wrote her false name and turned to look at her now officially wedded wife.

"Shall we leave?" Alexandra looked down at her and turned to her side.

Eleanor quickly grabbed hold of Alexandra's strong arm and stared at the exit of the church. She was married. She was really married and stuck with this handsome man for the rest of her life. She tried to let out a nervous smile, but she just let out another croak.

Larkin walked to Alexandra's side. She looked at him and smirked. "Get the carriage ready."

He nodded and walked past the couple, opened the door of the church again, and ran to the carriage.

"Are you ready to make a run for it?" Alexandra asked out loud, looking forward yet perceiving that everyone in the church was about to jump on them both to ask thousands of questions.

"What?"

"Yes or no, Lady Stownar?"

Eleanor didn't know what to respond. "Yes?"

"Alright..." She quickly pulled Eleanor close to her. She placed her arm behind her back and the other behind her knees and lifted her up like she weighed nothing.

Eleanor screamed, wrapped her arms around Alexandra's neck, and closed her eyes tightly. "Do not let go of me!"

"I would never do such a thing," she spoke softly before she ran out of the church, dodging the questions and people eyeing them strangely.

"Larkin! Is the carriage ready?"

"Yes, it is!" Larkin said, sitting right beside the carriage handler.

Alexandra placed Eleanor on her own two feet, opened the small door for her, and slightly pushed her with her toned body. "Jump in, Lady Stownar. It will be a long ride, and we do not want to get to the mansion at nighttime," Alexandra whispered to her ear and kindly pushed her inside.

Eleanor swiftly sat down and looked at Alexandra. "What about my things?"

Alexandra opened her mouth to answer her, but she really didn't have a clue. "Larkin! Where is Lady Stownar's things?"

"Everything is on top of the carriage. Hurry up and get in. The rats and snakes are starting to come out of the church."

Alexandra smiled at her best friend and jumped inside the carriage, closing the door. She hit the ceiling of the carriage, and without delay, she heard the handler hit the horses with the reins.

Eleanor stared at Alexandra. She was taking most of the space, leaving her little room to spread her legs a bit. Eleanor stared at Alexandra's leg. The dress pants were obscenely tight, showing off every single muscle she carried on them. She tilted her head to the side and just continued to look at her until she reached her stomach. Somehow the clothing became a bit loose when it reached the torso.

Alexandra opened her eyes and rubbed her own cheek before looking at Eleanor. She seemed scared, yet at the same time, curious. Alexandra spread her legs and leaned over her knees and stared at Eleanor. "Hi."

33

Eleanor jumped a bit. She was shaken out of her daydream, and now, she was staring at Alexandra's gorgeous green eyes. "Hi," she replied and watched the blonde lean back on the carriage. "H—how long until we reach the mansion?"

Alexandra pouted and closed one eye as she thought of her answer. "Around five hours or more," she answered. "I should have thought this trip through. Maybe we could have stayed at the town mansion until we moved your things to the country mansion. The town mansion is a couple of minutes away from the church."

"Town mansion? You own another mansion?"

Alexandra observed Eleanor, studying her every move. She sighed and rubbed her hands and nodded. "Yes."

"Why do you live so far away?"

"I do not like the town mansion. It brings back unwanted memories."

"What memories?"

Alexandra smiled. She was curious.

Eleanor noticed the smile and shook her head and leaned back on her seat. "I am sorry. I should not be asking so many questions at the same time."

"You want to get to know your husband. I will gladly answer your questions at the right time."

"Of course. Please forgive me."

Alexandra kept staring at Eleanor. She was dumbfounded by her beauty; also, being dressed as a bride just made her look even more beautiful. "You are a gorgeous woman, Lady Stownar." Alexandra blurted out.

"Thank you. You are pretty handsome yourself, Master Alexander."

Alexandra threw her head back and laughed. She was handsome. How ridiculously amusing. She closed her eyes and mentally thanked her father for all the training he put her through. "I must say this beforehand, Lady Stownar. I have two pets that might trouble you occasionally. When you get to the mansion, just ignore them. I will not let them hurt you at all."

"What are they? Dogs?"

Alexandra chuckled.

Eleanor shivered.

"More or less…

CHAPTER SIX

In all her twenty-six years of life, Alexandra had never seen such a beautiful creature. Well, there was Snow, her white stallion, but that was another thing. Eleanor had fallen asleep after the second hour they had been on the carriage. Maybe because she was bored since Alexandra didn't talk much or perhaps it was because she couldn't get enough sleep the night before. Alexandra couldn't blame her. She was tired of herself. She wanted to imitate Eleanor's action and take a nap as they made their way back to the mansion. Still, she just couldn't bring herself to fall asleep and miss every small detail of Eleanor's slumber.

She had crossed her leg and leaned over the window of the carriage, gazing at Eleanor. The latter was sloping against the corner with her mouth slightly opened and letting out small snores. She chuckled a bit and peeked outside the window. The carriage came to a subtle stop. Alexandra saw her mansion and then went back to glance at Eleanor. She propped forward and extended her hand to pat Eleanor's.

"My lady, we are here," Alexandra announced before squeezing Eleanor's fingers tenderly.

Eleanor opened her blue eyes and blinked a couple of times. She moved her free hand and rubbed her eyes before locking eyes with the woman in front of her. "Ah!"

Alexandra moved back, again her hands away from Eleanor. "I am sorry if I startled you."

"No. Sorry, I just..." she shook her head and looked away from Alexandra. "Did we arrive?"

Alexandra nodded and looked at the carriage door when it was opened. "Welcome to the Dowry Country Mansion, Lady Stownar," Larkin chirped and then flashed a grin at Alexandra.

Alexandra shot him an angered glare. She pushed his face away from the door and came out. "Stop acting like a maid."

"A maid? Now, that is just insulting."

"Get her suitcases inside," Alexandra spat before fixing her suit. "Go!" She sighed and pushed Larkin away from her. Quickly, she turned to face the small door of the carriage.

Eleanor was peeking her head out and staring at the vast mansion. Her mouth and eyes were opened wide as if she had never seen anything so beautiful in her life.

Alexandra couldn't help but notice Eleanor's dumbstruck look on her face. She guessed that after years of living in the mansion, she had grown used to it and wasn't affected by the sheer beauty of it. For a moment, she turned back and tried to appreciate the house with the same eyes as Eleanor's. "Do you like it?"

"It is gorgeous."

Alexandra wrapped her arms around Eleanor's waist as she pulled her out of the carriage. Eleanor let out a surprised gasp. She wrapped her arms around Alexandra's shoulder as the older woman settled her down on the ground.

As soon as she placed Eleanor on the floor, she offered the younger woman her arm and walked with her to the mansion's grand entrance. Larkin and the carriage handler were struggling with Eleanor's suitcase behind the newly wedded couple.

Eleanor thought she was dreaming something that started off as a nightmare and then turned into a beautiful one right after she saw Alexandra's green eyes. She squeezed Alexandra's arm and felt the muscles beneath the clothes. She looked up at the tall woman and smiled. "You have a lovely home."

"Well, Lady Stownar. Welcome home," Alexandra responded as she began to ascend the entrance stairs.

"Stick! Pebbles! No, down," Larkin yelled as he saw the two gray fur balls running from behind the mansion and over to him.

Alexandra quickly turned around and frowned. She let go of Eleanor's hand and took a deep breath. "Stick! Pebbles!" she barked at them.

The two wolves stopped, turned to look at Alexandra, and then to the person behind her.

"Wolves? You have wolves?" Eleanor asked in disbelief.

The animals began to growl and make their way up the stairs, staring at Eleanor the whole time. By the time Eleanor saw them bear their fangs; she had grabbed hold of Alexandra's coat from the back. Alexandra crossed her strong arms over her chest and looked down at the beasts. She frowned deeply and coughed loudly enough to take the wolves' attention from Eleanor. "Down."

The female, Pebbles, let out a soft whimper and sat down on one of the stairs while the male, Stick, kept snarling and eyeing Eleanor with a deadly glare.

"You touch her, and I will have your testicles cut off."

The wolf whimpered and backed down. Alexandra let out a relieved sigh and walked over to the two wolves. She kneeled in front of them and grabbed hold of their snouts and made the animals face her. "Listen!"

Stick growled but quickly stopped when she noticed Alexandra's intense and defiant stare.

"This woman is your new master. I will not tolerate it if either of you hurt her. You bite her, and I will kill you…slowly. Got it?"

Pebbles let out a pained whine when Alexandra squeezed their snouts. She tried to pull away, but Alexandra held her firmly. "Got it?" Alexandra watched her two pets before letting them go. They both laid on their backs at the same time in a show of respect, letting Alexandra know that she was the dominant one in the "pack."

"Are they dead?"

Alexandra laughed softly at Eleanor's question. "No." She then extended her hand towards Eleanor. "Come here, Lady Stownar."

"I am not getting near those animals."

"Please."

Eleanor sighed and stood beside Alexandra as they stared down at the wolves.

"Pebbles, Stick. Up." Both animals stood up and stared at Alexandra and Eleanor. Alexandra squeezed Eleanor's hand and turned to her. "Touch them."

"No." Eleanor's answer was terse and severe.

Alexandra smiled and squeezed Eleanor's hand again. "Touch them. I promised you I would not let you get hurt in any way, didn't I?"

"Yes, but you do not know how they are going to react towards me."

"Touch them."

Eleanor bit the inside of her cheek and looked at the wolves. She closed her eyes tightly and moved her hand, waiting for her arm to be snatched away by the beasts. Instead, Eleanor felt something wet and slimy on the palm of her hand. She opened her eyes and saw Stick licking her palm, followed soon by Pebbles. "Well. They seem to listen to you."

"They better."

"Alex!"

The grand mansion doors burst open. The wolves yelped and jumped back. Alexandra turned around to see who had called for her. It was Nana.

The old woman waddled her way to Alexandra and pulled the tall woman down to kiss her cheek. "Alex! My goodness, you look so handsome with your wedding suit! Oh! Is this the lucky young lady?"

Alexandra nodded. "Lady Stownar, this is Nana. She has been taking care of me in my mother's absence since I was a young boy," she then turned to the old woman and held Eleanor's hand. "Nana, this is Lady Eleanor Stownar," she looked at Eleanor and smiled. "She is my wife."

"It is so nice to meet you, dear. I am Nana!" the old woman said, pushing Alexandra out of the way and getting closer to the gorgeous young woman.

"It is nice to meet you too, ma'am," Eleanor smiled as she held Nana's hands, not before wiping her wet hand against her wedding dress, of course.

"Oh no! Do not you call me that! I am Nana!" The old woman teased, trying to act mad at Eleanor. She then chuckled and patted Eleanor's face. "You might want to change out of that uncomfortable dress and take a warm bath, am I right?"

Eleanor smiled and nodded. "Oh, you have no idea."

"Well! If you excuse us, I am going to help Lady Stownar freshen up!" Nana said to Alexandra and Larkin as she squeezed Eleanor's hand and pulled her away from the chuckling Alexandra.

"I will be in the living room, Nana. Bring Lady Stownar when you ladies are done."

"Yes, yes! You should change out of those clothes too, Alex," Nana said as she strolled over to the stairs.

"I will, Nana. I will."

As soon as Eleanor was out of sight, Alexandra let out a loud, relieved sigh and undid the collar of her suit and took off her coat and the tuxedo overcoat. She walked over to the living room and sat on the most massive sofa and lay down ultimately. "So far, so good. She hasn't noticed I am a woman at all," she let out a soft hiss as she pulled onto her collar and waved her hand in front of the heated skin.

Larkin placed Eleanor's suitcase near the sofa and then sat down on a nearby couch. "Well, what do you think?"

Alexandra placed her arm over her eyes and exhaled loudly. "She is absolutely gorgeous, sinfully gorgeous. She is the kind of woman I will have trouble keeping my hands off."

"Told you. I told you Eleanor is beautiful."

"I should have married an old woman."

"What? Are you daft? Look at her, Alex!"

"I do not want to love her." Alexandra gasped before looking at Larkin. "I do not want to be vulnerable, and I certainly do not want to hurt her."

Alexandra sat up on the couch, leaned over her knees, and rubbed her face. "She is so beautiful; I just couldn't stop staring at her all the way from the church to the mansion. Right now, I want to run upstairs and help her take that bath!"

Larkin laughed and stood up from the sofa. He made his way over to the famous small table with large glass bottles. He grabbed a small glass and poured some liquor and handed it to Alexandra. "Relax. Just do not talk a lot with her. Stay as far away as possible if you do not want to fall for her."

"Stay away from a woman like her?" Alexandra accepted the glass and stared at it. "It will be hard, Larkin."

"I know. The other plan is to make Eleanor fall for you. That way, when she gets to know your true gender, she will not mind and will actually keep her mouth shut."

Alexandra took a small sip and then handed the rest to Larkin. "I like the second plan a lot more than the first."

***

Eleanor had her arms crossed over her chest as Nana poured a warm bucket of water over her head. The young woman let out a happy whimper and then ran her fingers through her wet brown hair, moving it out of her face. "This is heaven," Eleanor whispered.

"How do you find the mansion?" Nana asked as she put some lotion on her hands and moved to scratch Eleanor's head.

"It is breathtaking. I've never seen such a lovely house in my life," Eleanor answered while relaxing completely.

"And what about Master Alexander?"

Eleanor opened her eyes and moved in the tub a bit uncomfortable. "Well..."

"You do not have to be so shy," Nana said as she poured another bucket of water over Eleanor.

She let out a soft yelp when the cold water fell on her. "Cold!"

Nana let out a soft laugh and moved away from Eleanor to clean herself. "I will be back. I am bringing you some new clothing."

Eleanor moved her hair away from her face again. She heard the door to the bathroom close and then she leaned in the tub. The silence in the room made her uncomfortable, mainly because she wasn't used to living in such a prominent place. There was no doubt in her mind that she was grateful for what her husband did, but the thing was, her upcoming new life terrified her to no end. She was separated from her old life, from her mother, her maids, her house, and her books. Eleanor shivered and examined the drops of water that fell from her hair to the tub. To her, Alexander was beautiful. Handsome, young-looking, and intense, but serious. There was a barrier she might just have to push over and try her best to destroy, but how?

She took a deep breath and rubbed her arms, feeling the goosebumps forming. "Alexander Dowry..." she said the name and bit her lower lip. She remembered the touch at the church and the kiss, the green eyes studying her as if trying to pick out all her inner demons and secrets. "Alex..."

***

Alexandra was lying on the sofa, playing with Pebbles' fur. The animal was resting right beside her on the floor, letting out loud snores occasionally. Stick, on the other hand, was sitting, keeping an eye on the grand stairs. Alexandra was staring at the ceiling as she waited for Eleanor or Nana to come back.

A soft growling sound interrupted the silence. Alexandra moved her head to look at a blushing Larkin. "Are you hungry?"

His answer was a nod.

"I forgot to have breakfast this morning." Alexandra groaned, sighing, and resting her arm on her forehead. "My nerves were eating me alive."

Larkin chuckled. "Oh, well. I understand. Getting married to a stranger can surely kill your desire to eat."

Alexandra nodded, not caring if Larkin saw her or not. At that moment, Stick let out a soft howl that made Pebbles jump up.

"Alex! Come see!" Nana yelled from the top of the grand stairs.

Alexandra pulled on Pebbles' ear playfully before standing up from the couch. "What is it, Nana?" Alexandra walked up to the bottom of the stairs and looked up before opening her mouth in awe. Stick sneezed. Pebbles let out an awkward grunt, and Alexandra was about to explode with anger. "Why is Lady Stownar wearing one of my mother's dresses?"

Eleanor jumped at the rage she perceived in Alexandra's voice. She looked down at the light-colored dress that Nana had brought for her. She wasn't expecting that at all. Nana shuddered at Alexandra's low voice. Nana looked at Eleanor and saw that same frightened expression on her face. The old woman grabbed hold of Eleanor's hand and tried to ease her fear.

"Doesn't she have dresses of her own?" Alexandra then quickly grabbed hold of one of Eleanor's suitcase and dragged it to the bottom of the stairs, slamming it harshly on the first steps. Both wolves let out a yelp and ran out of the mansion. "I know you are poor, Lady Stownar, but I doubt you didn't pack any clothing."

"I— I didn't know. I—"

"It is my fault," Nana confessed. "Her suitcases were downstairs, and I didn't want to trouble Larkin or you, sir, in bringing them up since I know both of you, young lads, are tired from the trip. These dresses haven't been worn in decades. And clearly—" She turned to Eleanor and showed her off to Alexandra by pulling her to the very top step of the stairs. "She looks stunningly beautiful."

"Try to calm down. It is not a big deal," Larkin muttered, squeezing her shoulder.

"It is not a big deal?" Alexandra pushed him and stared at him angrily.

"No. It is not," Larkin answered back, clearly not scared of Alexandra's temper.

Alexandra trembled in agitation. She closed her eyes and ran her fingers through her hair and exhaled loudly. She looked up at Nana again and then at Eleanor. Yes, there was no doubt in her mind that Eleanor looked gorgeous. She never knew that such an old dress could look so alive. The curves that were hidden in that colossal wedding dress were out and for everyone to see. The corset hugged her breasts, so she was sporting a seductive cleavage. Alexandra had to rub her lips harshly just to stop the need to kiss her.

"Nana, leave us alone. You too, Larkin. Go look for the wolves. I think I scared them a little too much," Alexandra gulped down the anger down her throat as she waited for everyone to leave. She noticed that Eleanor was about to follow Nana, but she quickly stepped down on the stairs. "I did not ask for you to leave."

Eleanor closed her eyes tightly and took a deep breath. She turned around and looked at Alexandra. "I am sorry. I—"

Alexandra raised her hand to silence her. "We will talk about this soon. Now, let me show you to your room." Alexandra grabbed hold of the suitcase she had thrown and went back to gather the rest.

Eleanor watched her. Larkin had had such a horrible time with the suitcases, and now Alexandra picked them up like they were nothing. Not to mention Alexandra was climbing the stairs with ease. Eleanor was impressed.

"Let me help you," Eleanor whispered as she grabbed one small suitcase with her trembling hands.

Alexandra let her do as she pleased. She slowly began to walk down the grand hall, stopping in front of the master chamber, which was the room at the end. As soon as she stopped, she took a quick glance at the large doors before turning to her right and staring at another big door. It wasn't as big as the master chamber's, but it showed that it belonged to someone important in the mansion. Alexandra placed the suitcases on the floor and moved to open the door before waiting for Eleanor to walk in.

"After you."

Eleanor nodded and walked inside the massive room. Her eyes began to trail the place, not believing what she was seeing. Alexandra turned around and pulled Eleanor's stuff inside the room before closing the door behind her.

Eleanor jumped when she heard the door close. She turned to look at Alexandra and saw the serious gaze she was giving her. "I can explain. Nana was just trying to be nice, and I did not know that the dress belonged to your mother and—"

"Be quiet."

Eleanor covered her mouth and looked at the floor.

"There are so many things you need to know about me, but we have the rest of our lives to get to know each other, so I guess it is fine. Never mind the dress. I just...overreacted," Alexandra muttered as she looked down at Eleanor. She was still covering her mouth and looking at the floor. Alexandra frowned. "You can talk now."

Eleanor gasped for air and dropped her arms. "I thought you were going to strike me."

Alexandra twitched. "I would never lay a hand on you."

"Some husbands do."

"I am not like other husbands." Alexandra thought that the last sentence was an understatement. She rolled her tongue over her lip and decided to change the subject. "Are you satisfied with your room?"

"My room?"

Alexandra crossed her arms over her chest and raised her eyebrows at Eleanor. "Yes, your room."

"Aren't married couples supposed to sleep in the same room?"

Alexandra cracked a smile. "Lady Stownar?"

"Yes?" Eleanor looked up at Alexandra's dark green eyes and felt like her air got caught up in her throat.

"Do you want to sleep with me?" Alexandra moved close enough to make Eleanor feel uncomfortable. Eleanor wanted to say "yes" because that was what married couples did, but at the same time, she wanted to scream "no" because she was terrified. She was terrified of being touched by her husband, but despite being scared, she was curious about how Alex's warm touch would feel on other parts of her skin.

"When was I born?" Alexandra suddenly asked, shaking Eleanor out of her thoughts.

Eleanor frowned. "I— I do not know."

"What is my favorite color?"

"I have no clue."

"Which do I prefer? Coffee or tea?"

"I do not know." Eleanor gave up and averted her eyes to the ground. She thought she was pathetic. She didn't know anything about her own husband.

Alexandra could feel the other woman's disappointment, and for a second, she felt guilty of what she was saying. She shrugged and rubbed her own arms apprehensively. "It is fine. I do not know anything about you either. I think you should know a bit more about someone before sharing a room and a bed. Give it time. I do not want to have you sleeping beside me, scared to death and nervous. Like I said earlier, I will not have you do anything you do not want to do," Alexandra said. She moved her large hand to hold Eleanor's chin. She lifted her face and made the younger woman look at her.

Eleanor let out an uneven smile. She was drawn to Alexandra. One minute she looked like she was about to snap her neck and the other she was treating her like a true princess.

"A smile suits you better," Alexandra whispered as she gazed at Eleanor's lips. Eleanor felt like this was the perfect opportunity for her new husband to kiss her. To fully press their lips together and make her tremble with need like in those books she had read when she was younger. "Lady Stownar?"

"Yes?" Eleanor waited for it.

"Would you be kind enough to change that dress? It is disturbing to see my wife wearing my late mother's clothes."

Eleanor blinked and pulled away from Alexandra as she blushed and nodded.

"Just leave it on the bed. Nana will come back later and place it where it belongs."

Eleanor smiled and turned around to unpack when she noticed three other doors inside the room. She quickly turned to look for Alexandra. She was about to leave the room. "Alexander?"

Alexandra grabbed hold of the door frame and turned to face Eleanor. "Hmm? What is it, my lady?"

Eleanor opened her mouth to talk but decided to point at the doors. "What are they for?"

"One is your private bathroom," Alexandra stated and walked over to one door that was facing the foot of the bed. "This one leads to Nana's chamber," she said as she touched the doorknob. "The one right next to the bed leads to my chamber."

Eleanor blushed deeply. "I— can I—"

"If my lady has some trouble and wants to talk to me at any time of the day or night, you can open that door, and I will gladly do whatever I can to help." She then chuckled. "Of course." She leaned over and whispered the rest. "Please knock first. I tend to walk around nude."

Eleanor blushed and turned away from Alexandra. She didn't want her husband to see her reaction to the image that had just been formed in her head. "Thank you."

Alexandra snickered and began to walk over to the exit door once again.

"Oh! Alexander?"

Alexandra turned around and looked at Eleanor. She placed her hands on her narrow waist and smiled. "Yes?"

"Who did this room belong to?"

Alexandra sighed and looked at the room. "It was mine. I moved to the master bedroom six months after my father died."

Eleanor's mouth made an "o" shape. She nodded and looked at the floor. "Thank you, and sorry for bothering you so much."

"I do not mind. Please, make yourself comfortable. I believe lunch will be served shortly. I will be in my chamber changing out of these pesky clothes," Alexandra babbled, pulling the collar of her wedding suit.

Eleanor smiled and bowed her head at Alexandra. "I will see you later, then."

Alexandra nodded and finally walked out of the chamber, closing the door behind her. As soon as she was out, Alexandra leaned against the door and closed her eyes. She had never felt so tempted to say "to hell with it" to everything she ever believed in and take the woman inside her old chamber. She had to control every cell in her body in order not to touch her more than she did when she rubbed Eleanor's chin. She pushed herself from the door and slowly made her way to the master chamber. She opened the large doors and then walked in. She stopped dead on her tracks when she saw Nana sitting on one of the edges of the massive bed. Alexandra let out a grunt and closed the doors. "Nana."

The old woman jumped from the bed and turned to look at Alexandra, pouting like a small child. "I am sorry."

Alexandra rolled her eyes and walked over to her. She wrapped her arm around her shoulders and pulled the small woman close to her. "It is fine. I know you did not intend to do any harm. I just…"

"I know, Alex. I know," Nana assured her by patting Alexandra's cheek with her wrinkly hands. "I promise I will not touch your parents' things without asking you first."

"That sounds wonderful," Alexandra answered before sitting down on the bed.

"Should I get out your usual attire?" Nana asked, wobbling over to the immense closet.

"If you please," Alexandra replied, removing her suit and uncomfortable boots, and unbuttoning the expensive shirt. "I hate dressing up." She took off all her clothing and stood in front of the bed with a tight bandage over her chest and shorts. "Nana, could you come over here, please?"

The old woman pulled her skirt up a bit and walked over to Alexandra. "What is it, my dear?"

Alexandra sat down on the bed and pointed at her back. "Today, it was tightened to the point I thought I was going to faint," Alexandra said, referring to the bandage. "Could you please take it off?"

Nana nodded and began to tug on the bandages, letting it loose. "This is what it feels to wear a corset, Alex."

Alexandra let out a relieved sigh once she was free from her prison. She hissed a bit and moved her hand to touch her left breast. "It hurts like crazy."

Nana patted Alexandra's muscle-bound back and moved away from her. "Who wrapped it up?"

Alexandra looked at Nana and then at her mirror. She coughed. "Larkin."

"What? Larkin? Where was I at that moment?"

"Nana. He is like my brother, and you were sleeping. You are old. You need to rest more than you used to. Besides, he was helping me with the whole suit," Alexandra informed her as she moved to touch her right breast. "Holy God. It was torture. He pulled and pulled until I literally didn't feel my breasts."

"Oh, Alex. I am not that old. But, I am glad he tightened your breast like he did! That teaches you not to let a man touch them," Nana told her as she placed Alexandra's clothes on the bed. "Do you want me to wrap them up now?"

Alexandra let out a sigh and leaned back on her bed. "I prefer to take a bath first and let them rest."

Nana nodded. "Oh, well. I will get your bath ready then."

Alexandra thanked the old woman and then looked over to her mirror. She licked her lower lip and then leaned back enough to lay entirely on the bed. "I am so glad I do not have to wear a corset every single day of my life."

CHAPTER SEVEN

The first day at the Dowry mansion was strenuous for Eleanor. There were so many different places that she needed to remember, many of which were out of use, not to mention the servant's quarters. Some rooms were closed off and no one could get in. She always wondered the reason for that.

After breakfast, she had decided to walk around the outside of the mansion. She saw the stables, the horses, and the wolves running around without a care in the world. It was so weird to see such ferocious beasts acting like tame pups. She made a mental note to ask Alexandra about them.

The lunch was rather pleasant since Larkin was a charmer. He loved making embarrassing jokes and talking about all the things he did when he and Alexandra were younger. Yet, Alexandra was silent most of the time, observing Eleanor's reaction to everything. She seemed to be enjoying herself and Alexandra was pleased.

After lunch, Larkin went out to work with the horses while Alexandra went to her study to read and be alone. Something that Eleanor found rather frustrating.

The young woman wanted nothing more than to be around her. Still, Alexandra thought that it wasn't time yet for them to start interacting freely. Alexandra believed that the less Eleanor saw her, the less opportunity Eleanor had to notice that she was a woman.

Eleanor had taken the rest of the day to take all her belongings from her suitcases and place them around the empty, yet well-furnished chamber. When she was done, it was almost dinner time.

Everything went smoothly, just like at lunch. Larkin tried to make Eleanor feel comfortable by making jokes. At the same time, Alexandra ate quietly at the head of the table, where her father used to sit. She would laugh at some of

Larkin's jokes, yet, she never said a word. That made Eleanor worried. Maybe Alexandra was still mad at the whole dress incident? Or maybe Alexandra was just quiet?

"It was delicious," Eleanor stated, referring to the meal as she wiped her mouth with one of the table napkins. She placed it beside her plate and stood up. Both Alexandra and Larkin stopped eating altogether and stood up at the same time Eleanor did.

"It is fine. You do not need to stand up for me."

"We were taught good manners, my lady," Larkin told her with a smirk on his face.

Alexandra gave him a look and moved away from the table. "Are you going up to your room, Lady Stownar?"

Eleanor nodded. "I am exhausted. I am going to head upstairs and just go to sleep."

"Sleep well, my lady," Larkin muttered.

"You too, Larkin," Eleanor told him as she turned around and walked away from the dining table.

"I will escort you to your chamber," Alexandra said as she began to walk right behind Eleanor. Alexandra kept her eyes locked with the younger woman as she climbed the stairs. She stopped right in front of Eleanor's chamber and rubbed her hands before she noticed Eleanor had turned around to look at her. She raised her eyebrow at her, wondering why she hadn't entered the room.

"Are you going to sleep?" Eleanor suddenly asked.

"Yes. I am also rather tired and I would like to rest. I must wake up early to check on the horses. There is a potential customer that wants to buy some of my stallions. I have to get them clean and ready to present them to the buyer."

Eleanor frowned. "Isn't that Larkin's job?"

Alexandra smiled. "I like to work around the mansion as well, Lady Stownar. I do not like to stay locked up in my chambers doing nothing." Alexandra then placed her hands behind her back and stared down at Eleanor. "Maybe tomorrow, if you do not sleep in late, I might show you the outsides of the mansion and its neighboring lands?" Alexandra half asked, half stated.

Eleanor nodded at that. "That would be wonderful."

"Good." Alexandra smiled then moved her hand forward, palm up.

Eleanor didn't know what to do. She guessed Alexandra was asking for her hand and so she slipped her hand on top of Alexandra's. Alexandra squeezed Eleanor's delicate fingers before leaning forward and kissing the back of her hand painfully slow. Eleanor blushed deeply and became paralyzed. She didn't move until Alexandra was standing up straight and looking at her with those dark green eyes. "Sweet dreams, Lady Stownar."

Eleanor gulped down and tried to hide her blush by looking at the floor.

"You, too."

Alexandra smiled and opened the door for Eleanor. "I will see you tomorrow."

"Right." Eleanor smiled and then walked in, turning to slowly close the door. When she did, she leaned over it and took a deep breath. She closed her eyes and then moved her hand to her face. She squirmed in delight and let out a soft squeal before jumping on her bed.

***

Larkin was sitting down outside the mansion's steps just like he did every morning. He chewed on one of the many mints leaves he found around the front yard and tried to avoid the wolves' gaze as he just contemplated the morning. He leaned back, resting himself with his hands as he spread his legs a bit and stared at the mansion's gates. Stick came to his feet and began to nibble his shoes while Pebbles started to lick and drool on his shirt. Larkin groaned and grabbed hold of Pebbles' furry neck and pushed her away from him before jerking his leg. "Get off, Stick."

The male wolf growled and raised his leg to Larkin's pants. A second later, Larkin felt his leg being sprayed with a warm liquid.

"You bastard!" Larkin yelled, making both Pebbles and Stick run off to the backside of the mansion. He watched them disappear behind the stables, not before letting out a snarl. "She should have left them to rot in that godforsaken forest. What use do we have of two stupid wimpy wolves that act like pups?" he whined and shook his pant leg. "And these were my comfortable pants."

"Stick is only marking his territory. You should feel loved."

Larkin jumped when he heard a sudden voice. As he turned, he saw the woman leaning against the grand doors, arms crossed under her chest, sporting a mischievous grin on her lips. Larkin rolled his eyes and patted his waist. "Loved. I should throw them to the forest and see if they can fucking survive on their own accord."

"I bet they can. Wolves are still wild beasts. I am sure they can tear apart a throat or two," Alexandra said as she walked down the stairs and moved next to Larkin.

"You trust those animals with your life, do you not?"

Alexandra smiled and nodded. "Of course. I trust they annoyed the hell out of you also."

Larkin frowned. If she was in the mood to tease him, then so was he. He mimicked Alexandra's pose earlier and crossed his arms over his firm chest. "So, tell me, how was your first night as a married... man?"

Alexandra raised her eyebrows and turned to face him. "Just like the night before," she said with a shrug. "Did you think that I was going to be this calm if I actually slept with her?"

"Really now? Nothing happened?"

"I gave her my old bedroom, Larkin. I wasn't going to force myself on her."

"But—"

"No. I will not get Eleanor intoxicated, though the idea sounds rather tempting and amusing. I would love to see that woman lose control."

Larkin raised his eyebrow and pouted in amusement and amazement. "Wow. Alexander Dowry. Such self-control!" Larkin bowed his head low and began to clap his hands. "I applaud you. You are nothing like us, filthy men. You are so… different."

"I am not you, Larkin." Alexandra chuckled as she stood from the stairs, gave her back to Larkin, and strutted over to the stables.

"If you were not going to consummate the marriage, why, oh why, did you follow her to her chambers?" Larkin asked as he ran a bit to be side by side to Alexandra.

"To wish her a good night's sleep. I want her to feel welcomed in my mansion, Larkin. I do not want her to fear me either. I want her to think of me as a confidant or her friend." She paused as she heard Larkin scoff. "I am serious."

"Her friend? Have you seen that woman, Alex? She is gorgeous. When I went ahead to ask her hand for you, I could not keep my eyes off her."

"That is you, Larkin. You are too obvious with your feelings sometimes. I can control myself." She grunted the last word as she opened both stables' doors. She walked over to her stallion Snow and pulled him out, patting his stomach affectionately.

"Alex, be honest with me? Do you actually like her?"

She focused her eyes on the large animal before darting her green eyes at the man next to her. She quietly nodded, her hands never stopping their caress on her adored horse. "She is my wife…" Alexandra began, paused, and licked her lips. "I never thought that I would find her so fascinating and beautiful. I am intrigued by her."

"If you find her so intriguing, why are you hiding in your study or out here with the horses?" Larkin asked in annoyance.

"Because I am terrified of falling in love with such a pure soul," Alexandra whispered before grabbing a bucket and a broad brush. "Can we stop talking and get to work? Please?"

Larkin grabbed another brush and began to move it against the animal's fur. His eyes trailed over to Alexandra and then went back to the horse before he spoke again. "Is it because you are afraid? Or maybe you do not really like women at all?"

Alexandra stopped her actions and stared at Larkin. "What is wrong with you?"

"Have you ever been with a man?"

"What the hell is wrong with you?"

"I am just asking. I mean, I have never seen you with a man."

Alexandra was about to throw the brush at Larkin and crack his head open. "Your fucking questions about my personal and sexual life are getting out of fucking hand, Larkin!" she spat at him.

"You do not have to get so agitated. It was just a simple question."

"Look. First, I am not going to risk it. Eleanor is not ready to have sex with me. How do you think she will react when she sees me naked?" She dropped the bucket and transformed herself into the most feminine woman she could possibly have mastered. She turned to Larkin and proceeded to act as if she was an exaggerated version of Eleanor. "Oh, my goodness me, my husband, my husband has breasts? Oh Lord Almighty, what is going on? I am so confused."

"Alex, do not ever do that again. That was terrifying."

Alexandra couldn't help but scoff. It was scary, indeed. She grabbed the brush and threw it all wet and sloppy over Larkin's face. "Also, I do not find men fascinating at all. Hell, Larkin. You are a handsome man, but believe me, you can walk around naked in front of me, and I will act like I am watching a horse run. I will feel nothing."

"I do not know about that; you get really fucking excited when you see Snow run around."

"Larkin!"

"Jesus Christ. Forgive me for insulting your manhood."

"Stop being sarcastic, Larkin."

"Stop being so sensitive."

For a couple of minutes, both friends grew quiet. The only sound between them was the sound of the brush against fur and the snorts coming from Snow. "Hey, Alex?"

"What is it, Larkin?"

"Do you find me handsome?"

"Oh, God! Larkin!"

"You just said I am handsome!"

"Go to hell!"

Larkin threw his head back and laughed. "I am just bothering you, Alex?"

She shook her head and raised her eyebrows at him, trying to act mad. "I am going to kick you out of this mansion one of these days."

Larkin chuckled and patted Snow's neck thinking of a way to change the topic. "By the way, your wife hasn't woken up?"

"No. I guess Eleanor was telling the truth when she said she was tired."

"Maybe, or maybe she is avoiding you just as you avoid her? I mean, come on, you yelled at her for wearing a dress."

Alexandra rolled her eyes and walked away from her horse, not before grabbing hold of a bucket. "You are annoying."

Larkin just chuckled and snatched Snow's snout. "Am I annoying?" The horse snorted loudly and tried to move away from Larkin. He, on the other hand, gave the horse a loud kiss on his snout. "I will take that as a yes!"

Alexandra was mumbling incoherent words as she walked out of the barn with the empty bucket. "He is painting me as if I were the most horrible person on the face of the Earth. Of course, I yelled, I was mad when people are mad at something they usually yell, it is a normal thing to do..." Before she could head over to the water pump, she heard a loud howl behind her. Alexandra jumped a couple of feet in the air and turned to see a tail-wagging Pebbles staring at her. "What in heaven's name is wrong with you?"

Pebbles made an awkward noise and sat down on the green grass.

"Oh, no. You are not playing the innocent act on me. Why did you howl at me just now? Hmm?" She was about to say something else to the "grinning" wolf, but something knocked the air out of her. That something had hit the back of her knees, making her stumble to the ground, landing on her back.

She quickly sat up, with the bucket still in her hands, and noticed that the male wolf was licking Pebbles' ear. "You better run, boy." The animal just panted and sat down beside Pebbles and tilted his head to the side. Alexandra placed the bucket beside her before she stood up and put her hands on her hips. "Explanation, if you please?" The wolves just rolled over into their stomachs and covered their eyes with their paws. "No. I already said that it is not going to work on me. It never does. We have gone through this."

She moved once again over the wolves only to have them run away from her, not before Stick taking the bucket and escaping with it. That alone made Alexandra madder. She yelled at them, cursed, and ran after her bucket. She didn't seem to notice that one of the mansion's windows had been opened and that a young woman was staring at her little pursuit.

Eleanor giggled and leaned over the windows as she just watched Alexandra run after the wolves. It was a hilarious sight. Alexandra, on more than one occasion, had fallen to the ground as she tried to trap the male wolf in a corner. She crawled on all fours, trying her hardest to get Stick to drop the bucket.

"Are they too fast for you?" Eleanor asked loud enough for Alexandra to hear.

Alexandra quickly turned around and saw her. Her breathing was hard, and she knew she had gotten her clothes dirty with mud and grass stains. She wiped her forehead with her arm and placed her hands on her hips as she tried to take control of her lungs. "No. Actually, I think they outsmarted me."

Pebbles howled at Alexandra, which made her jump, surprised. Stick placed the bucket on the floor and imitated Pebbles.

Eleanor smiled widely and shook her head. "I think they did."

Alexandra ran her fingers through her hair and grabbed hold of the bucket before giving the wolves an angry glare. "Thanks for making me look stupid."

Pebbles sneezed and Stick just stood up to wag his tail.

"Have you had breakfast yet?" Eleanor asked from the windows, trying to suppress her amusement.

"Yes. Yes, I have," Alexandra answered, turning to Eleanor again and trying to act as calm and collected as possible.

"Would you like to keep me company while I eat?"

Alexandra stopped dead on her tracks and nodded. She shrugged and smiled. "Of course."

***

Alexandra was resting her cheek on her knuckles as she watched Eleanor finish up her breakfast. She was so enthralled by the young woman; it wasn't until one of the maids took her plate that she noticed that Eleanor was done. For a moment, Alexandra slipped both her hands on top of the table and turned to stare at Eleanor. She just couldn't keep her eyes from her.

"I should give your cook a hug," Eleanor whispered as she grabbed hold of her cup of coffee and drank what was left. "Everything was delicious."

Alexandra nodded. "I'll let Alma know."

Eleanor smiled and placed her hands on her lap as she felt Alexandra's steady gaze on her. She cleared her throat and looked at Alexandra with the corner of her eyes. "You prefer tea."

Alexandra frowned. "Excuse me?"

Eleanor chuckled and waved her hand at her. "You asked me what you preferred better, coffee or tea? I must answer tea. Yes. I noticed right after a meal you ordered tea instead of a cup of coffee. Am I right?"

Alexandra nodded and smiled in amusement. "You are correct."

"Well! That means I know something about you! Are we still strangers?"

Alexandra tilted her head to the side and just stared at Eleanor. "Why do you want to get to know me so fast? To tell you the truth, I am not that interesting. I am just a boring rich man. I bet a peasant has more stories to tell you."

Eleanor couldn't help but blush at Alexandra's scrutinizing gaze. She went back to stare at her lap and shrugged. "You are my husband, and I am your wife. It is only proper for me to know you to have a happy marriage with you."

Alexandra scoffed and slowly leaned back against her chair, her eyes never leaving Eleanor. She crossed her legs and squirmed in her chair with excitement. "A happy marriage?"

Eleanor frowned and gathered enough courage to drill her blue eyes with Alexandra's dark green eyes. "Is there a problem with that?"

"Oh no, not at all, Lady Stownar."

"Then, may I ask why you are acting so amused?"

"Because of you, Lady Stownar. I find you amusing, intriguing, and…" She stopped to take a sharp look at the woman in front of her before whispering, "Gorgeous."

"Thank you for the compliment, Alexander. I find you rather attractive too." She licked her lower lip and looked down at the floor. "I never thought that the person I was to marry was going to look like you."

"We are on the same page. I guess we are lucky that our spouses are delectable to our eyes."

"You make me blush, Alexander."

"Forgive me, I do not mean to upset you or make you uncomfortable, but…" Alexandra exhaled loudly and shook her head. "I was going to ask you if you had any plans for the rest of the day, if not I would like to show you around the mansion, Lady Stownar."

"I would be delighted!"

Alexandra laughed softly and stood up from her chair. "Do you know how to ride a horse?"

Eleanor frowned and looked up at Alexandra with a confused expression on her face. "Ride a horse? Dear God, no. My father never let me get up on those things. He said it wasn't ladylike."

"Ladylike?" Alexandra chuckled. "Would you like to ride a horse with me?"

"I do not know. I do not want to be a nuisance to you."

"No, no. You are not a nuisance, and please, call me Alex."

Eleanor froze. It was kind of intimate to call someone by their first name, little alone by their endearing nickname. She swallowed hard and rubbed the back of her neck as she tried to avoid Alexandra's eyes on her. She looked back up and nodded awkwardly. "Alright, Alex."

Alexandra smiled and offered Eleanor her hand. Quickly, Eleanor stood up and grabbed hold of Alexandra's large, callused hand. She looked down at it and, in a second, had a flashback from the wedding day. She stared at the long rough fingers, and without thinking, she moved her other hand to touch the skin over the back of Alexandra's hand. Alexandra didn't move an inch. She thought that if she made any sudden movement, Eleanor might believe that she wasn't okay with the unexpected contact. However, also, she stayed still, enjoying the soft sensation of Eleanor's skin upon her own. That soft touch was enough to make Alexandra's mind race with different scenarios in which Eleanor's delicate hands were touching her in different places. God, were Eleanor's hands as soft as the rest of her body?

Alexandra cleared her throat nervously, yet Eleanor wasn't done with the soft exploration of Alexandra's hand. Eleanor's fingertips trailed over the veins on the inside of her wrist as they disappeared into Alexandra's white shirt. The skin there was soft, too soft yet the hands looked roughed up, tanned by the burning sun. Eleanor's blue eyes turned to Alexandra's face. Eleanor noticed how the person in front of her appeared to be having trouble breathing.

Alexandra's lips were parted, her chest was rising and falling slowly as her eyes traced Eleanor's hand movement. Were her fingers skilled when it came to giving some form of a caress? She had to swallow hard and squeeze Eleanor's hand to go back to reality.

"Does my husband work outside among the servants?"

Alexandra was about to snatch Eleanor's hand, pull her close, and plant her lips on Eleanor's and finally give her that real kiss that she had been yearning for since that day she saw her blue eyes at the church. Eleanor was testing her grounds while seeing how far she could go with Alexandra.

"I— I do not like to be lazy, Lady Stownar. I take pride in working alongside my servants and Larkin. They are good workers. Besides, I enjoy supervising them."

"Yes, but I can sense that this is not only outside work," Eleanor said, frowning and slowly caressing Alexandra's palm with fingers. "Swords?"

"I am impressed." Alexandra exhaled. "I practiced fencing for years."

Eleanor chuckled. "I have a good eye for details."

Alexandra raised her eyebrow and gave her a teasing grin. "Do you now?"

Eleanor felt Alexandra was just about to start making fun of her, so she quickly cut their intimate contact and changed the subject.

"Can we get back to the subject matter, Alex? You were talking about riding a horse?" Eleanor asked before hiding her hands behind her back, stopping the torture she had made Alexandra endured.

The older woman, on the other hand, let out a saddened sigh the moment she broke contact with Eleanor. She dropped her hand and her shoulders in defeat before tilting her head to the side. "Would you accompany me to one of my favorite places in the mansion?"

"Oh, you mean the study?" Eleanor asked teasingly.

"Oh no, it is definitely not the study…"

***

Larkin was staring at the whole scene. He was holding to one of the many horses in the mansion while Alexandra steadied Snow for Eleanor to get on it. He was holding his laughter in and trying to keep a serious face in front of Eleanor and Alexandra. He was scared that Alexandra would kill him if she saw him laughing. "Do you need help, Alexander?"

Alexandra shot him a glare. Mentally, she asked him to stay quiet until she told him to speak again. She turned back to the blushing Eleanor and let out an uneven nervous smile.

"Alright. This is not hard." She sighed and ran her fingers through her hair. She pushed her sleeves up to her elbows and grabbed hold of the black horse's reins and steadied the animal. "The best way to ride horses is to have one leg on each side."

Eleanor gasped and jumped away from Alexandra. "I beg your pardon?"

Alexandra frowned and looked at Eleanor with a confused expression on her face. "What?"

"One leg on each side? I've seen women ride horses and they do not ride that way."

Alexandra tilted her head to the side and scratched the animal's jaw. She licked her lips and shrugged as she thought of something to say. "Lady Stownar, that is the safest way. You will not lose your balance."

"I will not ride in such a way," Eleanor said, and she crossed her arms under her ample chest and looked away.

Alexandra let out a loud sigh. She threw her arms up and then placed her hands on her hips as she thought of something. "It is that or riding with me."

Eleanor opened her eyes wide and felt the upcoming blush rise to her cheeks. "Ride together?"

"You can ride sideways if you wish. I will be behind you to steady you, so you will not fall," Alexandra informed as she played with the short blonde hairs that tickled the back of her neck. "Only if you want to."

Larkin's upper lip twitched. He cleared his throat and stood up straight. His shoulders were shaking and he was about to choke on his own breath if he didn't laugh.

Alexandra's jaw tightened as she saw this. She walked over to him and pushed his shoulder aggressively. "Get the other horse back to the stables and stop laughing."

"I am sorry, but I want to stay. This is the most fun I've had since you brought the wolves home."

"Larkin. This is no time for jokes."

"I am not joking," he said with a wide grin on his face.

Alexandra took a deep breath, looked up to the sky and shook her head. "Give me strength," she whispered before turning and walking back towards Eleanor. "Are you coming with me or not?" Alexandra asked as she patted the animal's neck. "I assure you there is nothing to be worried about. Snow is the most docile horse I have met. He will do nothing to harm you."

Eleanor looked at the horse who snorted loudly and then back at Alexandra. She unfolded her arms from under her chest and gave up. There was no use fighting. Alexandra didn't seem like she was about to be lenient.

Alexandra smiled arrogantly before grabbing hold of Eleanor's hand, which she placed on top of the saddle's horn, making her squeeze it tightly. "Grab hold of the horn, then place your foot on the stirrup." She ordered and waited for Eleanor to follow her instructions. "Good, now at the count of three you are going to pull yourself up and sit on the saddle and do not worry about the animal. He can hold you steady," Alexandra commanded as she moved behind Eleanor and grabbed hold of the seat and the horse's mane. She steadied the horse, trapping Eleanor between her tall body and the horse. "At the count of three…"

Eleanor was out of herself. The feeling of the person behind her, almost grinding their body together was too much for her to handle. Her hands trembled as they reached for the horse seat, her breath got caught in her throat. She could feel Alexandra behind her, breathing into her neck, speaking close to her ear. Eleanor was sure that she would faint if she didn't get some cold air on her. She shook her head a bit and totally ignored Alexandra's small count. When it came down to three, she was standing in the same position she had been three seconds ago.

"Are you alright?"

Eleanor looked at the floor before nodding. "Yes. I was just preparing myself physically just in case I fell," she lied. She was too fixated in the heat emanating from Alexandra's body to even notice that she was talking.

Alexandra rolled her eyes and shook her head. "Again. At the count of three. One…" She looked at Eleanor and noticed she wasn't listening again. The younger woman's lips were parted as if she was in some sort of a trance. She scoffed in annoyance, grabbed Eleanor by her waist, and without any warning, she lifted her up and placed her on top of the horse, ignoring Eleanor's surprised scream.

"There we go, see? Easy!" Alexandra said before patting the horse's hind, making the animal move forward.

"You want to scare me to death; I just know it." Eleanor let out a soft yelp as Snow took a couple of steps forward. "Wait. No, no, stay!" She turned to Alexandra, who simply stared at her, hands on waist, chuckling at how petrified she was. "Do not just stand there! Make it stop moving."

"Lady Stownar," Alexandra whined. "Grab the reins." She directed before moving to Snow and grabbing his mane and stopping him from moving altogether. "You have to know that the horse will only do what you want it to do. Also, do not scream, or it will become nervous."

Alexandra turned around to look at Larkin. The man was red like a tomato, his eyes were filled to the brink with upcoming tears, and his shoulders raised and fell. She walked over to him, poked his chest enough to make him hiss.

"Will you stop poking me so hard? That's going to leave a bloody mark!"

Alexandra ignored his complaint and grabbed him by his vest. "If you dare laugh, I swear I will take Stick's biggest dump and leave it under your pillow tonight. Are we clear?"

"Crystal," he answered before rubbing his chest.

"I do not know when I will be back."

"Where are you taking her, Alex?" he asked with a hint of teasing and raising his eyebrow.

She didn't answer, she went back to Eleanor and tried not to smile at how stiff the woman looked on the saddle while the horse swayed from side to side, not used to the weight it was carrying. "I am coming, Lady Stownar,"

"This thing will not stop moving, and I cannot get down, so you better get over here and stop it!"

Alexandra chuckled as she grabbed the horn and pulled herself up quickly until she was sitting behind Eleanor and strapping her securely with her legs. She moved one hand over her waist and pulled her in closer to her chest. "Are you comfortable?"

Eleanor wanted to scream "no!". She wanted to slap Alexandra across the face for touching her in such an intimate way, she wanted to push Alexandra for being so close to her and violating her personal space, but she didn't. She was enjoying having Alexandra this close to her and taking control of the situation. "Yes. I am quite comfortable even if I am sitting sideways…" she looked down at the ground and closed her eyes. She turned around and hid her face on Alexandra's shoulder. "I really do not think I can get used to the height."

Alexandra shrugged. "We are up on a Shire stallion. This is one of the biggest and tallest horses around." Alexandra explained before tugging the reins a bit. She clicked her tongue and kicked the horse to get him going. "Other than the fact that you have basically done something against your will, are you feeling alright?"

"I feel lightheaded."

"Do you want to cancel our little outing?"

"No! I—" Eleanor groaned and rubbed her forehead in frustration. "I've never done this before. This is my first time on a horse."

"I see. Well, I can assure you that you are in good hands. I will not let you fall; I truly hope you enjoy the place I am about to take you. It is rather beautiful. My mother used to love it."

Eleanor raised her gaze up and stared at Alexandra's handsome face. "What is it?"

"Now that is a surprise, I do not want to spoil it."

"A surprise?"

Alexandra chuckled and looked down at Eleanor. "Do you like surprises?"

"If it came from someone else, then maybe. I do not know what is going through that head of yours, and I do not know what your idea of a surprise is," Eleanor said, earning a heartfelt laugh from Alexandra. Eleanor was taken aback by the sudden burst. It was a rather refreshing change from the usual serious demeanor.

Eleanor studied her husband's face. She examined every expression line on Alexandra's face. She mostly noticed that her husband had the smoothest skin she had seen in her life. It was impressive for someone that is supposed to shave. She also noticed that Alexandra's face, other than being incredibly striking, had some delicate features to it. For example, the lips. Eleanor gulped as she stared at them. They were fine yet soft on the sides. They seemed to go up a bit, forming a soft and subtle cat-like curve that Eleanor wanted to touch with her fingertips.

"What is it? Do I have something on my face?"

Eleanor gasped and shook her head. Her face grew red by the embarrassment of thinking that she was just caught gawking at Alexandra. "Oh, no. Nothing at all."

"Alright, then."

Eleanor looked in front of her and saw the sudden dense vegetation around them. She frowned at that and looked up to see the trees' canopies covering the sky. "It is a forest."

"Yes, it is. But this isn't what I wanted you to see."

Eleanor nodded and placed her hands on her lap as she kept looking around. Yet, as much as she wanted to stop herself, her eyes went back to gaze at Alexandra's face. "Why are you so quiet?"

"Quiet? I think since you came to my house, I've been pretty talkative."

"Maybe I am comparing you to Larkin."

"Larkin never shuts his mouth," Alexandra mumbled before snuggling close to Eleanor.

Eleanor chuckled and nodded. "Yes, but I feel like you do not want me to notice something about you."

Alexandra grew tense yet shrugged, trying to act natural. "Because I am quiet?"

"Of course."

"What do you want to talk about?"

"Well, for once, why did you decide to marry me? I mean, I have never heard of you back in town."

Alexandra faced her and tilted her head to the side as she gave her a questioning gaze. "You never heard my name? Now I feel insulted."

"My mother said that you were one of the richest men in town, but I never pay attention to those things." She sighed. "I guess I was too preoccupied with my father's gambling to be paying attention to the latest gossip."

Alexandra nodded, satisfied with what she said. "Well," she began before clearing her throat, "I do not have a good reputation in town."

"Oh? And why is that?"

"I am not sure. I guess it is the fact that I never attend any sorts of gatherings."

"Ah. You do not enjoy socializing?"

"Not at all. I do not like to be surrounded by hypocrites talking about how perfect their lives are." Alexandra sighed and moved on the saddle as Snow walked over a tall mound of dirt, making Eleanor grab hold of Alexandra's forearm to steady herself and not fall. "You do not seem to be like the people in town, though."

"I wasn't much out there either. I was always locked up in my house reading."

"You read?"

"Yes, my father taught me."

"I am happily surprised by this. What do you like to read?" Alexandra asked, slipping her hand over Eleanor's stomach once again, holding her steady as Snow walked over a large tree branch. The heat coming from Eleanor made her want to get closer, to smell her in, and wonder what she felt like when she was pressed against her.

"Anything really, but my favorite genre is romance," Eleanor answered as she relaxed in Alexandra's arms while absentmindedly rubbing the hand that was over her stomach. "What about you?"

"Mostly business-related stuff."

"How boring!"

"You got that right, but I enjoy it. It— it helps me keep my mind busy."

"You like to stay in the study a whole lot. I wonder what troubles you so much that you want to keep your mind busy at all times?" Eleanor shuddered as she felt the vibration of a deep chuckle escape from inside Alexandra's chest.

"You will know eventually, Lady Stownar. I think it is too early in our marriage for me to burden you with unnecessary problems. Especially when those problems are my own." Alexandra looked down and noticed that Eleanor was still looking up at her. A hint of empathy glistened into her blue eyes, which made Alexandra, futilely move away from her. "What?"

"I know that our marriage was completely out of nowhere, not planned, not thought through, but we are stuck together, Alexander. I cannot live knowing that my husband is going through tough times and that I in no way helped to ease those troubles. I am not like those women back in town who wait on their husbands to fix everything. I am indeed different, and I will protect what is mine."

Alexandra raised her eyebrow and leaned back. "Yours?"

"Are we married?"

"I believe so."

"Then, Alexander, you are mine as I am yours. You are going to have to face that fact one day. Your problems are mine, and my problems are yours. Let us try to make this as easy for both of us as possible. I can see the strength that you have inside of you but believe me." She smiled and leaned closer. "I am stronger."

CHAPTER EIGHT

Time was dull and slow when Alexandra wasn't around. The mansion went on with their routine, like a city alive with their town's people. The maids cooked dinner and the male servants made sure the horses were taken care of. Some servants doubled as guards for the night, yet today, they went on with the chores as if daylight could mask bad things that could happen in a secluded mansion.

It was a matter of time before something would happen. In the meantime, the only thing left to do was to wait, as Larkin did ever since he found Alexandra in the town mansion's stables.

He waited at the front door of the mansion. He sat on the stairs, his hands lazily petting the grey fur of the female wolf while his eyes were glued to the grand gates that surrounded the mansion. He moved his foot from side to side, with the same rhythm as a watch's second hand.

His sole duty in life was to protect the Dowry family. He had a lot to repay Alexandra's father for after he took him in when he was a boy. That was all he knew. His only determination in life was to keep Alexandra safe even if it meant forgetting about his own personal needs.

Larkin sighed, grabbed his pocket watch, and looked at the time. "They have been gone for quite some time, right?" Larkin asked the wolf next to him. The only thing he heard as a reply was a single whine. "I am bored too, pup," he added before pulling on Pebbles' fur. "I guess we should make a round."

He stood up from the stairs and patted his trousers. Pebbles quickly stood beside him and began to wag her tail as if waiting for a command from the second leader of the "pack."

"Where in heaven's name is Stick, Pebble?"

She whined before circling around him.

"Go look for him," Larkin commanded, and without time to spare, the wolf darted to the east side of the mansion's front yard. For a couple of minutes, Larkin heard the rustling and yapping of both wolves until noticing something wasn't right. The male wolf ran over to him, holding something in his snout. Larkin frowned, got on one knee, and studied Stick. The animal was quite excited over something. "Stop. Stop it. Stay still, Stick!" he almost growled as he grabbed him by his ear and held him. "What is this?" he asked as he snatched a piece of cloth from Stick's snout.

"Where in heaven's name did you get this from?" he asked as he looked at the ragged piece of clothing. Larkin decided that it was white, but it was so defiled with blood and grass stains that it was hard to tell what it was from. The man frowned, pulled out his powdered gun, and held it close to his chest. "Stick…" He looked down at the wolf and placed the cloth near his snout. "Where did you find this?"

Both wolves were looking up at him, panting with their long tongues rolled out of their snouts. They seemed to be having a wonderful time like when they went hunting in the woods. Stick, on the other hand, sprinted back to the trees and bushes outside of the mansion with Pebbles and Larkin close behind. As Larkin ran after both wolves, he kept going over his head what he was supposed to do, just in case someone came to attack him. Should he have let the wolves do their job? Should he have shot? Should he have screamed for help? He frowned and then began to slow down as he saw Stick sniffing the ground.

"What is it, boy?"

Pebbles turned to him, barked, and then went back to sniff the ground near Stick. The male wolf scraped the ground with his front paws.

Larkin walked over to them and looked down at the land underneath him. "Someone was here," he whispered as he got down and saw bloodstains on the floor. "Could it be the man that tried to get inside the mansion some nights ago?"

Stick barked and moved closer to Larkin as if wanting to get a reward for his excellent investigation.

"I will take that as a yes." He smiled and patted Stick on his neck. "Good boy. You scared him off and got a good bite out of him too."

Pebbles pushed her snout to Larkin's face, demanding some attention as she reminded him that she had also protected the mansion nights before.

"Yes, yes. You too, Pebbles. Good girl." He pulled her snout close and kissed it, earning a growl from the jealous Stick. "What? I do not see a ring on her finger." He chuckled and stood up straight as he looked around the forest. "We better tell Alex."

***

"How much longer?" Eleanor asked. She wanted to finally be able to untie herself from this awkward situation. After her sorry attempt to get her husband to open up, she did exactly the opposite. Alexandra was quiet and red, but what bothered Eleanor the most was the fact she wasn't sure of the cause of her crimson face. Was it heat, anger, or embarrassment?

"Soon," Alexandra answered, trying to act as collected as she possibly could. This woman was going to be the death of her. She sentenced her own execution the moment she signed those wedding papers at the church. Eleanor was very extroverted, everything that Alexandra wasn't, and damn it, she was moving against her way too much. She couldn't even think straight. Alexandra would never admit it, but she had passed the same tree five times already.

"My bottom is growing numb."

"Mine too, but I am not complaining."

"Your bottom should be used to this kind of seat. Mine is not. I have all the right to complain."

"True, but you are not making this enjoyable for either of us with your complaining," Alexandra refuted before letting out a relieved sigh when she saw the meadow opening. She quickly stopped her horse, which earned a surprised yelp from Eleanor. "We are here."

Eleanor raised her gaze from her lap to the row of dense trees in front of her. She frowned and turned to look up at Alexandra. "I do not see anything."

"And you will not. Not yet," Alexandra said before taking out a handkerchief from her vest.

"What are you doing? What is that for?"

Alexandra raised the handkerchief and looked at Eleanor. "Can I?"

Eleanor sighed and closed her eyes before nodding. "I guess we will not start moving forward unless we start to trust each other, right?"

"Whatever you say. I just want to take advantage of this whole situation," Alexandra said before covering Eleanor's eyes with the handkerchief and tying it behind her head. "Is it too tight?"

Eleanor shook her head as she touched the soft cloth over her eyes. She also enjoyed the scent it carried. It smelled like pure wet wood with a hint of a clean floral scent.

"It is fine," she whispered before inhaling the natural perfume once again.

Alexandra grabbed hold of the reins again and clicked her tongue. The horse began to walk again, making Eleanor lose her balance. The younger woman's hand came to tightly grab Alexandra's forearms. She leaned on her, resting her cheek on Alexandra's chest as she gasped. "I was about to fall!"

"I guess we will not start moving forward unless we start to trust each other, am I right, Lady Stownar?"

Eleanor couldn't help but smile and pinch Alexandra's arm. "Touché, but still! I could've fallen backward and just died."

Alexandra had to shake her head and ignore Eleanor's words as she walked past the last tree that was used as the entrance to the grand meadow.

As always, Alexandra had to take a moment to admire the vast and gorgeous site of the green and natural floral rug. She took a deep breath and swiftly jumped from Snow.

"Lady Stownar, I am going to help you off the horse," Alexandra announced, knowing that the younger woman was going to get anxious if she grabbed her and placed her on the ground.

Eleanor moved her hands around as she waited for Alexandra to hold hers. Instead, she felt two strong arms wrap around her waist. She let out a surprised yelp and quickly wrapped her own arms around Alexandra's broad shoulders as she set her down. This was Eleanor's perfect opportunity to surround herself with that beautiful scent this person carried, so she pressed her nose to Alexandra's shoulder and inhaled again. Never in her wildest dream did she think that she would have been attracted to the smell that this person carried. It was intoxicating, to say the least, and soothing. She could imagine herself being wrapped in that scent every single night as she settled to sleep, knowing that her husband would be close to her.

Alexandra felt a sudden rush of heat pool in her stomach. The closeness of their bodies was inebriating. Her hands became tense. She was on the verge of planting her lips on her and devouring her amidst the meadow, wanting only to see and hear this woman writhe in pleasure. The vivid vision rushed through her like a bolt of electricity, blinding her of all common sense.

She shuddered as she inhaled shakily and slowly pulled Eleanor away. She needed to take hold of her own actions before she did something that she would regret. As she shifted away from Eleanor, she thought of something to make her wake up from her daydream.

"Do I smell funny?" She almost had an aneurysm knowing she had just asked the most mood-killing question in all existence.

Eleanor was slapped back to reality by Alexandra's voice. Still blindfolded, the brunette took a couple of steps back, but was stopped with Alexandra's iron grip. She held her in place, knowing full well that if Eleanor continued walking, she would probably fall.

"Lady Stownar. It is not wise for you to be walking around with your eyes closed. I am going to ask you to please, take it nice and slow," Alexandra whispered, still lightheaded by the sudden closeness. She exhaled loudly and commanded her body to pay attention and stop acting like a hormone raging teenager. She squeezed Eleanor's hand, pulled her away from the horse and led her to the middle of the large field. "Are you nervous?"

"Why do you ask?"

"You are shaking."

Eleanor sighed. "Well, maybe I am nervous, but just a bit."

Alexandra had to smile. She stopped walking altogether and then she let go of Eleanor's hand. Slowly, she moved behind her and took off the blindfold.

Eleanor's face lit up the second, her blue eyes roamed through the immense space of flowers and grass. The trees circled the place as if guarding it of any human that might dare and damage the pristine and unaltered beauty. Her jaw dropped in awe as she turned around, admiring every inch of this magical place.

While Eleanor took in the beauty of the place, Alexandra's eyes were fixated on the beauty of the woman in front of her. She studied the younger woman's expression carefully, seeing if she was indeed happy with the place. Finally, their eyes locked together and everything went silent inside Alexandra's mind. All that mattered was the laughter coming from Eleanor Stownar.

And just like a switch, Alexandra shuddered at the idea of losing this sense of happiness that had invaded. She took a step forward and moved her hands to Eleanor only to have them clasped by the smaller woman. She didn't want this moment to escape or be damaged by words. She simply watched and admired how someone she had just met a couple of days ago, had managed to dig into her core.

"I take it you like the place?" Alexandra asked, her eyes never leaving Eleanor's amazed glance.

"Are you joking? This is the most beautiful thing I have seen in my life!"

Alexandra smiled and whispered, "Yes, it is." Her eyes were fixated on Eleanor's parted lips. Finding herself so vulnerable brought her back in time and space. She shook her head and slowly moved away, giving Eleanor enough space to let her investigate and roam. She, on the other hand, sat down on the sea of flowers and leaned back, crossing her legs and resting her head on her arms as she faced the clear sky.

"Is this part of the mansion, Alex?"

"Yes. Larkin showed me this place ten years ago. I am used to its beauty by now."

"I do not think I could ever get used to this," Eleanor whispered as she began to walk around the immense field.

Alexandra turned to her side and leaned her face on her hand as she watched Eleanor looking down at the flowers. It seemed that she was trying her best not to step on any of them.

"On second thought." She saw Eleanor turn to her with curiosity on her face. "I think the meadow looks a whole lot more beautiful today."

"Oh, really? Why is today different?"

"It is because you are here today with me, Lady Stownar."

Eleanor quickly looked away and tried to hide her red face. "Thank you for bringing me here."

"It is my pleasure," Alexandra said as a clear understatement.

Eleanor sighed and looked up to the sky before shrugging. She raised her arms over her head and threw herself back, falling on the flower-covered ground. The flower petals rose when she landed, covering both Alexandra and her. Eleanor giggled and brushed them off her dress but froze when she saw Alexandra staring down at her. "What is it?"

"I am still wrapping around my head the idea that we are married and that you truly want to get to know someone as boring as I am."

"Wouldn't it be better if we did know each other, though?"

Alexandra couldn't help but grin. She leaned on her side and moved her hand to pull a flower petal out of Eleanor's hair. Alexandra thought her words over as her eyes trailed a path over Eleanor's hair down to her lips. She stopped there, spellbound, and curious about how soft they were. "My name is Alexander Dowry III. I own a small, yet successful, horse-trading business that my father started along with my grandfather. I inherited the business when my father passed away ten years ago."

"Wait," Eleanor interrupted, grabbing Alexandra's hand. "You inherited the entire thing when you were a teenager?"

"That is correct."

"How did you manage?"

"Larkin was my father's right hand. He helped me along the way, teaching me the basics, and after I was old enough, I took the reins of the business, no pun intended."

Eleanor snorted and rolled her eyes.

"And I have managed it from then on."

"What about your mother?"

Alexandra sighed, grabbed hold of Eleanor's hand, and rubbed her thumb over the wedding ring. "My mother died when I was a child, Lady Stownar."

"Oh. I— I am sorry to hear that. I bet your mother was good with you. You are very protective of her memory."

"My mother was a saint. She was the epitome of what a good parent should be. My father was always busy, but my mother..." Alexandra moved back and finally laid back on the ground. "I can still remember her voice when she read stories to me, her laughter, her piano lessons..."

"You play the piano? Are you joking?"

"I haven't touched a piano since my 14th birthday, but I can assure you that if I decide to touch one again, I will play it."

"Well, we have something in common. My father thought that all ladies should learn how to play an instrument to entertain their husbands. So, he enrolled me in violin classes."

Alexandra's eyebrow twitched a bit. "To entertain?"

"Oh, yes. On those boring nights, a husband and a wife should look for a way to entertain themselves, and what better way than with some music?"

Alexandra couldn't help but laugh. She covered her eyes with her arm, trying her hardest to contain herself. She wasn't used to laughing, at least not so loud.

"What is it? What's so funny?"

"Lady Stownar!" Alexandra turned and took in a deep breath and patted her chest before continuing. "Lady Stownar, please. There are many ways a husband and a wife can entertain each other."

"How should I know, Alex?" Eleanor asked this time she moved forward enough to pull some grass away from Alexandra's hair. "We haven't been together that long."

"Well, then. I guess we can entertain each other."

Eleanor's cheeks became crimson red.

"I can ask the servants to dust the piano."

"Oh." The disappointment in Eleanor's voice was too comical for Alexandra to handle. She truly looked like she was pained by Alexandra's joke.

"Lady Stownar, I was joking."

"Oh, I know you were." She sighed and closed her eyes.

"What about you? It is your turn to talk."

Eleanor raised her shoulders. "I am an only daughter. My mother married a man that was twenty years older than she was. They met the day of their marriage." She stopped to look at Alexandra. "Ring any bells?"

"Continue."

"There is nothing more to say, Alex."

"What about your mother? What is she like?"

Eleanor pursed her lips. "She is like any other rich woman in town. Greedy, angry, and thinks too much about what people would say."

"Ah, yes, I know a couple of those."

"Really, I just—" Eleanor sighed and locked eyes with Alexandra, who seemed to be a bit distracted by Eleanor's lips. "Alex?"

"Hmm?"

"Are you listening to me?"

"A bit."

Eleanor chuckled and pushed herself up into a sitting position. "Thank you for bringing me here. It really is a beautiful place."

"You really liked it, huh? Well, we can always come back again some other time. We can bring some food and have a little picnic. You can bring your books and read or even your violin."

"My old violin broke some years back, and all my books are back at my mother's house."

Alexandra frowned at that and sat up also. "I see."

"It is getting late, Alex. Shouldn't we go back?"

Alexandra tilted her head and looked up to the sky. Some clouds were starting to gather, and it appeared as if it would start to rain soon. She nodded understandingly and stood up swiftly. She patted her pants and then offered her hand to Eleanor. "Let us go home."

***

Larkin heard the door of the mansion opening and closing, followed by Eleanor and Alexandra's laughter as they talked amongst themselves. Larkin stood from the living room sofa and made his way through the dining room, over to the grand entrance next to the stairs. As he walked in, he frowned in confusion as he saw Alexandra and Eleanor talking so freely and smiling at one another as if they had known each other all their lives.

He scoffed, crossed his arms over his chest, and leaned on the entrance of the dining room in pure awe.

What kind of magical spell did Eleanor use to make Alexandra smile like that? It has been too many years since he had seen a smile paint the face of that woman. He cleared his throat loudly, which made both women jump in surprise.

"Larkin!" Alexandra was the first one to react.

"Have fun?"

Eleanor looked down to the ground and moved away from Alexandra and over to the large stairs. "I am going to retire to my chamber for now."

Alexandra's neck almost snapped as she turned to look at Eleanor. She frowned and licked her lips nervously. "W—will you be joining us for dinner?"

"Of course, Alex. See you then!" Eleanor said, and without much ado, she left.

Larkin raised a skeptical eyebrow and stared at Alexandra; his lips pursed teasingly. "Well, I take it you had fun."

"Oh my God." She took her overcoat off and placed it hung on the coat rack next to the door. "That woman…"

"Shh!" Larkin waved his hand to shut her up and grabbed her by the vest, pulling her closer to him. "Before you start gushing about her, we need to talk about something more important," he whispered close to her face.

"What's wrong, Larkin?"

"Someone was snooping around the mansion again," he told Alexandra before pulling the piece of cloth from his pockets for her to see. "And Stick took a bite out of him."

Alexandra nodded, acknowledging, and turned to the stairs. She made sure that Eleanor was out of sight before she jerked her head at Larkin. "Let us go to my study."

Before leaving, Larkin opened the door to let the two large beasts out of the entrance. He thought it would be better to have them running out and about just in case someone else got the idea of entering the perimeters of the mansion. Then, he turned to follow Alexandra to her chamber, where he closed the door behind him once they entered.

Alexandra moved to the desk that once belonged to her father, sat down, and let out a tired sigh before turning her green eyes to Larkin.

She watched how he tiredly sat down on the leather seats in front of the desk. "What is it?"

"We had an intruder. We are not sure who it was or how many." He stopped, grabbed the cloth again and placed it on the desk. "What I know is that Stick gave him a new one."

Alexandra took the cloth and stared at it for a couple of minutes before bringing it to her nose.

"Alexandra," Larkin resumed his explanation, yet calling her by her real name made the woman quickly turn his attention to him. She knew well when he was in a serious mood and when he was joking.

This time, he was dead serious.

"A couple of weeks before your wedding, one of the servants that guards the backyard told me that someone tried to sneak inside. Luckily, it was Pebbles who attacked whoever tried to get in."

"This is a cheap fabric," Alexandra stated as she rubbed her thumb over the cloth.

"Alexandra, the only person that keeps popping in my head is Cassius."

"My cousin?" She snorted. "It is not my cousin. When Uncle William died, I am sure that he left something for him. Why would he try to sneak and rob my home?"

"Are you stupid? He is not going to come here himself and try to get in. Robbing is not even the purpose. Your uncle planted a seed in that boy. He is as curious about you as your uncle was. William Dowry was a lazy son of a whore, and his son, I am sure, is just like him. They didn't work for the business like your father did, and they or should I say, Cassius, wants in on that money you are generating through your father's horse-trading business."

"Obviously."

"Cassius is probably sending spies to see any vulnerability. He wants to hurt you. Maybe he heard about your marriage, and since your uncle knew about your mother only having one child, Cassius is just as curious."

"You know what Larkin, if you would've told me this a couple of days back, I would've just let it pass as if it was nothing, but now—" Alexandra scoffed and threw the cloth back at Larkin. "I have been working on this business for over ten years now. My father worked hard."

"I should know."

"Double up the servants at night. The wolves shall always remain outside. No more babying them."

"Finally," Larkin teased.

"Yet, you must understand we are not sure if it is really Cassius. It could be a common thief."

Larkin nodded. "Yes, of course, but we have to have an idea of whom it might be."

"We cannot point fingers. As soon as we find out something else, then we will do what needs to be done, alright?"

"Sounds good to me, Alex." He smiled and tilted his head to the side. "But tell me, how was your little escapade?"

Alexandra grinned back at him, leaned back on her seat, and placed her boots on top of the desk. "Wonderful."

"Well, well, what is with the change of attitude? If I remember correctly, you were not really up for the idea of getting married."

"You were right, Larkin. She is..." She stopped to think her words over. "Annoying, yet perfect."

"If she is annoying, then she is not perfect, Alex."

"No, you do not understand. That woman is so centered into digging out all my secrets, and I just find it hilarious how she keeps asking."

"You do not sound annoyed."

"I do not?"

"No. Hell, I would even dare to say that you sound in love."

Alexandra pursed her lips and waved her hand. "Shut up. In love? I just met her."

"Well, when you are in a good mood, you can be rather lovable."

"Oh, Larkin, thank you," Alexandra said, placing both her hands over her heart and pouting at Larkin. "But my heart belongs only to Nana."

Larkin snorted and leaned his head back as he laughed. "I am serious. You are a good person. If anyone got a chance to know you for who you really are, they would have no problem falling in love with you, and, of course, I bet the same goes with Lady Stownar."

Alexandra sighed and dropped her arms before looking away into a random spot on her desk. "She is lovable, but— Damn it, Larkin, I cannot get that close to her! I just cannot. What would happen once she asks for more? For intimacy?"

"How should I know?"

"I cannot fall for her. I just cannot."

"Clearly, you are already lusting for her. I mean, I cannot blame you. That woman is gorgeous. Hell, if you ever get a divorce I—"

"Do not dare say what you are about to say, or I will blow your head off with the gun I have right here inside this desk."

Larkin closed his mouth quickly and swallowed hard. The darkness that spread over Alexandra's face was enough to make a jolt of fear run down his spine. He raised his hands up in defense and shook his head. "Forgive me. That was out of line, Alex."

Alexandra's face relaxed suddenly as if she had just acknowledged what had just happened. She exhaled loudly and leaned back on her chair. "I— I am sorry, I overreacted."

"No, I should not have said that. I would have reacted the same way," he muttered before silence consumed the study. "I am going to go now."

"Larkin, wait—" Alexandra called out before standing up and walking towards him. Without warning, she threw her arms around him and brought him in for a tight hug. "I am sorry."

"Do not fret it, kid," Larkin told her as he patted her back softly, confused by the sudden display of affection.

"I do not want a girl to come between us," Alexandra said with a hint of tease in her voice.

Larkin snorted. "Nothing can come between us. So, relax." He moved away, touched her face, and grinned. "I just want to see you happy, that is all that matters to me."

"I will try to be."

Larkin sighed, nodded, and opened the door of the study, leaving Alexandra alone.

***

Nighttime came, digging through the mansion like a thief. Creeping in through the crevices of the old stone walls, blowing off the candle flames that illuminated the long halls that were witness to the whispers and wonderings of the servitude. The whispers came and went as the servants moved their things to sleep in their respective chambers. Their yawns echoed in the last hall of the forgotten stairwell. They moved like a mouse, wanting nothing more than to leave in the quietest matter. They didn't want their master to come out screaming for peace and quiet.

Yes, the master is married.
He is?
Didn't you hear?
So, that gorgeous lady is his wife?
Wait, have you seen her?
Oh yes…

Doors closed and the whispers began to die down as each minute passed. Everyone mumbled their last words of the conversation before the tiredness of the day fell upon them.

The important people on the other side of the mansion moved about their chambers tiredly. Each one had their own routine that they followed religiously. Larkin would clean his boots and set them aside for the next day. Nana would pray silently, sitting on her bed.

Eleanor brushed her hair a hundred times, Alexandra stood in front of her window, which faced the large mansion gates.

Alexandra undid the binds of her chest and let out a pleasurable sigh as she unbound her breasts. She closed her eyes and inhaled as the night air engulfed her, undressing her, and leaving her as what she really was. She walked around her chamber, barefooted as she pulled out what she thought might be her outfit for tomorrow morning. She then sat down on her bed and ran her fingers through the tangled mane until she was satisfied.

Nighttime was here and Alexandra dreaded to go to sleep due to the unapologetic nightmares that haunted her very core. The images would repeatedly play in her tired mind like an endless time loop. She was constantly opening another door to escape and saw the same scene of her mother begging her to run. Yet this nightmare was different.

Alexandra leaned back, closed her eyes, and let her body relax on her bed. She was finally free of all the stress of pretending throughout the day. As her imprudent thoughts came to a slow, the voices of fear and anger quieted down and in came the sound of piano chords.

She sighed as her fingers moved slowly and clumsy at first but then harder and more secure. The song in her head began as a whisper of a long-forgotten memory and then turned into raging emotion. Her fingers became alive with the black and white teeth of the grand piano. Her eyes now opened, trailed over each note, analyzing, thinking, and mastering it repeatedly as her head bobbed up and down and from side to side.

"That is enough for today, Alex."

Alexandra froze and sat up straight. She rubbed her sweaty hands over her dark pants, not before closing the piano and standing up. Her eyes searched for the person who had just spoken to her, but she found herself inside a dark living room. She swallowed hard and found the entrance of the dining room slightly open. She heard footsteps; people were running from side to side.

"Hey."

She jumped and turned around only to look eyes with dark blue eyes. "Lady Stownar?"

Eleanor frowned and moved her hand to close the dining room door behind Alexandra. "I am here. Relax," she ordered before her hands met Alexandra's sweaty cheek. "Do you have a fever? Are you alright?"

Alexandra frowned in confusion. "What are you doing here?"

"What do you mean, what am I doing here? I live here."

The lights were on now. Alexandra saw and quickly recognized the furniture of the living room of her own home. She turned back to Eleanor whose hands were now clasped securely on the nape of her neck. "I am sorry, I-"

"I am here," Eleanor interrupted while her eyes traveled down to Alexandra's parted lips. "I am here," she repeated and pulled onto Alexandra. Her soft lips rubbed against Alexandra's quivering ones. Alexandra's hand came to rest on top of Eleanor's hips as she pulled her in...

The silence in the air was cut with the sound of a gunshot that echoed inside Alexandra's mind and pierced her ears, leaving the aftermath of a deafening shrill.

Her screams woke her up.

Alexandra pushed herself into a sitting position. Her heart pounded inside her chest and in her head like a drum. Drops of sweat rolled down her face and neck while the heat of her body asphyxiated her. She pulled the covers off and stumbled to the ground as her shaky legs gave out underneath her.

"Fuck!" She gasped for air and coughed as her sharp intakes got caught up in her throat. Slowly, her heartbeat dropped down to its normal rhythm while her legs stopped shaking altogether. She looked up at the window and saw the new shades of orange that painted the once dark sky. Grabbing unto her bed, she pulled herself up and grabbed hold of her pocket watch. It was already morning, and once again, she couldn't get a good night's rest. This time, the nightmare had decided to change characters.

With a groan, she threw herself into her bed and covered her eyes with her arm. If she was lucky, she could catch a few more minutes of sleep before Nana woke her up, yet a soft knock interrupted her train of thought. She propped herself up on her elbows and listened attentively.

"Alexander?"

She swallowed hard and stood up. She padded her way to the door that connected her chamber with Eleanor's. Her hand lingered over the doorknob, yet she didn't open the door. She rested her head on the hardwood as she thought if she should answer or not.

"Alexander, are you awake?"

Alexandra sighed and nodded before clearing her throat and answering her with her deep voice. "Yes. I am here."

Eleanor smiled from the other side of the door. "Are you alright?"

"I had a nightmare, I am fine now," she lied, the flashback of her nightmare hit her at full force. She felt Eleanor's kiss and heard her voice. Alexandra opened her eyes and touched the wood of the door with her open palm as if wanting to touch Eleanor's face. "I am sorry I woke you up."

"I am fine, do not worry," Eleanor whispered before sighing and moving away from the door. "If you need anything—"

"I know. I— I am going to try and sleep a bit more, if that's alright with you, Lady Stownar."

"Oh, of course." Eleanor frowned at the sudden change.

"I am sorry, I just really need to rest," Alexandra clarified as she pushed herself off the door. She clearly heard Eleanor wishing her a good night, yet the fear of her nightmare crept back on her. She slipped under her covers and laid on her back. She whispered a soft prayer, begging to whatever deity was up in the heavens to release her from the nightmares and to not have Eleanor be the one in those dreams.

***

The awkwardness during breakfast was suffocating. Larkin noticed it right away and decided to stay quiet and not say any of his jokes unless one of the two women started talking. He ate quietly while eyeing both Alexandra and Eleanor.

Alexandra's baggie eyes exposed that she hadn't had a good night's sleep. Eleanor's body language signaled that she was upset about something. He cleared his throat and grabbed his cup of coffee before taking a long sip.

"Alexander, did you have a good night's sleep, after all?"

Larkin turned his eyes from Eleanor to Alexandra.

Alexandra was in the process of chewing a piece of toast before she swallowed. "Yes, thank you for asking."

Larkin then looked at Eleanor.

"I am glad I was rather worried when I heard you last night."

"That's quite alright," Alexandra answered before noticing Larkin's eyes on her. "Larkin, is there something wrong?"

"Oh, no, I just. Noticed that you both were quiet."

"I am always quiet."

Eleanor chuckled as she noticed that both Larkin and Alexandra were about to start arguing. Suddenly one of the wolves outside let out a loud howl that made her jump in her chair.

"Still not used to the wolves, Lady Stownar?" Larkin asked with a mischievous smile painted on his lips.

"How did you manage to get those animals under control? Where did you get them?"

Larkin gulped down a piece of cheese before pointing to Alexandra. "Alexander just came out of nowhere with these two pups wrapped up in his coat. That was ten years ago, since then, Stick and Pebbles became part of the family. Am I right?"

Alexandra nodded. "Yes. I found them in the forest behind the mansion," Alexandra added before looking down at her tea.

"That's cute. I bet they do not bother you a lot," Eleanor stated.

"Oh, they do. They are animals after all, but the key here is to let them know who the leader of the pack is. I am the one that feeds them and the one that disciplines them. They are good receptors of emotions too, so when they see me angry they know they have to leave me alone."

"Are they overprotective of their pack leader?" Eleanor asked with a hint of teasing in her voice. She dared not to look at Alexandra since she knew that there was a subtle smile on her lips. She wouldn't want her husband to think she was mocking him.

"I would like to think that they are. They have always been my companions when I am outside, but I am sure they will be your guardians too,

Lady Stownar. Those animals can tell when someone is special to their master," Alexandra said before eyeing Eleanor mischievously.

"I can be another pack leader?"

Alexandra shrugged and said, "Two is always better than one. Of course, you must keep in mind that if you act like them, if you are rolling around with them on the dirt like Larkin does, then they will think you are just like them. Meaning," she looked over at Larkin and laughed, "they will piss on your pants."

"Are you calling me an animal?" Larkin asked.

"More or less…"

"Excuse me, Master Dowry. You've received some mail."

Alexandra turned around to look at one of the maids in the mansion. Larkin, on the other hand, stood up and walked over to the maid, taking the letters from her hand, and bowing his head to her, letting her know she could leave.

"Long time since we've got any mail," Larkin muttered as he sat down on the dining table, on Alexandra's left side, facing Eleanor. He waved the letter at Alexandra and raised his right eyebrow.

"What is it?"

Eleanor looked at Alexandra's serious face and then at Larkin. She patted her lips with a napkin and stood up from her chair. "I should leave you, gentlemen, alone."

Both Alexandra and Larkin stood up at the same time, but then frowned when they heard Eleanor's words. "Please stay, Lady Stownar," Alexandra cajoled Eleanor as she fanned her exposed neck with the letter. "You are not bothering us at all, is she, Larkin?"

"Not at all, Lady Stownar."

"Well, if you insist."

As soon as Eleanor was seated, both Larkin and Alexandra sat down. She fanned her neck one last time and then opened the letter, which was sealed with blue candle wax. She pulled the letter out and traced her eyes over the cursive written letter before frowning. "What in the world?" she murmured as she felt the heat of her temper rise like a fire.

"What's wrong?"

Alexandra looked at the letter again and then at Larkin. "My cousin wants to meet me at the town mansion up the state to talk to me. Here he is saying that he believes that the town mansion is part of the inheritance his father left him."

"That doesn't make sense. Cassius knows damn well that house belonged to your mother and, therefore, to your father."

"Well, the stupid man says that William told him on his death bed that the house belonged to him because his father gave it to him as a gift."

"Bollock!" Larkin yelled, slamming his fist on top of the wooden table.

Eleanor jumped a bit and placed both of her palms on the table as she tried to steady the plates and glasses. "I will put my hand on the fire for this. Your father would never give his wife's home as a gift! That house was too important to him!" Larkin sighed, rolling his eyes in annoyance.

"Is there any way to prove what he says is a lie?" Alexandra asked.

"The property titles are back in the town mansion. We can go and get them and slap your cousin Cassius with it."

Alexandra's gaze was blank. She heard Larkin's words and felt her breathing get caught in her throat. She swallowed hard and shook her head before placing the letter on the table. "He will be in the town mansion in a few days. He wants to meet there." Her eyes averted to Larkin back on Eleanor and then back to Larkin again. "I do not... I do not want to go to the town mansion."

Larkin's face went from confused to upset. The pain in Alexandra's voice made him regret his words, yet what hurt him was Alexandra's reaction when he said, "You have to face the mansion one way or another. Why not now? I can lead the way."

She shook her head a couple of times before taking a deep breath. She folded the letter back and then turned to glance at Eleanor.

The young woman's face reflected confusion and worriedness. "Alex?"

"Lady Stownar. I must take care of this... family matter. I guess Larkin and I will be going to the town mansion today and be back in a few days. We really need to do a thorough search of those papers."

"That sounds understandable. What I do not understand is the fact that it looks like you have seen a ghost. Are you alright?"

"I am fine, but I really need to get going."

"You do not want me to come with you?"

"No!"

Eleanor moved back a couple of steps before tilting her head to the side like a confused pup.

"I— umm..." Alexandra sighed and ran her fingers through her hair. "I am sorry. I just do not think that is a good place for you to go. The place has not been cleaned in almost two decades. I wouldn't want you to get sick."

Eleanor nodded and decided that it was smart to simply drop the subject and continue with her day. It looked like the town mansion topic wasn't one that Alexandra liked to address.

Eleanor's sudden change in temperament made Alexandra nervous. She thought it would be better to give her a glimpse of what had happened in the town mansion. "Lady Stownar, will you follow me to my study room? I need to talk to you."

"Of course."

"Larkin, prepare the carriage and pack some clothing for a week. We do not know how long all of this nonsense will take."

"Yes, sir."

Alexandra grabbed hold of Eleanor's hand and almost dragged her up the stairs before pulling her in her study, closing the door, and locking it. She ran both of her hands through her hair and turned around to face Eleanor. "Do not be nervous."

"How can I not be nervous when you just locked the door behind you and have been acting so strange?"

She decided to ignore the insult thrown her way. Alexandra crossed her arms and stared down at Eleanor before addressing her. "Remember in the carriage when we had just left the church? You asked me why I did not like going to the town mansion. You remember?"

"Yes, I do," Eleanor answered as she began to relax under Alexandra's gaze.

Alexandra rubbed her forehead as she thought of some ways to voice out her fear. Her lip quivered as she remembered the smell of blood, and the screams silently echoed in her head. "My mother was killed and raped in that mansion."

Eleanor's eyes grew wide. "Alexander, I am so sorry."

"I was there and I saw it all. I haven't been to that house ever since the incident happened." She rubbed her neck and closed her eyes. "I wouldn't feel comfortable if you were to go there."

"I told you I wasn't going to go."

"Still, I thought you might think I did not want to be near you."

"I did not think that."

"Good," Alexandra sighed and placed both hands inside her pockets. "One day, I might take you there. You own half of my property now."

"Not really. The law doesn't give me the right to anything."

"Fuck the law."

Eleanor raised a skeptical eyebrow and crossed her arms under her chest. "Alex, language."

"I am sorry, but one of these days, you will see that I have no respect for those stupid laws."

"I can already see that," Eleanor chuckled.

Alexandra pushed herself from the door and took a couple of steps forward until she towered over Eleanor's short frame. "Will you miss me once I am gone?"

"Well, I am not sure. We haven't been together that much, and besides, you, sir, have not given me much to miss." Eleanor smiled up to Alexandra mischievously.

Alexandra scoffed and raised Eleanor's chin as she studied her face. She was amazed at how a single woman could be as gorgeous as Eleanor. Her young face gleamed with joy; her red lips curled up in a teasing grin while her blue eyes shone with playfulness.

Alexandra was so enthralled by Eleanor, she didn't notice she was cupping her face with both hands. It was as if she was holding a treasure box. Her body had come close to Eleanor that she could feel the radiating heat between them.

"Lady Stownar, I am sensing that you want me to kiss you, am I right?"

"Lord Dowry, I would love nothing more than that."

Alexandra chuckled and decided that kissing her forehead rather than her lips was the best idea for now. So, she did, yet the disappointment that Eleanor felt as if electricity had just struck her made the younger woman move away rapidly. Eleanor ignored Alexandra's confused gaze and crossed her arms, turning away to face the window. "You better get going, Alexander."

Alexandra frowned at the sudden cold shoulder. "Lady Stownar?"

"I do not want to hold you back from your personal things," Eleanor added before drawing out the distance between them.

"Have I done something to offend you?"

Eleanor scoffed. "You have not done a thing."

"You have to understand one thing, Lady Stownar, and that is that I have never in my life been around a woman that I have respected as much as you. Which makes me wonder why you want to have such intimacy with someone that you barely know?"

"Because I want that intimacy. I want to get to know you, but if you continue treating me like a child, how am I supposed to react?"

Alexandra felt a fire ignite inside of her very core. Her posture became rigid as her eyes studied the woman before her.

Truth be told, she wanted nothing more than to pin the younger woman down, plant her lips upon hers and devour her without a care in the world.

Alexandra wanted her and it was getting so hard to ignore the fact that her heart skipped a beat every time they locked eyes together, and every time, they had even the slightest intimate contact.

Just holding hands drove the blonde mad with want. Not only that, but she was also presented with a woman that wanted the same thing as her, intimate contact.

Yet, the fear was there, latent, and touchable, as touchable as the woman before her.

Absentmindedly, Alexandra rolled her tongue over her lower lip while her green eyes trailed over Eleanor's mouth. She squeezed her own hands together and decided to place them inside of her pockets just to feel control over her actions. She needed to keep her hands busy, or else they would sneak their way around Eleanor's waist.

"Forgive me, Lady Stownar. I want nothing more than to see you happy. Clearly, I am not capable of giving you that happiness right now."

"Why? Why is it so difficult for you to open to your wife? Are you not attracted to me, Alexander?"

Alexandra couldn't help but laugh. She covered her lips with her hand, thinking that Eleanor might find it rude that she was making fun of her question. "You are beautiful, Lady Stownar."

"Thank you for the compliment."

"I still think that we need to know each other before having any type of intimacy."

Eleanor nodded and averted her eyes away from Alexandra. "I wish I could understand."

"You will, someday. Hopefully, soon." Alexandra turned on her heels and walked out of the room.

CHAPTER NINE

"Alex!"

It felt like she had just woken up from a nightmare and was able to breathe and think again. Her eyes focused on the dark orbs in front of her that stared down with compassion. She shuddered and looked over the moving houses outside the window.

Alexandra took in a shaking breath and blinked away the tears that were pooling in her eyes. "I am sorry."

"You were gone for some minutes there. Are you alright?"

Alexandra cleared her throat and nodded, deterring her eyes from Larkin. "Yes, I was daydreaming, I guess."

Larkin glowered apprehensively before moving back on his seat. "We are almost there."

"I know."

She felt a knot in her stomach the moment the carriage came to an abrupt stop. The feeling of short breath came rushing back at full force. She saw Larkin getting out of the carriage. The older man looked at her from the window before opening the door for her. She stepped out, took off her hat and gloves, and took in the state of the mansion. The paintings were scraped off. From the windows, you could make out the torn curtains that once decorated the gorgeous house.

She took a deep breath and walked inside.

The place was a mess. Every piece of furniture was covered with white sheets and dust. The pine floor had lost its shine and the wood seemed cracked. The picture was completely different from what she remembered, yet her mind seemed to go back in time. She recalled when the house was alive.

As she moved in further, she could make out where her mother used to sit in the living room. She would have a book in her hand and Alexandra in her lap as her hands trailing the words she enunciated for Alexandra to repeat.

Next to the door that led to the living room was the grand piano covered with yet another dusty white sheet. Alexandra saw herself sitting down, her mother by her side as awkward and clumsy notes were played repeatedly.

"Let us go," Alexandra led as she walked past the living room to the dining room, stopping at the doors. She moved her hand to the knob but stopped when she heard a commotion on the other side. She could still hear the footsteps of people running and the sound of men laughing as they discussed who was going to go first.

At the same time a woman's whispers. They were ghosted into Alexandra's mind. She opened the door and saw her there, eyes dead, hands covered in blood.

Vivian Dowry-Thompson swallowed a mouthful of blood, turned to her daughter, and reached out for her. "Run, Alex, please."

Her frantic eyes searched for the woman on the ground, yet she found nothing but the bloodstain plastered, like a horrid painting. She turned to face Larkin, who had managed to walk in just in time to see her stand in a trance.

He had called her more than once, yet she was lost in her own memory to hear.

Tears welled up in her eyes and without speaking a word, she collapsed in his arms while her hands clung to his vest for dear life. Her open mouth let out sob after sob of insufferable pain as she tried to control herself.

Larkin held her and didn't say a word. His hat fell by his feet, forgotten. His attention was with the woman in his arms who became undone by the memories of her past. He couldn't fix her and he didn't want to. He held her steady and waited for her to release all that pent-up sadness she had accumulated all those years.

"I am here," he whispered to her ear, squeezing her strong body to his. "I am right here."

***

Eleanor held the bed pillar for support as she cringed and groaned every time Nana pulled the laces of her corset tighter.

"Raise your arms over your head and let out that breath you are holding," Nana ordered. Eleanor did as she was told while Nana pulled on the laces tighter and tied them into a bow. "All done."

Eleanor gasped for air and felt like she was going to explode. She turned to look at Nana and quickly sat down on the bed when she felt dizzy from the lack of oxygen. "I will never get used to this."

"No. You will not," Nana muttered as she walked back over to Eleanor with her dress.

Eleanor didn't think Nana was looking at her, so she took the opportunity to look outside the window.

"You miss Alexander."

"Well, he is my husband. I miss his company."

Nana smiled and helped Eleanor slip her dress on. "I think you are starting to fall for him and I do not blame you. Alexander is a handsome, strapping young man. One kiss from him and you are done for."

"I cannot know. Alexander hasn't kissed me properly yet."

Nana was surprised by that and looked at Eleanor before moving away and opening her jewelry box in front of the younger woman. Eleanor quickly picked a discrete necklace and gave it to Nana.

"Explain to me, for I am old, and maybe things have changed since I was young like you. What is a proper kiss?" the old woman asked as she watched Eleanor pull her hair up so she could put the necklace around her neck.

Eleanor felt her cheeks turn red. She looked at the floor and began to rub her hands together as she tried to find a proper way to answer the old woman. "Well, you know. Like those kisses in romance novels."

"I do not know how to read."

Eleanor looked up at the ceiling and released a sigh. "You know. How does a man and a woman kiss properly?"

"Hasn't Alexander kissed you at all?"

Eleanor smiled and rubbed her hands. "He did kiss the corner of my lips in the church. He has kissed the back of my hand on two occasions and… the day he left, he kissed my forehead."

"Well! Then he has kissed you properly."

"No! No, Nana. No. He has not!" Eleanor stood up and grabbed hold of the bed pillar again, looking down at the old maid. "I've read in books how a man that loves a woman kisses. He is demanding, sweet, dominant, yet submissive at the same time. He cups her cheeks and lets her know how much he wants her with just one kiss. Alex… Alexander has not kissed me that way!"

"Are you telling me that you want Alexander to kiss you like he loves you?"

Eleanor moved back from the bed pillar and lowered her gaze. "Yes."

"My child. You have only been married to Alexander for less than a week. Do you expect him, a man that has been alone all of his life to just kiss you like he truly loves you?"

"I want him to kiss me like a husband kisses his wife!" Eleanor finally stated.

"I think you are just feeling lonely sleeping in your bed all alone. I get it."

"What?" Eleanor blushed and her mouth hung open when she heard the old woman's words. "That is called lust and that is a sin!"

"Is it wrong to want your husband? Isn't that how it works? You want someone, you ache for that someone to touch you, and slowly you start falling in love with that person. Hell! You do not even notice when you have completely fallen for the person until you notice that you cannot live without them. That is when you become aware of your own feelings." Nana smiled. "Lust? Call it lust! I call it true love! And if love is a sin, then we are all going to hell!"

"Nana, do not say such a thing!"

"Tell me what you felt when you first saw Alexander at the church! Be honest! Lying is a sin!" She winked.

Eleanor rolled her eyes and looked at the bed. She rubbed her elbows and then shrugged. "I love his hands. I do not know, I just thought they were different. They are delicate, yet strong. They are beautiful because of the soft tanned colored but ugly because of all the calluses. Then his eyes…" Eleanor stopped to collect her thoughts. She rubbed her shoulder blade and looked at Nana. "He does have nice eyes," she continued. "I thought he saw right through me at first, but— Oh well! You know! You are basically his mother, why should I be saying this?" she said, sitting beside the older woman.

"Because you see him with the eyes of a woman. I see him with the eyes of a mother. Yes, I do see he is handsome, but I do not see what you see." Nana smiled and poked Eleanor's nose. "Now. Let us stop all of this chit-chat and decide what are we going to do with that wild hair of yours today?"

***

"This is completely unacceptable. How could you have let the mansion come to this? When was the last time someone came here to clean?" Larkin asked as he waved a cloud of dust away from his face.

Alexandra ignored him as she grabbed hold of yet another drawer and emptied its content on the ground. She kneeled and collected each yellow paper in her hand, overlooking the rat excrement and dead cockroach that came along with it. Her face was of utter disgust, but it was hidden behind one handkerchief which she had tied behind her head.

They had been in the mansion for a day now and they had come empty-handed. Anxiety was starting to creep in and it was evident by the aching sensation on the back of her neck.

Her cousin was going to be there soon and if she wanted to answer him with full evidence, she needed to find those papers.

She stood up, pulled the collar of her white button shirt, and moved to the window. She took a deep breath of air as she tried to get her stomach under control. While she was rubbing her abdomen and mumbling something about having a weak stomach, she saw the gate to the mansion being opened by her carriage driver. Alexandra frowned and stuck her whole torso outside of the window and squinted to see who was entering her property.

"Larkin…"

The older man was too preoccupied, pulling out a large dossier from a broken-down bookshelf to listen to her words. He sat down on the dirty ground, flouting the fact that his pants needed to be thrown out after meeting the floor. He left through the dossier and pulled out a delicate yellowed paper. His eyes lit up with excitement.

"I found your parent's marriage certificate."

"Larkin."

"I guess this is good! The mansion documentation must be around here somewhere…"

"Larkin!"

"What is it?" He asked as he turned to look at Alexandra. "What are you staring at?"

"He is here."

"Who?"

"My cousin," she answered as she closed the window. "Go and greet him! Try to stall him as much as you can while I continue to search for the documents! Go!"

Larkin placed the paper he found on top of the desk and patted his dirty clothes, sending clouds after clouds of dust into the air. Alexandra pushed him away from her and the older man ran out of the study room. Alexandra then looked back at the dossier Larkin had just desecrated and began to pull the papers out harshly, turning the folders upside down and throwing their contents on the floor.

"Come on! Come on!" She threw the empty case away and got out of the study room. She ran to the next room. The door appeared to be locked, so she took a step back and raised her knee up, slamming the sole of her boot on the wood and busting the door open.

She looked around the room and noticed it was a guest chamber. She wiped her dirty nose with her arm and began to give the drawers in this chamber the same treatment she gave to the ones in the study room. Once again, she came out of the room, empty-handed.

"Well, hello! You came a day early, sir. I am Larkin Ward. I am Master Alexander's right hand!" Larkin said with a handsome grin on his face. The façade that he has put on was the one he always used to get his way with whatever life presented before him. Smile and nod, act like a gentleman, and everything would fall into place. At least that's what his late father used to tell him. Up to now, the advice has worked.

Instead of getting a greeting as enthusiastic as the one he had given, he received a disapproval grunt in return.

The man who stood beside him didn't look a year older than him. His clothes revealed that he was indeed in the same social status as Alexandra. The difference was that Alexandra was raised to be polite. This man was anything but a gentleman.

"Let me guess, summer cleaning?"

Larkin raised his dark eyes. They met a couple of darker green eyes that looked down at him as if he was just a pest like the cockroaches Alexandra found in the study room. He stood up straight and wiped the smile from his face and replaced that happy-go-lucky smirk with an angry frown. The man took off his hat and gave it to one of his three servants together with his baton. He pulled his white gloves off and gave it to the second servant as he looked down at Larkin. He ran his fingers through his short brown hair and cleared his throat. "Where is your boss?"

Larkin crossed his thick arms over his chest. "He will be down shortly."

"He came here all alone with you and the carriage driver?"

"I believe we did."

The man smirked and shook his head. "Aren't you going to ask me to sit down?"

"No," Larkin simply answered.

He placed his hands on his hips as he tilted his head back, trying somehow to look taller than Larkin. "I am Cassius Dowry. I am your boss's cousin. His blood. Do not treat me like I am your equal."

Larkin couldn't help but smirk. "Who said I am treating you like my equal? If I were treating you like my equal, you would have been sitting down with a glass of lemonade in the palm of your hands, sir." Larkin's words made Cassius's upper lip twitch in anger.

The last chamber! A servant's chamber. There was only one drawer. Alexandra closed her eyes and took a deep breath before grabbing hold of the drawer and turning it upside down. Like magic, sheets after sheets of paper came floating down from it like feathers. Alexandra felt like her heart was stuck in her throat. She got down on her knees and began to look at each paper one by one, reading over its contents out loud. "Stock, stock, a list for the weekly grocery shopping."

She began to panic before she grabbed hold of one yellow and delicate piece of paper. Her green eyes traveled over the ink, imprinted letters, and let out a sigh of relief.

"Documentation of the house property... Mansion Thompson."

She felt like jumping and so she did. She looked down and saw both her father's and mother's signature, and once again, she jumped higher.

"Damn it!" She looked upwards and closed her eyes. "About time you got on my side, huh?"

Suddenly, the sound of a heavy book hitting the ground made her reopen her eyes and looked at the source. She tilted her head, got on her knees, and grabbed hold of a pocket-size book, with its cover eroded by the humidity. It appeared that the drawer had a false bottom, which became loose with her shaking.

Without putting much thought into it, she placed the book inside her back pocket and ran out of the room.

"You are testing my patience. Either you tell your master to come down, or I will tell my servants to go look for him."

"I will take your servants down with my bare hands if they try to do anything," Larkin threatened him before hearing the stairs cringe in a rapid rhythm. He turned around and saw a dust-covered Alexandra running down the stairs. "Master Alexander! Your cousin is here to see you, sir," Larkin said, changing his usual familiar tone with Alexandra into a more professional one. "He was getting impatient."

Alexandra smiled at her best friend and waved the paper in her hands. She gave him a wink and patted his back, sending millions of dust particles into the air once again. "You are here early," Alexandra remarked as she bowed her head. "I take it you are Cassius Dowry," she said, extending her dirty hand. "It is a pleasure to finally see you. Alexander Dowry III. Always nice to meet family."

Cassius looked at Alexandra's hand and placed his glove on just to shake her hand with a disgusted look on his face. "Pleasure."

"He doubted your ownership of this mansion. I guess you found the right documentation to prove it belongs to you," Larkin told her as he gave Cassius a dirty glare.

"I believe you are right, Larkin." Alexandra teased before showing Cassius the piece of paper. "My parents owned this house. Meaning, as soon as they both died, it became part of my property and heritage."

Cassius had to bite his tongue. He looked at the paper and then gave it back to Alexandra. "To be quite honest, that wasn't the only reason I came here." He opened his brown frock coat and stuck his hand inside before pulling out a small envelope. "I wanted to finally meet my cousin, Alexander. Father spoke so much about you."

"I am sure he did." Alexandra chuckled before handing the documentation to Larkin.

"A friend of mine is holding a ball to introduce his daughter to society, Alexander. I was asking myself if you would be interested in coming to that ball. It will be held at my house since my friend's house is being remodeled. What do you think?" Cassius asked as he gave Alexandra the invitation attached to the address of his mansion. "It would be nice if the family spent some time together, do you think not?"

Alexandra grabbed the invitation and nodded. "I will try to be there," she answered as she studied the man's expression. Her eyes went back to the three servants behind him. The middle-aged men eyed her from head to toe, squinting their eyes as if studying her. Alexandra couldn't help but feel a cold shiver run down her spine, making her skin crawl and her stomach squirm.

"Please, be there," Cassius requested as he looked at Alexandra's hand, noticing the gold wedding band. "Bring your wife." He placed his hat and gloves back on. He grabbed the baton the servant was holding for him and bowed while tipping his hat forward. "Goodbye, cousin."

Alexandra simply bowed her head and watched the four men leave. "That went well," Larkin chuckled after a long silence.

Alexandra looked at Larkin and then at the invitation in her hand. "What do you think?"

Larkin gave Alexandra a reprehensible shrug before answering, "It is a great opportunity for you to show off Eleanor in the society's balls, Alex." He nodded at his own words. "I will take this as the chance to shut down the rumors your own uncle started. Not to mention, it would be nice to get out of the mansion."

Alexandra raised a skeptical eyebrow, folded the invitation, and placed it inside her dirty pants, that's when she remembered the book. She pulled it out and looked down at it with newfound curiosity.

"What did you get there?" Larkin asked as she walked closer to Alexandra.

She shrugged and the front. Her mother's maiden name was written in her own handwriting.

"A diary?" she whispered in wonderment. She leafed through it and sneezed when dust particles invaded her nose. "I will take a look at this later on, not now," she announced before turning to Larkin. "Let us go home."

***

Nighttime always made her feel uncomfortable, especially if it was raining the way it was tonight. The loud thunder shook Eleanor out of her sleep with an audible gasp. Her blue eyes flew open wide, scared that the sound that she had heard was something more than just nature being feisty.

"What time is it?" she asked herself while she rubbed her tired eyes with the back of her hands. Another lightning hit the ground around the mansion, and the atrocious thunder that followed it made her whimper in fear. She pulled the bedsheets away from her body and walked to the foot of the bed, grabbing hold of her robe, and hiding her naked body. She moved to the window and pulled the curtains open and looked outside.

The moment that she saw the carriage arrive was the exact moment that she felt a blanket of unstable nerves envelop her from head to toe. Absentmindedly, she rubbed her arms, closed the curtains, and decided to head downstairs.

Alexandra was having a battle of her own. She had gotten out of the carriage and was trying her hardest to pull the horses past the mansion gates. The animals wouldn't listen. The shocking lightning strikes were scaring them. Therefore, she needed to take them to the barn before she lost control of them and hurt someone.

Larkin came to her aid. He pulled onto the reins and steady the two horses enough to draw them in. The rain, the sound, and the lightning were making it difficult for Alexandra to hear Larkin's words. He pleaded for her to get in, that he would deal with the horses and that she better not get sick before the ball. Alexandra answered with a grunt, turned on her heels, and walked in the direction of the large doors of her mansion. Her first preoccupation was the diary. She pulled it out of her drenched clothes and noticed that it was wet but not to the point of being ruined. She let out a relieved sigh as she set it aside. She was drenched and cold, and she wanted nothing more than to change, warm herself up, and head to bed.

As soon as she stepped inside the mansion door, she looked over to the entrance hall and saw Eleanor standing right in front of her, eyes wide open and excited to see her back.

Alexandra tried to ignore her presence. During her ride home, all she could think about was the fact that she had left on bad terms and that as soon as she walked in, Eleanor would fight with her. The last thing that she wanted to do was get into a silly argument. So, Alexandra thought that maybe if she dismissed the younger woman, she wouldn't have to deal with her.

Eleanor noticed Alexandra's circumventing gaze, and yet, she stood by the long hall relinquishing the fact that Alexandra was home and that she was in front of her in all her serious glory. She swallowed hard and flinched when the large doors were slammed shut. She didn't know if she should take that as an "I am mad back off" kind of action, so she stood there, and waited.

"Good evening, Lady Stownar."

Eleanor let out a sigh of relief when she heard Alexandra's voice. It had been days since she had heard that voice call out to her, and if she was honest with herself, she missed it.

"Good— good evening," she replied shyly, admiring the way Alexandra looked when she was dead tired.

Alexandra walked towards her, but it was only to head to the living room, where she sat down on the ground, not wanting to damage the expensive sofas. She took off the waistcoat and threw it aside before taking off her black boots.

Eleanor clung to her every movement as if waiting for something. The candles inside the living room illuminated Alexandra's face, enhancing her frown, and wet blonde hair, which glistened like pure melted gold. Eleanor rubbed her hands together before Alexandra's booming voice made her jump startled.

"It is pouring outside. I will command the maids to bring more wood for the fire since it will get colder into the night." Alexandra sighed and ran her hand through her hair, moving it away from her face.

"Of course."

Alexandra pushed herself up and turned to look at her wife. The young woman never looked as delightful as she did now. With only her robe, dazed, sleepy, and confused. "I do not want you to catch a cold."

"Alexander?"

"Would you like for me to put more candles in the hall as well?"

It has been too long since she last heard her husband's voice. The absence was evident and she had never felt so bored. She missed looking for conversation and the feeling of being protected that only her husband could give her. She swallowed hard; her fingers rubbed the wedding band on her left hand while her brain tried to form some coherent sentence that would explain how she was feeling due to Alexandra's return.

Eleanor couldn't believe it, but she was about to say how much she missed her husband. "Alex... I—"

Alexandra closed her eyes tightly and let out a soft curse under her breath. She didn't want to get close to Eleanor, she knew that if she did, she would lose any type of self-control that she had been holding onto for the past week. Yet, when Eleanor called out to her again, she felt compelled to turn and stand before her. "Yes?"

Eleanor looked up at her. Her eyes shined with an unspoken question that dried up at her lips, unable to come out. Yet her hands sneaked their way away from her chest to become entangled in Alexandra's wet ones. Taking a hesitating step forward, she trailed the contour of Alexandra's lips. The soft touch of their hands was enough to make Eleanor shudder as she felt the electricity course through her and pool in her lower stomach.

Alexandra frowned, towered over her, and squeezed Eleanor's slender fingers before pressing her cold forehead against Eleanor's heated one.

"I am so sorry, Lady Stownar," she whispered as if it was a secret.

Eleanor slipped her hands away from Alexandra's grip and cradled her face. "Why?"

Alexandra opened her mouth, yet an aching groan escaped from deep within her chest. "I do not want to hurt you."

"What if I want to be hurt?"

Alexandra opened her eyes just in time to see Eleanor stand at the ball of her feet and pulled her into a scorching kiss.

Alexandra froze petrified by the notion that if she moved just an inch, if she moved in a certain way, if she spoke, Eleanor would know, and this pleasant torture of having those sweet lips on her own would end just like that.

Yet, as soon as she felt the second brush of Eleanor's lips, her hands slipped their way to cup Eleanor's face. Alexandra closed her eyes and exhaled the breath of pure fear that she was holding in.

With her thumb, she caressed Eleanor's cheek, earning a soft sigh from the brunette. Alexandra took this opportunity to slide her tongue inside of Eleanor's warm mouth. The young woman found a determined tongue slip into her mouth. It swiped passionately against her own, sending an electric shock down her spine and into the pit below her navel.

The soft moan that escaped from the back of Eleanor's throat made her suddenly open her eyes and push herself away from Alexandra in a mixture of confusion, shock, and uncontrollable pleasure. Her breathing spiked up, and she could hear her heartbeat inside her head.

"I'm sorry!" Eleanor gasped for air. She touched her husband's arm and looked down, hiding the redness of her face. "I am so sorry. I didn't mean to."

Alexandra was still in a daze. She placed her hands on top of Eleanor's shoulder and tried her best to straighten herself. Did she hear it correctly? She didn't mean to? Alexandra shook her head and slid her hands down Eleanor's arms.

"Wait. No, no, do not say that," Alexandra whispered. Her body was warm compared to seconds ago when she was trembling from the coldness of the night and the rain outside.

Eleanor pushed Alexandra's hands away from her. The less contact she had, the better. Her mind was spinning with scenarios of what might happen if they continued, and even though this was exactly what she had wanted, she had to confess that she bit more than she could chew. She never knew that she would react the way it did. It terrified her. "You do not understand…"

"Then make me, because I do not get it," Alexandra murmured as she tried her best to get a hold of her senses and to go back to acting like the detached individual, she portrayed herself to be. Yet, she could still feel the warmth not only of Eleanor's lips but of her body also. She rolled her tongue over her lips, wanting nothing more than to relieve and indulge in the taste that was Eleanor.

Eleanor looked up and locked eyes with Alexandra. She was slowly inching away from her. She was embarrassed enough as it is, and now this person was pulling her close enough to touch each other's forehead once again. Eleanor shuddered while her blue eyes went from the suddenly dark green eyes to the warm, parted lips. This closeness was dangerous, if she didn't stop this, she would probably consummate the marriage right there and then, in the living room.

"I really have to go, Alexander. I am sorry." She jerked herself away from her grasp and hurried back to her room, clutching to the robe, and making sure that her body was never exposed to hungry green eyes.

"Wait! No…" Alexandra called after her, but it was already too late. She let out a low curse. She didn't want to scream and wake the entire mansion up. Alexandra closed her eyes, sucked her lower lip, and then leaned sideways against the wall.

"Alex!"

Alexandra opened her eyes and sighed as she saw her maid, holding a candle up. "Nana. What are you doing up? It is late." Alexandra pushed herself from the wall and walked over to the elderly woman.

"I heard that you were back! I just wanted to know if you needed anything."

Alexandra let out a gentle smile before patting the woman's wrinkled face. "I am fine, but you might want to check on Lady Stownar."

"Oh?"

"Yes. I am terribly tired. I would like to just go up to my chamber and sleep until late."

"I will arrange for that," Nana said. "What happened between you and Lady Stownar?" She looked around the hall to make sure they were alone and then proceeded. "Did she find out...?"

"No! No, no. Dear God if she knew I would probably be dead by now."

"Do not say such things!" Nana said, stomping her foot.

Alexandra smiled. "We kissed."

"How?"

Alexandra couldn't help but widen her smile. "Nana, what kind of a question is that? We kissed. Like a married couple should kiss."

"What is with you, young people, and kissing? It is the 19th century, not the 12th century."

Alexandra shook her head in amusement but shuddered. A reminder that she was still wet and cold. "I should change."

Nana nodded at that and extended her hand to the tall woman. "Come now." She was sure no one was seeing her. A maid wasn't supposed to act this way with the master of the house, but this was Alexandra. Her Alexandra, the woman she had raised like her own daughter. "Come on, Alex! I do not want you to catch a cold!"

Alexandra couldn't believe that she was smiling so much. She moved her hand and grabbed hold of Nana's wrinkly one and led her to the stairs. "Now, this brings back memories. Remember when you used to drag me by the hand so I could get washed."

"I still do."

***

She looked at herself in the mirror. Her cheeks were so red and her lips looked swollen. Eleanor couldn't believe she had done that. She looked down at her lap and licked her lips. She had read about lip-to-lip kisses, but what

Alexandra did tonight was totally different. It felt so strange yet so good at the same time.

"Eleanor! Goodness gracious, stop it!" she said out loud and leaned over her beauty table on her elbows as she covered her eyes. "He should know how to kiss a woman! He is older than you, and surely, like any other man, he must've been with other women in the past."

The thought made her twitch with a fit of illogical jealousy. She sighed and ran her fingers through her hair, getting some wild strands away from her face. She looked at the mirror again. This image of her, red, shook up, and just plain shocked seemed to fit her quite well. She wiggled her nose and looked at the desk. She grabbed the brush and slowly began to untangle her hair. Maybe focusing on one task would help her ease her mind.

Eleanor smiled at that. Of course, it was going to help. After all, that's what she would do back at home when she was having a rough time or if she was anxious. There is no need to be thinking of how Alexander kissed her, slipping his tongue inside her mouth, letting out those low rumbles of pleasure and pressing his tall body to-

She threw the brush on the desk when she was about to give the third stroke. "I am going to sleep!" She announced to no one and took off her robe, threw it on the chair in front of the night table, and slipped under the sheets. "Not like he is thinking about it as much as me!"

***

Alexandra was in a complete state of bemusement. The only thing that was on her mind was the feeling of Eleanor's lips on her own. Her delicious taste, her hands on her face, and the feeling of her body pressed to hers. She couldn't help but rub her lower lip absentmindedly, trying to somehow recreate what she had just experienced.

She was so overcome by the fact that Eleanor was the one to initiate the incident. She chuckled and placed her arms behind her head as she closed her eyes. She pondered if she was Eleanor's first kiss. That thought alone made her squirm under her bedsheets with delight. Yet, even thinking about Eleanor kissing someone else before she made her stomach turn. She found her eyebrows knitted together in annoyance.

She let out an exasperated sigh before blowing out the candle on her nightstand. There was no need to be thinking of anything related to Eleanor. The woman still went about her way, not knowing that she had married another woman. If Alexandra wanted something more than fervent kisses, Eleanor needed to know the truth.

When would it be the right time to tell her? How would she react?

Alexandra shrugged and succumbed to the image of a smiling Eleanor, leaning over to give her another kiss.

CHAPTER TEN

The smell of blood was intoxicating to the point that it got stuck in her throat and lungs. It was abrasive, she couldn't breathe. Anxiety swept her senses, numbing them.

She stuck her index finger between the collar of her shirt and her neck and pulled, trying to release herself from the tension.

She looked at herself in the large mirror in the living room that was connected to the wall and the ceiling, giving it the perfect angle to reflect everything in the place. It was such a perfect touch for narcissistic women that adored looking at themselves. But something wasn't right.

Alexandra looked at herself once again and frowned deeply confused. She touched her brown vest and looked down at herself. She undid the scarf around her neck and pulled the collar of her white shirt in a last attempt to cool down her heated face and neck. She threw the tie away and pulled her pocket watch out from her vest.

"Nine," she whispered out loud. It was nine o'clock in the evening and she was standing in the town mansion's living room.

The confusion started to build upon the back of her neck which she rubbed anxiously while she looked around the living room. It was dark, the only thing that illuminated the place were chandeliers and some candles. Her eyes trailed over to the large hall that led to the dining room.

She heard some movement and her heart skipped a beat. She placed her watch inside her pocket and slowly began to walk to the dining room. Her shaking hand pushed the door slowly and she saw the body of a woman lying on the ground, her back to Alexandra. At the same time, a man left using the other door, pulling his pants up and laughing.

The scent of death snaked its way into her nostrils, making her cough. She took out a handkerchief from her back pocket and placed it over her nose before she kneeled in front of the woman.

"Ma'am?"

She received a soft and pained groan as an answer. Alexandra threw the handkerchief away and slowly turned the woman around so she could face her.

Blank blue eyes looked up to her as brown hair covered most of the bruises on her face. With a slow movement, the woman grabbed hold of Alexandra's shirt and pulled her harshly against her as she wheezed. "Run, Alexandra, please!"

Alexandra let out a loud gasp as she sat up on her bed. She could hear her own heart beating strongly in her ears as her whole body shook with fear. She looked around the room and noticed she was in the country mansion. She let out a relieved sigh and placed her hand over her heart as she commanded it to go back to its regular rhythm.

"Just a bad dream. It was just a bad dream, Alexandra." She repeated the mantra that she had designed years ago to appease her mind. This time it wasn't working. The dream was different. She gulped and panted. She ran her shaking hand through her sweaty hair and pulled the sheets from her.

She covered her naked body, and with shaking hands, she grabbed her pocket watch, which laid on the night table.

It was early in the morning, but the sun still wasn't up. Alexandra was sure that some maids were up fixing breakfast and getting the mansion ready for when she and Eleanor woke up. She opened the curtains and looked outside, staring at everything she owned.

A flash of her nightmare hit her at full force. Those blue eyes looking blankly at her, that brown hair covering the reality of inevitable death. Alexandra frowned while calling out Eleanor's name. She closed the curtain, put her boots on, and turned to look at the door that connected her chamber with Eleanor's.

Alexandra had the sudden urge to just walk into that chamber and demand another kiss. After all, she could do so; Alexandra was Eleanor's husband by law and by the church. She smirked. Still, she decided not to be as harsh. It just wasn't in her nature to do those sorts of things. She instead let Eleanor come to her of her own volition.

She stood up straight and took off her robe. She looked down at her chest and noticed that Nana had kept her bound even though she was asleep. Alexandra sighed and put one of her many vests just in case the bind wasn't that tight. She had to hide her curves one way or another. She buttoned her black jacket and grabbed the pocket watch, hiding it where it belonged. The only thing visible of it was the small platinum chain that connected it to one of the buttons on Alexandra's vest. She grabbed a brown tie and wrapped it around her neck, tying it the way her father taught her to. Still, she never got the hang of it, so she gave up and threw it on the bed. Besides, she liked it better to expose her neck for the world to see.

She went back to look at the door and let out a loud sigh. She could still feel Eleanor's warm lips pressed against hers and she could even recall the way she felt when she ran her delicate fingers down her neck. She felt as if her whole body became alive after years of longing for affectionate touches. She placed her hand on the doorknob and stopped. She warmed the cold material with her warm touch before she turned it and pushed the door open.

Alexandra peeked her head in and saw the curtains closed, and the candles that once illuminated the room were out. She walked inside and closed the door behind her. She looked over the bed and saw Eleanor under the covers. Alexandra couldn't help but smile. She slowly and quietly walked over to her and stood at the foot of the bed, watching her sleep.

The bedsheets were covering her up to her mouth. The only things visible were her nose, eyes, and hair. She made her way over and sat down on the edge of the bed, resting her elbows on her knees. She turned and looked over her shoulder and watched the sheets rise and fall with every breath Eleanor took.

Alexandra rubbed her hands nervously before taking a deep breath. She had never, in her life, wanted to touch someone as much as she wanted to touch Eleanor Stownar. This feeling of breathlessness was overwhelming. The images of Eleanor's lifeless eyes haunted her. She had to take a deep breath once again to stop herself from crying.

What has this woman done to her?

***

"It was kind of awkward, right, Mia?"

"I just waited for those pesky dogs to get the man. I was not going outside to get in trouble or get hurt. Nuh-uh!" The maid snorted as she batted the eggs inside a deep bowl and blew a strand of brown hair from her face. "Did someone tell Larkin about it?"

"Larkin is always cleaning the damn horses and sniffing Master Alexander's ass!" another maid said as she checked the temperature of the boiling water.

"Now, Alma, do not be so rough on him! I know you just want to marry the man," Mia said as she wiped a smudge of flour from her face.

"Never! I'd rather die than let him touch me." Alma gasped as she felt a hand touch her lower back. Quickly, she turned around and found the bearded Larkin looking down at her with a wide grin on his face.

"Morning, Alma."

"Larkin! Get your filthy hands off me!"

The rugged man just rolled his eyes and walked away from her and sat down on the servant's dining table, watching the young kitchen maids prepare breakfast. "I would like a nice, black coffee."

"Get it yourself!" Alma shouted as she poured herself a cup of tea.

"I'll get it for you, Larkin."

"Such a nice girl you are, Mia. I think Alma could learn a few things from you. It is a shame that at such a young age, our dear Alma acts like a sixty-something-year-old woman." He shrugged as he accepted the coffee from Mia and flashed her his trademark smile. "Thank you, sweetheart."

"You are much welcome, love."

Larkin raised his cup to her as if he was making a toast. "Even Nana is more playful than you, Alma."

"Then marry her," Alma mumbled as she drank the hot liquid in one fast gulp and turned back to prepare the bread for breakfast.

"Oh, that's right. Larkin, the other night a guy tried to sneak in using the back door," Mia said as she sat down beside the handsome man. "We thought... Well, at least I thought we should let you know. I saw the wolves going after him."

"Yes, I know. Pebbles and Stick went after them. I really think you girls should be careful. Lock the doors, and if someone you do not know wants to come inside the mansion through the kitchen, just say no. Even if he says he is a messenger. Call me and I will see to it, alright?"

Mia leaned on the table and rested her cheek on her knuckles as she watched Larkin drink his coffee. "So, tell me, Larkin. How is Master Alexander's wife? We have heard of her, but never even seen her! Now that is a bit pathetic."

Alma clapped her hands together and watched as the flour went to the air. She turned around and leaned on the counter, waiting for another maid to take over what she was doing. "I heard she was a beauty. Is she nice?"

Larkin shrugged. "She is nice and beautiful," he whispered as he blew on his coffee and took another sip. "Alexander seems to like her a lot."

"That's got to be rough! Marrying someone without knowing them," Mia said, wiggling her nose and leaning on the chair. "I wish some upper-class man would sweep me off my feet and carry me into the sunset on his white horse and marry me, giving me the life I've always wanted! I always thought I was born to be a lady, not a maid."

"Sure, Mia. Keep dreaming," Alma said, wiping her hand with a damp cloth and going back to cooking. "Shut up and help us over here."

Mia growled, sat up, and patted Larkin's head. "I bet you think the same thing. You are rather smart, Larkin. You know how to read and write, and you look like a gentleman even if you have a caveman's beard." Mia giggled. "I bet you could just marry anyone you want, right?"

Larkin stared at the middle of the table and just nodded. "I guess," he whispered before letting the cup sit on the table and getting up. "I guess I could've married anyone I wanted, but I presume I am a bit too late for that."

Alma and Mia tilted their heads to the side and watched Larkin leave the large kitchen. The younger maid, Alma, looked at Mia and nudged her ribs with her elbow gently. "What did you do? He is depressed now, all because of you."

"I wasn't the one that treated him like trash when he came in," Mia responded to the accusation.

"Bah! Get those eggs ready!"

***

Eleanor exhaled painfully slow as Nana jerked her with the strings of her corset. Eleanor held onto one of the bed pillars for dear life before she felt Nana pat her bottom. "There we go. You are done."

She lowered her arms and touched her stomach, checking if she was still able to breathe. "Thank you, Nana," she whispered before watching the old woman waddle around the room, gathering Eleanor's dress and shoes. It was already late in the morning. She had woken up around ten. She couldn't sleep at all due to her mind replaying last night's events.

Nana noticed this; she saw the young woman looking around the room apprehensively, especially the door that connected Eleanor's room with Alexandra's. Nana couldn't help but chuckle in silence.

"Is everything alright, Lady Eleanor?"

Eleanor nodded and whipped her sweaty palms against her corset. Her nervousness was evident through her fidgeting, her hands kept rubbing her wedding band, and she kept bumping on Nana as she walked around.

Nana was in the process of helping Eleanor with her dress when both women froze in place.

A soft melody invaded the silence in the room. Nana let out an audible gasp and let the dress she was holding fall to the floor. Eleanor turned to face the old woman whose face had lit up to the point of tears. She covered her mouth and closed her eyes tightly before letting out a delighted squeal.

Eleanor frowned in confusion. "What is it?"

"Do you hear that?"

Of course, she did. The sound of a piano was heard loud and clear throughout the mansion. "Is that Alexander?"

"It has been years since he touched that piano! Years!" Nana swallowed hard and clapped her hands.

Eleanor couldn't help but laugh and grab hold of the older woman's hand. She looked like a proud mother, excited over the fact that her baby had learned how to walk.

"I must say, Lady Eleanor, I am so happy that you are here. It has been so long since I have seen Alexander smile. I do not know what you have done, but I cannot thank you enough."

Eleanor felt the heat rise to her cheeks and an involuntary chuckle escaped her mouth. "I haven't done anything."

Nana scoffed and patted her cheek. "Then, thank you for simply existing."

Eleanor leaned into the old woman's hand. She missed that kind of touch, a mother's touch. Her heart shuttered with nostalgia as Eleanor wondered how her mother was doing. She hadn't been able to talk to her since she got married.

Nana left her side and helped her get ready for the day while the background silence was filled with the soft melody of the piano. Eleanor hid her amusement. She had been able to bring forth something different from her husband with just a kiss.

Her stomach fluttered with butterflies, and she held her giggles by covering her mouth. She always read about the whole "butterflies" in the stomach thing but never experienced it until now.

She wanted to hurry up, get dressed, and join Alexander so she could bear witness to her husband playing the piano.

Eleanor almost ran out of her chamber as she followed the sound. She found herself standing outside of an unknown room. When Alexandra had given Eleanor a tour, she didn't say anything about that room. The door was unlocked, and Eleanor took the opportunity to push it open. Her breath got caught up in her throat.

Alexandra was sitting down in front of a grand black piano, staring down at the keys as she played them, moving her head with the rhythm of the soft song. The morning sun rays that were coming from the open window illuminated the room, giving it a surrealistic atmosphere to the scene in front of them.

Eleanor had to swallow hard and hold her breath as she watched how Alexandra raised those green eyes at her.

"Sorry to disturb you," Eleanor quickly said as she opened the door and stepped inside. "I heard the music and—"

"I was not disturbed," Alexandra responded, nervously rubbing her clothed thighs.

"Nana said it has been a long time since you played."

Alexandra stood from her chair and headed towards Eleanor, hands behind her, completely open. "She was not lying."

The moment she saw Alexandra heading her way, she could feel her breathing became labored and her knees quivered with nervousness. She moved her trembling hands to her back, yet she couldn't help but smile up to the tall woman. "Alex, about last night, I..."

"I want to believe that you enjoyed it as much as I did."

"That's an understatement, but it took me by surprise."

"I was the one that was taken aback."

Eleanor averted her eyes from Alexandra and looked from the door down to the floor in embarrassment. "I am sorry."

"Lady Stownar," Alexandra said as she moved closer and cupped Eleanor's chin, locking her eyes with hers once again. "Whatever we do together, in mutual agreement and with consent, is never wrong. If I made you feel uncomfortable, I beg only for your forgiveness, and I swear I will do everything in my power to take it back."

"No— I just…" Eleanor sighed and grabbed hold of Alexandra's hand and pushed it away. "The sensation…it was too much."

Alexandra chuckled and rolled her tongue over her lower lip. "The sensation?"

"Do not mock me, Alexander, I swear to God."

"Oh, I am not mocking you, Lady Stownar. If anything you are the one teasing me, talking about sensations…" Eleanor shrugged as she heard Alexandra laugh. She moved away, but the taller woman quickly grabbed her arm and pulled her in again. "I am sorry, I will stop."

"You better stop, or I will never let you put a hand on me again."

"Are you threatening me?"

Eleanor swallowed hard and raised her chin up. "Maybe." Eleanor shuddered as she saw that same spark of lust ignite in Alexandra's eyes as they had done last night.

Alexandra held her steady, looked down at her lips, and backed up at her gorgeous blue eyes. The question was there, unspoken, all she needed was a quiet answer.

"Kiss me already."

That was all Alexandra needed. Alexandra pressed her firm body to Eleanor's, pushing her to the door. Eleanor looked at Alexandra's green eyes and quickly placed her delicate hands on Alexandra's shoulder.

Alexandra let out a pleasurable sigh. Having Eleanor's soft body squeezed with hers was proving to be more delicious than in her dreams. Her hands touched and caressed Eleanor's face as she approached her forehead to Eleanor's. "You have no idea how gorgeous you are, Lady Stownar."

Eleanor swallowed hard as she listened to Alexandra. She had never been this close to anyone before in her life. Maybe that was why she was starting to sweat, perhaps that was the reason why she was feeling out of breath. No, wait; actually, that was the corset.

"I still cannot believe that I am the one that gets to hold you like this…" Alexandra had to chuckle as she pressed her body closer to Eleanor's, letting out a soft groan when she felt the younger woman's chest so intimately close to hers.

98

She could feel the warm breath on her lips, the scent of Alexandra was intoxicating her, and she wanted more. God forbid, she wanted so much more than a simple stroke to her face and such intimate body contact. She wrapped her arms around Alexandra's shoulder and pulled her closer, if it was possible, and closed her eyes as she waited impatiently.

As soon as she captured her lips, Alexandra felt heat spreading through her like a wildfire. Eleanor tasted sweeter than last night. She felt so much softer and right, Alexandra thought she was sucking the life out of her. Alexandra had closed her eyes and rolled them into the back of her head. She felt how Eleanor's hesitating tongue traced her lower lip and without thinking twice, she opened her mouth and using her tongue, she invited Eleanor's inside. She let out a gasp, moved one hand to Eleanor's lower back.

Eleanor had to breathe, or else she was going to make a fool out of herself by fainting. She pulled away, looking at Alexandra's swollen lips. Eleanor had undone this person to the point that the only thing in her mind was that she wanted to give her body and soul away to taste those precious lips again. She closed her eyes tightly and pushed herself off the door. Both her hands held onto Alexandra's hair as she tried to steady her and went to dive for another soul kiss.

"I want to kiss you everywhere, Lady Stownar," Alexandra purred.

Alexandra's voice managed to cut through the fog in Eleanor's mind. She opened her eyes and tangled her fingers with blonde hairs, latching to the roots and making the taller woman pull away.

"Have I given you permission?"

Alexandra's smiles take on a devilish tinge. "Am I hearing correctly? Permission?"

"Am I stepping in uncharted territory?"

Alexandra moved closer, her leg coming to rest securely between Eleanor's. The heat was now emanating from the junction of her thighs, and Alexandra wanted nothing more than to taste that warmth.

Eleanor gasped and pressed her open palms to the wall behind her. She raised her eyebrows, surprised, scared, excited.

"That question is an understatement, Lady Stownar."

Eleanor chuckled as the nervousness slipped away to be replaced with a thirst she didn't quite understand. "I want you to kiss me everywhere too, Alexander. I wonder about the things we could do alone, yet, it is such a shame that your gentleman manners are stopping you, or us, from exploring each other."

"Exploring," Alexandra scoffed.

"Why are you still answering?"

"Is the husband ordering his wife around?"

Alexandra steadied her and grabbed her jaw to study her gorgeous blue eyes. "Forgive me," she said before leaning in and kissing Eleanor fiercely and possessively, the kind of kiss that made Eleanor shudder with the excitement of what might follow if they continued.

The two women didn't notice when the door to the room was pushed open. An apple chewing Larkin walked inside, looking at a letter in his hand.

"Alex breakfast is rea—" His eyes grew wide as he saw the scene before him. He felt how the half-chewed piece of apple fell from his mouth and he began to stutter his words. "I…! I am sorry! I did not know you… argh! See you downstairs, sir." He closed the door quickly and smacked his face. "Knock! Knock on the damn doors! Knock!"

Eleanor stared at the closed door and then went back to look down at herself. She had her arms around Alexandra's shoulder. Her chest raised and fell with every deep breath she took. She raised her eyes to meet Alexandra's and saw her husband looking at the closed door with a calm expression. "You can let go of me now."

Alexandra's arms unwrapped themselves from Eleanor's waist and slowly, she stood up and straightened her clothing. She ran her fingers through her now wild hair and coughed, trying to get her body under control.

Eleanor pulled away and turned her back to Alexandra. "We shouldn't have done that."

"I can do whatever I damn please in my mansion," Alexandra said, almost snarling as she fixed her vest and then rubbed the back of her tense neck.

Eleanor ignored the sudden change of demeanor from Alexandra before her eyes caught sight of a piece of paper. "What is this?" she asked out loud and kneeled to pick the document up. "I think Larkin dropped this." Eleanor turned around and gave Alexandra a look.

"What?" she asked and snatched the paper away from Eleanor's hands before reading it. "Oh. This." She cleared her throat and turned to look at a grinning Eleanor. "I guess he was going to remind me of this," she whispered as she turned the paper around. "It is an invitation…"

"Oh, I read what it is. So?"

"So?"

"Are we going?"

Alexandra scoffed. "No."

"Oh, thank you so much! You do not know how long it has been since I've gone to a— wait, what?"

Alexandra tore the paper in half and walked out of the room "We are not going to that ball."

Eleanor's jaw fell and so did her shoulders as she stared at Alexandra's back. "Why? I mean, it is a good opportunity to relax and meet people! Besides, isn't it your duty as my husband to take me to those things?"

Alexandra turned around to look at her wife. She stopped walking suddenly and watched how Eleanor bumped against her. "You think I like showing you off like a damn show horse? I am sorry, Lady Stownar, but I am not like normal husbands in this society."

"I want to go!"

Alexandra let out a loud sigh. She placed one hand on her waist, and with the other, she massaged her temples. "Lady Stownar..."

"I want to go, Alex," Eleanor said, stomping her foot on the floor and crossing her arms under her chest. "I do not wish to be trapped in this mansion for the rest of my life! I want to go out. I want to meet people! I want to have fun with my husband. Is that too much to ask?"

"Yes."

"I knew you would unders—" Her happiness was short-lived when she heard Alexandra's answer. She couldn't help but frown at the blonde. "You are not going, are you?"

Alexandra shook her head.

"But why not? I do not understand!"

Alexandra let out a frustrated groan. She ran her long fingers through her hair and closed her eyes before leaning on the wall. "It is quite simple," she began not before she cleared her throat, stood up straight, raised her chin, and looked down at Eleanor. "I do not know how to dance. Also, before you start complaining, I will not take you to a ball, so you can dance around with other people while I sit down and watch you."

Eleanor let her arms fall to her side. She stared at her husband with incredulous eyes before looking at the ceiling. "I cannot believe this!"

"Me neither," Alexandra said before walking away from Eleanor and heading to the stairs.

"Wait, wait, wait! You are not turning your back on me! We are going to fix your little problem, and we are going to the ball." Eleanor ran after Alexandra and grabbed her strong arm, stopping her from going down the stairs.

"I thought I made myself clear, Lady Stownar."

"But it is such a foolish excuse! Clearly, you must be joking!"

"Do I look like I am joking?" Alexandra asked as she slipped her arm away from Eleanor's grasp. "We are not going—" She was silenced by a pair of perfectly formed lips. She had to grab hold of the stairs handle to hold Eleanor and her weight also. She kept her eyes open, though. It wasn't every day that a woman as gorgeous as Eleanor shut you up with a kiss as sweet yet as strong as the one Alexandra was receiving.

"Can we please give it a try?" Eleanor asked as she stared at Alexandra's eyes.

"Try what?" She had forgotten the whole conversation after that kiss.

Eleanor smiled and rubbed Alexandra's neck before bumping their noses. "I can teach you how to dance."

"How cliché." She chuckled into her face and slowly pushed her off the stairs with her own body.

"I love clichés," Eleanor answered, placing her hands on top of Alexandra's chest.

Quickly, the older woman grabbed her wrist and lifted her hands away from her.

"Clearly," Alexandra said before clearing her throat. "Either way, we haven't had our breakfast yet. We cannot start our day without breakfast." She then turned and began to descend the stairs.

Eleanor stood at the top of the stairs and just watched how Alexandra walked away from her. Did she do something wrong? "Alex…"

Alexandra turned around to face the brown-haired woman and frowned, confused. "Are you not going to join me?"

"Oh! Of course!"

CHAPTER ELEVEN

I saw him again and, as always, I felt sick to my stomach. How can a man who is related to Alexander be this disgusting? The way he looks at me makes my skin crawl. And his advances are getting out of hand. It has been two weeks since the wedding, and he simply does not give up. I told Alexander about William's obnoxious "playfulness" as he calls it. Still, my husband believes that his brother's words are empty. How much do I have to endure?

Larkin rubbed his hands nervously as he heard the words being read to him. He moved uncomfortably in his chair as if he wasn't supposed to be listening.

Alexandra closed the diary and hid it in one of the many drawers near her desk. She was fuming. Larkin could tell by the way her lips were pursed tightly, and the muscles on her jaw moved as she clenched it.

"You weren't even born then," Larkin said, thinking that it might help Alexandra calm down. The glare that she gave him in response said otherwise.

"This is the father of the guy I will be visiting in a couple of days. How can I look him in the eyes and act as if nothing happened?"

"Well, nothing has happened."

"I haven't finished reading the darn thing, Larkin." Alexandra pushed her chair back, making a shrill noise in the process. Larkin hissed as he heard it and closed his eyes in annoyance.

"I do not think it will do you any good to read your dead mother's diary."

"Oh, like you know what's good for me?"

"I got you a wife..."

Alexandra opened her mouth to give him a smart-ass remark but was

103

interrupted by a soft knock. "Lady Stownar...Hi."

"Hello, Alex. Ready for your lessons?" Eleanor asked, flashing Alexandra a mischievous smile.

"Lessons?" Larkin couldn't help but chuckle.

Alexandra sighed. "The woman wants to teach me how to dance because she wants me to go to that ball my cousin is holding for his friend's daughter."

Larkin let out a snort and quickly covered his mouth when he noticed that both women were glaring at him. "I am sorry. I just— I am sorry!"

Vexed by Larkin, Alexandra stood intimidatingly next to him and snarled. "Go and wash the horses."

Larkin's snickering suddenly came to an end. He snapped his head to look at Alexandra and shouted. "What?"

Alexandra took a deep breath before feeling Eleanor's hands on her shoulders. She swallowed hard and moved her attention to the younger woman.

"You shouldn't pour your frustrations on Larkin. I would be laughing at you too."

"Lady Eleanor. If I were you, I would watch my words."

Eleanor rolled her eyes and shook her head before patting Alexandra's face. "Alex, you really do not need to be yelling at poor Larkin." She chuckled and averted her eyes towards Larkin. "Go on, Larkin. This monster will not be bothering you anymore."

Larkin cleared his throat and stood. "I will see you both later," he said before leaving them alone.

Alexandra clenched her jaw and eased Eleanor's hands away from her, not before noticing how the other woman's grin spread out from ear to ear.

"Lady Stow—" she began before seeing that playful spark in Eleanor's blue eyes. Alexandra felt her upper lip twitch. It was going to be hard to say no to Eleanor. Alexandra could already feel her serious gaze slipping away and being replaced by an amused pout.

"You are not escaping from the lessons, if that is what you are thinking."

"I was not thinking about that. I was actually pondering the fact that you are giving Larkin orders."

"Does that please my husband?"

"Oh, greatly." Alexandra chuckled and watched Eleanor pull her by her hand and down the stairs. "What are we doing exactly?"

"I am going to teach you how to dance."

"Oh, come on! I thought that was just an excuse to get me out of the study."

"That too."

"You really do not have to do this, Lady Stownar."

"Oh, but I do—" Eleanor smiled and placed her arms akimbo. "Well?"

Alexandra frowned in confusion. "Well?"

"What are you waiting for? Move the furniture."

"Excuse me, but isn't this enough space for you?" Alexandra said, stretching her arms out as if she was trying to prove the room was big enough to be occupied by ten stallions and still have room to have a drink.

Eleanor just crossed her arms and didn't move an inch. Alexandra stared at her for what appeared to be a full hour. Eleanor was starting to feel the pressure of the stare and became nervous. She moved a bit uncomfortable and cleared her throat, looking away. Alexandra turned away from her, took off her coat, and threw it over to one of the sofas before rolling up her sleeves to her elbows.

"This better be worth it. Or we are going to have a problem here," Alexandra whispered before pushing the large sofa to the side, followed by the living room table and the loveseats.

Eleanor looked around and just nodded. "I think this will do."

Alexandra stood in the middle of the room and simply stared at Eleanor. "I am waiting."

"Please. Be patient!" Eleanor mumbled and stood in front of Alexandra. She grabbed hold of Alexandra's thick wrist and placed the calloused hand on her own hip. "Stretch out your other arm and hold your palm up," Eleanor said. When Alexandra did so, she placed her delicate hand inside Alexandra's rough one. "This is the basic posture."

"Why are you so stiff?" Alexandra asked as she looked down at her.

"Stiff?"

"Hmm." Alexandra groaned as she moved her extended arm and squeezed Eleanor's hand a bit. She pulled Eleanor a bit closer, but every time she took a step forward, Eleanor took a step back. "What—"

"Why are you moving closer?" Eleanor didn't let her finish.

"I am sorry, but aren't we supposed to be close to each other?"

"Yeah, but I—"

"I told you not to feel uncomfortable around me, what's the worst I could do?"

"I do not want Larkin walking in on us again. That was embarrassing."

"So?" Alexandra frowned and slipped her hand from Eleanor's hip to her lower back, pulling their bodies dangerously close.

"Alexander!"

"What is it?"

"Please, take a step back! You are invading my personal space!"

"Oh, for goodness sake, Lady Stownar. Weren't you the one that wanted intimacy?"

Eleanor gasped and pushed Alexandra away with her free hand. "Enough. Do you want to learn to dance or not?"

"To be honest. No." Alexandra said and noticed Eleanor's pained expression. She groaned and rubbed her temple before sighing. "I mean, yes. I wish to learn to dance. I just…"

"Say you are sorry."

Alexandra's neck almost snapped. Say that she was sorry? The audacity! When did this happen? Eleanor was the one that was always scared of her. She trembled every time she got near her or if she even raised her voice. Now she was calling the shots?

"Excuse me?" she asked in disbelief.

"That will do!" Eleanor smiled and quickly moved to Alexandra and repositioned her hands. "Now, if you act nicely, I might just teach you the basics today."

Alexandra scoffed and felt Eleanor's hand on top of her shoulder. "Fine," she mumbled and shook her head again and relaxed under Eleanor's embrace. "Hurry up. I have things to get done."

"All right, now. Look down to your feet if you please?"

Alexandra did just that while Eleanor kept looking at Alexandra's messy mane. "I am going to take a step back. When I do, I want you to follow it with your foot, moving forward. You will follow my lead…"

Alexandra grunted. "Your lead?"

"For now. You do not know how to dance, remember? Just do exactly what I do, but with the opposite foot," Eleanor said before squeezing Alexandra's shoulder. "At the count of three, are you ready?"

Alexandra nodded as she squeezed Eleanor's hand and waist.

"One…two…three." Eleanor took a step back and looked down at her feet. "One."

"One what?"

"That is the first step of a ballad, Alexander. I'm sure you have heard the tempo."

Alexandra's gaze told her otherwise. Frustrated by her stubbornness, Eleanor stood beside the taller woman. She directed Alexandra into following her lead as Eleanor showed her the basic moves.

Alexandra's eyebrows were knit together as she tried to keep up with Eleanor. Her father never danced; her mother never got to teach her how to dance. She saw people dancing and knew that there needed to be proximity between bodies. Therefore, she had checked out the idea of dancing with anyone. Still, the fact that Eleanor was the one that she was going to dance with made her both frightened and excited.

After Eleanor was done explaining what her feet were supposed to do, Alexandra let out a frustrated groan. Still, her frustration was washed away as soon as Eleanor glided to stand in front of her with a broad smile painted on her lips.

"Hold me like I taught you," she said and Alexandra couldn't help but smirk as her callused hand, held Eleanor's soft one. Her other hand came to touch Eleanor's back. "Perfect! Now, we move, just like I said before. Let us start off slow." She nodded her head and began to count as she took a step back, then to the side, and once again another step forward.

Alexandra stumbled at first. The fear of stepping on Eleanor made her stiff, and Eleanor could sense that. As the minutes passed, their tempo became quicker. Alexandra relaxed enough to stop looking down and focus on Eleanor's face.

Eleanor was on cloud nine. The happiness her face radiated was evident and contagious enough to make Alexandra chuckle and pull Eleanor closer. In a manner of seconds, their dancing lessons were interrupted by a gentle and warm kiss. The basic posture was forgotten, the tempo became slower. Alexandra wrapped her arms around Eleanor as she sighed happily upon the other woman's parted lips.

Eleanor chuckled and rubbed her nose against Alexandra's before sliding away from her embrace. "You did well for a first-timer. We can practice some more later."

"Sounds like a plan."

"We should do this more often. Dance, I mean. You seemed to enjoy it more than I did."

"Where do you get that idea from, Lady Stownar?"

"Oh, I do not know. Maybe it is the fact that you haven't let go of me yet."

"Can you blame me, though?"

"Not at all." She sighed and pulled Alexandra from her nape to savor another soft kiss. "I actually enjoy the fact that I am falling for my husband."

Feeling butterflies in her stomach wasn't something that Alexandra was used to. Her heart dropped as fear crept its way into her mind, whispering the uncertainty of the words that Eleanor had just spoken. Even if that was something that Alexandra wanted, the fact that she was close to having Eleanor's love petrified her and sent a cold shiver down her soul.

Her grip grew stronger, and yet, Eleanor's blissful ignorance shined through as she pressed her chest tighter against Alexandra's and deepened the kiss. If only she knew that Alexandra was squeezing her harder to make sure that she was still awake and that this was not a nightmare.

Alexandra closed her eyes as her body reacted to the tenderness that Eleanor provided tenfold while forgetting about that one detail her wife didn't know about her.

If she were to tell Eleanor now, what would be her reaction? Should she tell her now? If not now, when?

Eleanor's moan woke her up from her daydream and made the taller woman take a step back and release Eleanor from her grip. Her eyes, dazed from the waves of lust that spiked her arousal, stared at Eleanor's half-closed and confused blue eyes.

"Alexander?"

"Are you in love with me, Lady Stownar?"

Eleanor tilted her head and reached out to Alexandra, but she took another step back. Eleanor scoffed nervously. "Well, I— I mean. I am certainly attracted to you. How could I not be?"

"Then, that is not love. That's lust."

Eleanor rolled her eyes in exasperation. "Oh, Alex please—"

"No. You must know the difference, and that's fine by me." She exhaled loudly, trying to get a grip on her own emotions. She fixed her vest; she ran her hand through her blonde hair and went back to her serious demeanor. "I will be attending to my horses until dinner time," Alexandra announced as she walked to the sofa and grabbed her coat. "We will continue this later."

Eleanor was left alone in the middle of the enormous living room with only her thoughts to accompany her. She was frowning deeply, anger flaring up like a fire in a forest. Her hands would've been trembling if it wasn't for the fact that Eleanor was absentmindedly touching her wedding band. She was growing weary and tired of catering and ignoring Alexandra's sudden mood swings. Her mind raced rationales for Alexandra's motive, and she still couldn't put her finger on the reason.

Her thoughts were interrupted by some footsteps coming from the long hall. Eleanor turned around quickly and saw Larkin walking in, chewing, yet again, on a piece of herb. She raised her eyebrows at him and cleared her throat loud enough for him to hear.

He stood up straight and swallowed the piece of weed, quickly regretting the action. "Lady Stownar."

"Larkin…" Eleanor whispered and looked at the closed doors of the mansion. "Care to have a talk?"

Larkin frowned and looked behind him and then back at Eleanor. "You want to talk to me, Lady Stownar?"

She simply nodded and moved her hand, signaling him to sit down. "Alexander is out with the horses, right?"

"If he isn't here, then, I guess he is," Larkin whispered as he sat down on the out of place sofa.

"He loves his horses, I see."

Larkin stared at the gorgeous woman in front of him as she moved about the living room until finally sitting down beside him. He shifted uncomfortably before Eleanor waved her hand at him. "What is it that you want to talk about?"

"You know Alexander more than I do. I wonder if you could talk to me about him. He seems to be… closed off."

He coughed a bit and moved away from her and crossed his legs. "What about him?"

Eleanor frowned and raised her shoulders. "Let us start with his past."

"I really do not think I should be talking about him behind his back. He has quite a temper as you know," Larkin said, rubbing his eyebrow.

"It is an order." Eleanor gave Larkin an intense glare that made the older man go stiff.

He hesitated before licking his lips and answering. "I do not remember much about Alex when he was a boy. He was always quiet and did not talk much. He did, however, go horseback riding a lot and usually would ask me to race him."

"What about his father? What was he like?"

"He was strong. He was a good, loving father, but really strict," Larkin answered, touching his knee, and looked at Eleanor once again. He took her in. It was in his nature to stare, especially when such a gorgeous woman was sitting right beside him at arm's length. Any man would want to discover every single part of her white skin, and her full lips were so inviting. Larkin had to take a deep breath and control his raging male desire, but of course, that only made it worse. Her smell was intoxicating. She smelled so sweet, so womanly so...untouched.

"I do not know much about his mother. I only saw her corpse," he added and stood up from the sofa before he did something foolish. "His father used to breed horses and also sold them to farms, to rich families to use as entertainment or to simply embellish their carriages." He cleared his throat and moved to the small table with tall glasses filled with whiskey and other types of alcohol. He poured himself a drink and then turned to look at the beautiful nymph.

Eleanor was staring at him. She was studying his face, trying to figure out if even once he lied to her or not. He knew a lot. She was sure of that, but since he was the right hand of her husband, she doubted this man would say something way too personal.

"After Alexander II died, Alex took over the business. He continued with his father's affairs."

Eleanor looked down at her skirt and thought of her next words. "Did Alexander have any other fiancée before me?"

Larkin choked on his drink. He quickly placed the glass back on the table and turned around to cough. When he was sure he had enough oxygen to answer, he turned to face Eleanor again and let out a nervous chuckle. "Now, why would my lady want to know about those sorts of things?"

"Because I am his wife."

Larkin frowned and took a deep breath. "No. He did not have any type of serious relationship with any woman. He was focused on his horses and on his mansion."

"Why did he suddenly wish to get married?"

Larkin let out a sly smile. He looked down at the table, and slowly, he traced his callused finger over the glass' edges. "A man...or in any case every human begins to grow tired of waking up alone so he—"

"Why didn't he get a whore?" Eleanor asked, standing up from the sofa and walking to Larkin. She crossed her arms under her chest and looked up at the tall, handsome man before her. She smiled, imitating him, and raising her eyebrow. "If he wanted some kind of sexual company, there are always the town whores."

"With all due respect, my lady, but would you be kind enough to let me finish what I was saying?"

Eleanor looked at his chest and then back at him. "Go on."

"He was brought up by a very religious family. He is no man of taking mistresses to his bed. So, he decided to marry a woman that seemed to need his help," he whispered before leaning closer to look down at her. "And he is no man of forcing himself on women or damsels in distress…" He grinned. "I bet my right arm he hasn't consummated the marriage."

Eleanor's neck almost snapped when she looked away from Larkin. She took a step back and rubbed her exposed shoulder before turning around. "That is none of your concern, Larkin. This conversation is over."

"As my lady wishes." He bowed to her and left the room using the same door as Alexandra.

"The nerve!" Eleanor shook her head and looked down at the small table. She grabbed the glass of whiskey and took a quick shot of it before slamming it back on the table. She hissed and covered her nose before letting out a cough, all the while wondering how in heaven could anyone drink that?

CHAPTER TWELVE

Is it wrong to hate my husband's brother? Because, to be honest, I cannot bring myself to do anything else but to hate him. I am tired of his eyes, his smirk, his stupid insinuating jokes... I hate the fact that Alexander ignores me when I tell him he has insinuated himself on me. William even had the audacity of saying that I would look even more beautiful if I was pregnant with his child rather than Alexander's. I almost puked on the spot. Yet, I must confess, I am growing weary of his words. Not only weary, but frightened. The other day he grabbed my elbow harshly when I turned to walk away from him. I want nothing to do with him. He does not seem to get it. I love Alexander; besides, I never gave him a motive or reason to believe that I was interested in him... On a good note, Alexander told me he was going to take me to the country mansion. I have missed the meadow and the library greatly.

"The library..." Alexandra sighed and stretched her arms over her head. "It has been closed ever since..." She shook her head and went back to the broken-down diary before a loud bark made her turn her eyes from it. She inhaled tiredly and turned to look at the window behind her. Something was amiss. Both Stick and Pebbles were acting unrested as they barked and growled at something outside the gates. "What's wrong with you too? Is someone outside?"

As she stood up, she heard a soft knock. "Come in."

"Excuse me. We are about to close the kitchen for tonight. I was wondering if you would like a cup of tea or something before we do."

Alexandra turned to look at the young maid before letting out a polite smile. She shook her head and waved her hand. "Thank you, Mia, but no. I am fine for the night."

"All right then. Have a good night."

"You too, Mia."

The maid turned back and slowly began to close the door before Alexandra called for her. "Yes?"

"Would you be kind enough to see if Lady Stownar needs anything?"

"Alright." She closed the door this time and let out a loud sigh. She was finally going to meet and talk to the mistress of the entire mansion. She looked down at her maid uniform and quickly wiped the stains of food from her apron as she made her way down the hall to Eleanor's room. She raised her hand and slowly knocked on the door.

"Who is it?"

Mia cleared her throat before speaking. "Mia, my lady. I am a kitchen maid." She took a step back when she heard Eleanor unlock the door and open it.

"Well, hello there, Mia. I believe we haven't met, haven't we?"

Nervousness crept its way into the young girl. She stared at Eleanor dumbfounded before articulating words. "Good morning…"

Eleanor giggled. "You mean good evening, right, dear?"

"Ah! I—" She cleared her throat again and tried to concentrate on her words. "My lady, we are going to close the kitchen soon and I was wondering if you would like something to eat or drink before we do."

"A cup of hot milk would be nice," Eleanor whispered, nodding at her own words.

"Alright then. I will be back shortly." Mia bowed her head and jogged down the hall and down the stairs as she made her way to the kitchen.

Eleanor stared at her, smiling. When she was finally out of sight, Eleanor closed the door and walked over to the small table in front of her bed. She sat down and ran her hand through the slick wood before hearing another knock, but this time it came from the door that connected her room with Alexandra's. She frowned a bit and let out a sigh. "Who is it?"

"It is me."

"I do not wish to see you right now."

"I have a surprise for you."

Eleanor clicked her tongue and stood up from her table. "It better be a nice surprise," she mumbled before opening the door. "Good evening."

"Likewise," Alexandra replied before stepping inside her former chamber. "I've noticed you do not do much around the house."

"Do you want me to clean it?"

Alexandra stood up straight and looked down at Eleanor. "No." She let out a sigh and moved her arm to Eleanor. "Care to join me?"

"Sorry. But I believe it is a bit too late for our dancing lessons."

"Would you please stop acting like a child and come with me? I want to show you something you might just like."

Eleanor muttered something under her breath about her not being a child and wrapped her arm with Alexandra's. "Fine."

"I do believe you told me once you like to read."

Eleanor looked up at Alexandra and nodded at her words.

"Yes, of course. I am usually busy, and I am not good at keeping you company, am I?" Alexandra assumed.

"You are fine. I understand that you need to work."

"That still doesn't excuse my behavior." She released Eleanor's arm and dipped her fingers in her pocket, pulling a small, rusted key. She placed the key into the door's slot and slowly turned it until she heard a click. "My mother," Alexandra began before opening the door. "She was kind of like you. She loved to read." She chuckled and pushed the door open for Eleanor. "This is the house library. All the books that the Dowry family has ever owned are in here. I am sure you will have your entire life to finish them."

The smell of dust and fungus was evident when the door was open. The moon's light poured in from the windows as dust danced around the streaks. Alexandra let out a nervous chuckle before turning to Eleanor. "Forgive me. I did not think this through. I should have asked the maids to clean it before I—"

"I love it. Thank you," Eleanor interrupted her as she took a step in and looked at the tall walls filled with books.

Alexandra watched her, studying her expression, wanting nothing more than to make sure that Eleanor really did enjoy the surprise.

"It is not that big but the books are good. I haven't been here in a while, but I am sure you can find something to entertain yourself."

"Thank you…" Eleanor said as she turned her back away from Alexandra. "Thank you so much."

Alexandra stared at Eleanor's back before slowly walking over to her. Her hands moved forward and almost touched her wife's waist. Almost.

"Are you all right?"

"Yes, I am fine, Lady Stownar, and thanks for asking. I think I am a bit tired though. Today was a rough day with the horses, the dancing—"

"About that…"

No, no, please do not make her talk about that. "What about it?" Alexandra asked and seconds later she kicked herself mentally.

"Are you still hanging on to the idea that what I feel for you is lust?"

"Yes," Alexandra quickly answered and closed her eyes as she cursed herself.

Eleanor chuckled and shook her head before walking towards Alexandra. "If this is lust, then I will be so damn happy to go to hell for it."

Alexandra swallowed hard. Control was slipping away way faster than she thought. To the point that her movements were involuntary. Her arms would circle around Eleanor's waist, while her lips would find hers like a magnet. But now her actions seemed to be more violent as she heard Eleanor's soft protest, her mouth and her hands pushing away.

"What in the world are you doing, Alexander Dowry, let go of…"

"You have no idea how hard it was for me the night of our wedding," Alexandra said right on her face, stealing the oxygen from her. "You are something out of this world, and all I wanted to do was you." Alexandra swallowed hard as Eleanor gasped, eyes wide. Vulgarity wasn't something that Alexandra was normally used to, but this woman was anything but normal. "I want nothing more than to see you underneath me, screaming my name," she groaned as she felt Eleanor's warmth through her pant leg. "To be between your legs and taste you."

"Alexander!"

"You are wet aren't you, Lady Stownar?"

Eleanor couldn't do anything except stare at Alexandra, who had managed to rub her knee even closer to Eleanor's core, catching her by surprise and making her release the sweetest most velvety moan Alexandra had ever heard in her life.

This was too much for Eleanor to handle, too fast for her own good. She was still getting used to Alexandra's breathtaking kisses, how could she get used to this new sensation that was coursing through her stomach, coming in jittery knots of pleasure. Eleanor's grasp on Alexandra's arms became tighter, pushing away. She needed space, she needed to breathe, she wasn't going to succumb, not in a dirty library! "Get off of me."

"You do not like physical contact?" Alexandra asked as she placed both of her hands on Eleanor's waist, pushing her against the large shelf and holding her in place. "Yes or no?"

She could lie, but then again what would happen after she said "no"? Alexandra would release her from the sweet torment she had Eleanor under. She would walk away, forgive herself from acting so recklessly and Eleanor would stand there, alone, in a dirty library, hot and bothered with only herself to fix that.

If she said yes, God only knows what will happen and that excited her even more. "Yes, I like it. To be honest, I quite enjoy it, but this is not the place to be…" The intense, burning sensation that brushed her lips made her forget what she was supposed to say next. Alexandra's slow open mouth kiss made her let out sounds she didn't even know she was capable of. And then there was Alexandra's hands, which touched and caressed her neck, leaving a trail of goose bumps along the way. Now, she found herself holding unto the person in front of her for dear life and she grew scared. Scared of the unknown. Was she ready? Eleanor breathed in hard and deep, oxygen wasn't reaching her brain, for she saw only white sparkles behind her eyelids. "How can you do this to me?"

"I ask myself the same questions every time I look at you," Alexandra exhaled, and shook her head, trying to think clearly. "We are both in this too deep, Lady Stownar. I do not know how long I can wait…" she pressed her strong and muscular leg closer to Eleanor. "Oh my God, you are so warm."

"Alexander Dowry!" Eleanor protested, embarrassed, face red and hissing as she pulled on Alexandra's blonde locks.

"Make up your mind, Lady Stownar. Do you want me to leave you alone, yes or no?"

"No."

Alexandra sighed on the side of her face and brushed her lips against her earlobe before pressing them on her neck. "It is rather exciting how you tremble against me."

"Stop talking."

With a low grunt, Alexandra placed Eleanor's hands around her neck and her own hands came to rest under Eleanor's supple thighs, raising her to attack her lips again. The soft and surprised gasp that escaped Eleanor's lips made Alexandra tremble with need. She could not wait to hear what other sounds she could make.

Holding on to the loose blonde strands, Eleanor tried to steady her movements to deepen the kiss. It wasn't until she felt Alexandra's rough hand against the skin of her leg that reality gave her a strong slap to the back of her head… or was it the bookshelf?

Eleanor pulled away, looked down at the blushing person in front of her, and sighed. Eleanor closed her eyes and hit her head softly against the bookshelf.

Alexandra simply stared in pure awe as if Eleanor was a goddess and she had been blessed with life only to experience having her in her arms at that precise moment. "You are so beautiful…"

Eleanor was too preoccupied in trying to regain as much control as she had left to even notice that Alexandra had uttered any type of words, Eleanor herself was having trouble talking due to all the electricity that she was coursing through her.

"How you are presented to me right at this moment. Your face is alive with color, your lips are swollen and red, your hair is simply wild and seductive, and your chest…" Alexandra licked her lips and grunted loudly as she lowered her enough to plant an open mouth kiss to the exposed cleavage. "Your chest is just begging to be touched and worshiped."

Eleanor let out a soft whimper. Her hands came to cup Alexandra's heated cheeks and pushed her husband away enough to look at Alexandra's darkened green eyes. "Are you satisfied?"

"No, not yet." To tell her right there, to undo her vest, press her small chest to Eleanor's, to let her feel her as she was and just take her would've been the greatest thing in Alexandra's whole existence. But, then what? How would she react? What would Eleanor do? Alexandra simply wasn't thinking about that. The only thing she was concentrating on was Eleanor's mouth, her own shallow breathing and how good Eleanor's soft skin felt against her hands.

"*He isn't in his chamber and neither is Lady Stownar!*"

"*Then find him!*"

Both women turned to look at the closed door of the library when they heard the voices of the butlers and maids running down the halls. Alexandra quickly set Eleanor down to her feet again and fixed up her attire before opening the door and stepping out.

"What is going on?" she demanded one of the young maids.

"There you are! You must come down to the kitchen! Someone has entered and hurt young Mia!" the maid said, forgetting completely of any law of respect when she grabbed Alexandra by her sleeve and pulled her out of the library.

"What?" Alexandra turned around and stuck her torso inside the library. "Lady Stownar, go back to your chamber and lock yourself up."

"Wait, what happened? What is going on?"

"Please, a maid was hurt by a burglar and I need to see if she is all right. I do not know if the perpetrator is around, and just go to your chamber and stay there!"

Eleanor walked to Alexandra's side and looked down at the frightened maid. "I am sorry, but I am coming with you."

Alexandra let out a loud grunt and grabbed her hand. "Let us go then."

***

"Mia! Mia, for God's sake please, wake up!"

"Alma, take it easy, it was only a bump on the head."

"But a bump in the head could kill you!" Alma yelled as she shook the unconscious Mia. "Come on, wake up!"

Alexandra pushed the large kitchen door open, she pulled Eleanor inside and looked around at the mess. "What the hell?"

Alma turned around and released a soft whimper when she saw Alexandra. "Master! Mia— she is—"

"She is unconscious, that's all there is to it," Alexandra said as she kneeled in front of the two young maids. "Try to calm down, Alma," she ordered, picking up the unconscious girl and turning around to one of the butlers. "Take her to one of the guest rooms and leave her there for the night."

"Yes, sir!"

"Now, what happened here?"

A soft hiccup came from Alma before taking a deep breath and answering Alexandra's question. "Mia came down and said that she was going to prepare a hot cup of milk for Lady Stownar. We started to talk for a while and then I went ahead to clean the counter tops before leaving when I heard Mia struggling with someone and— when I went back, she was lying on the floor and a boy was looking down at her. I yelled at him 'What have you done?' and he ran out."

"A boy? What did he look like?" Alexandra demanded, putting her hands on her hips.

"I say, twelve, thirteen years-old, brown hair, white shirt and dirty slacks."

Alexandra nodded and turned around to look at Eleanor. "Go back to your chamber and stay there until I come back."

"Where are you going?"

"To get that boy. If he left on foot, he should be around the forest somewhere. I am sure Stick and Pebbles can sniff him out."

"But Alexander, what if he is armed?"

She sighed, cupped Eleanor's cheek, and silenced her with a strong peck on the lips. "I will not die just because of a boy..." She chuckled as she stayed close enough to get a nervous reaction from Eleanor. "Now go upstairs and lock yourself up in your chamber. I will let you know when I come back."

"Fine." One of them had to give in and it sure wasn't going to be Alexandra.

Alexandra turned and called out to one of the maids. She gave her the instructions to stay and usher Eleanor to her chamber. She quickly ordered the butlers to get her horse ready and once again, she ran up the stairs, not before stopping in front of a chamber.

"Wake up!" Alexandra yelled as she pushed the door open. She saw how Larkin let out a surprised scream and covered himself with his bed sheets. She chuckled and shook her head at the pathetic sight before her. "Get yourself clothed, Larkin, and bring your gun! We are going hunting."

***

"A kid?" Larkin asked as he struggled with his knee-length tight white pants.

"A boy," Alexandra corrected him as she grabbed hold of the reins of her horse and jumped on him. "Where are the wolves?"

Larkin struggled a bit with his own horse before he was finally on him. "You could at least wait for me to put a shirt on," Larkin said, shivering. "It is way too cold for me to be like this!"

"Shut up." Alexandra placed her thumb and index finger inside her mouth. She let out a loud whistle and seconds later she heard both of her wolves running from behind the mansion. "Stick!" She called out to the male and struggled with her horse. The animal always got nervous when the wolves were around him. Instincts. She made eye contact with the animal and jerked her head to the woods. "Go get him!"

Pebbles sneezed and playfully bit Stick's ear before taking off into the woods with Stick following close behind. Alexandra kicked her horse to get the animal going.

"Slow down!" Larkin yelled as he kicked the black mare and took off.

"Oh, now you are asking me to slow down?" Alexandra turned back and shook her head at her best friend. "Get going!"

Hunting and running. Just a few of Alexandra's favorite things. She could almost smell the fear and she could just make out the sounds of the whimpers coming from the boy. The wolves were near him, snarling and barking ferociously as they made eye contact with their victim. Clearly it was a boy, and he was running for his life at full force, ignoring the pain of having branches and bushes ripping through his skin and clothes.

"Stop and they will not hurt you!" Alexandra yelled, just in time to hear a wounded cry. One of the animals must have gotten to him. "Too late." The two large grey fur balls were on top of the kid, holding one leg while the other snarled and sniffed his face. Alexandra let out a loud shout as she got off her horse and held tightly one of the wolves' tails as she pulled him off the boy.

"Stay put before I put a bullet between your eyes." Alexandra almost snared as she pushed Pebbles' snout away from the boy's neck.

Larkin stumbled with the reins of his horse as he descended from it. He looked down at Alexandra and then toppled to the ground. "This is it? This runt!"

Alexandra grabbed the kid's leg and pulled him towards her. "Who sent you?"

The boy quickly squeezed Alexandra's hand and tried to push it away, stammering and whimpering in fear. Alexandra clasped the bite wound on his leg. His screams would surely be heard back in the mansion. "I do not know! Some men paid me five coins to see if everyone in the house was asleep!"

"Why did you hurt my maid?" Alexandra asked, giving the leg another squeeze.

"Ah! I did not know there was someone there! I simply opened the door and I accidentally hit her head! Please, sir! Let go, you are hurting me!"

Alexandra looked at Larkin before going back to the kid. She let out a loud snarl and pushed the boy away. "Get going before I get the police."

"What? You are letting him go."

"Yes. He doesn't know what the hell he was doing." Alexandra murmured before moving to pet Stick's neck. "Run, boy. My wolves are awfully hungry today."

The boy nodded, turned around on his stomach, and crawled away from Alexandra before standing up and running through the woods.

"You let him go? Just like that? Where is my gun?"

Alexandra patted the dirt off her knees and turned away from Larkin as she walked to her horse. "You left them with your clothes, remember?"

"We can follow him and see where he goes. Maybe we can meet with those bastards that gave him the order to come to the mansion."

"Or we can go back to the mansion and go to bed. Aren't you tired?" Alexandra asked as she pulled herself up from the ground and sat on the horse's back. "He was just doing as he was told. I am sure they've already fled anyway."

Larkin let out a frustrated groan. "Why are you so at ease? You know damn well that they can just get in again!"

"Double up the guards."

"We only have so many." Larkin sighed and ran his hands through his hair before taking fistfuls of it. "We have to keep our eyes open, Alex. This is getting out of hand."

"Nothing has happened, Larkin."

"Are we going to fucking wait for something to happen? Is that your plan? Because it is a shitty plan. We should fucking kill your cousin and get this thing over with!"

"We do not know if it is him."

"Well, we will definitely know if he isn't. Jesus Christ, Alexandra!"

"Shut the up, Larkin! Someone might hear you."

"Your father was smart enough to kill everyone involved with the little switcheroo. How come you are not smart enough to eliminate the one person that might screw everything up?"

"Because!" she yelled at him as she tried her hardest to settle Snow down. The animal had grown restless due to all the screaming and it was probably sleepy. "Because I am not my father. I refuse to go around killing just for the sake of keeping things quiet."

"You do not have to do it. I can—"

"You will not dirty your hands for me!"

"I would fucking kill myself for you, you dumb bitch."

Silence fell between them. The night's air grew dense and colder while little by little the animals of the forest began their routine of embellishing the silence of the night with their chorus.

Alexandra stared down at Larkin as she thought of words that might calm his eager breathing and rage, yet if she said something along the lines of, "you shouldn't do that for me," she knew that she would not hear the end of it.

Larkin mare let out an awkward snort and pressed her cold nose to the side of his hairy face as if trying to appease the man's wrath. Somehow it worked. He clicked his tongue in annoyance and moved his hand to pet the animal's jaw before turning to Alexandra. "Sorry for saying 'dumb bitch'."

Alexandra shrugged. "I can be dumb sometimes."

"And a bitch," Larkin added.

Alexandra nodded. "And a bitch."

***

She tried so hard not to bite her fingernails, so instead she was chewing on her thumb, while staring at the gates of the mansion from her window, in her long nightgown. She believed it would've been so much better if she went to sleep and waited for any news in the morning, but even laying down proved to be difficult. Her mind raced with images, amalgamations of scenes. Kisses, grunts, gasps, warmth, and skillful hands that undid her. And pulled her in to fear, and desperation, and liquid pleasure that pooled between her thighs.

She tried to sleep, she really did, but the moment she opened her eyes and found herself breathing hard, skin covered in goosebumps, she knew that even closing her eyes was a mistake.

Waiting proved to be the best thing to do. Even so, she found herself doing a lot of that for the past couple of days after her wedding. Waiting had been her preferred, albeit unwillingly, activity.

She waited for her husband to wake up, to invite her for breakfast, to take her out and show her around their mansion, to teach her how to ride a horse, to kiss her, to hold her, to undo her.

Waiting had become the most annoying thing that she had learned to do, but the rewards of her patience had been more than she had ever hoped for.

God, she hated to wait….

That was why the second she saw the two horses run through the gates with their respective masters, she felt a wave of relief hit her. And finally, she was able to breathe normally again, though she didn't notice she was doing otherwise. Closing her eyes and thanking God came on instinct and so did the ticklish sensation in the pit of her stomach when she heard running footsteps heading towards her door.

Eleanor stood up, brushed her hands against the cold wood of the door, and heard a person outside who was probably having an inner battle monologue of whether to wake her up or head to bed.

Eleanor answered the question for them.

She opened the door just in time to see Alexandra turning away, running that large hand through her blonde hairs, making Eleanor jealous that she wasn't the one doing so.

Questioning blue eyes met green ones. No words were said, they didn't need them.

Alexandra wanted to talk, to voice that everything was fine, that it was just a boy that had entered the home, but the woman that stood in front of her was wearing a mundane nightgown that covered up all the delicious curves that Eleanor showed off with her daily dresses.

And yet, she felt her breath stuck in her throat, her pulse accelerated, and her hand trembled with the need to take her in her arms.

"You are here," Eleanor whispered, as a secret that she shouldn't say even to herself. As if by Alexandra being there, she was committing some sort of a crime.

"I wanted to see if you were fine," she responded, eyes going back to Eleanor's face out of respect. It wasn't polite to ogle, not a woman who was wearing such little clothing, and so she decided to look for a topic of conversation before her mind trailed to other matters, like, perchance, what they were doing in the library before they were interrupted.

Not thinking, or maybe deliberately, Eleanor opened the door wider and stepped aside, inviting the older woman inside her chamber as her hands trembled and voice cracked. "Co—come in."

If she walked in that room, if the door was shut, if she kissed Eleanor again, she would seal her fate. She wouldn't be able to contain herself, and she would somehow act upon what she told Eleanor.

"Please?"

But how could she ever deny her anything, especially when she said please in such a soft manner. Clearing her throat and swallowing hard afterwards, Alexandra found herself striding into the room, fidgety.

Out of the corner of her eyes, she saw Eleanor padding her way to the bed before slowly sitting down on the edge. "What happened? Is everything fine?"

Yes, that would work. Talking about what happened outside would take her attention away from the other thoughts that were already sneaking their way in from the corners of her mind. Alexandra sighed tiredly and sat down next to Eleanor.

"It was a boy, like Alma said. He snuck in using the backdoor."

"Why was a boy trying to gain access to the mansion? A thief?"

"I do not think so. Too young to be one."

"Oh please," Eleanor scoffed. "I didn't know there was a minimum age requirement to become a thief."

Alexandra chuckled. "True, but he was not a thief."

"Then why was he here?"

"I am still not sure, Lady Stownar."

"Where is the child?"

"Oh, I sent him away."

Eleanor opened her eyes wide, dumbfounded. "You sent him away?"

Alexandra looked at Eleanor before nodding.

"This doesn't make sense. Why would a child be lurking about for no reason and why, in heaven's name, would you let him get away?"

"Lady Stownar…"

"He can come back! He can come back with people!"

"Lady Stownar, please—" Alexandra stopped talking the moment she noticed that tears had started to pool around Eleanor's eyes. "If you are worried about me—"

"Of course, I am! I am worried and I am even more worried now!" She reached out and cupped Alexandra's face. "What would I do if something ever happened to you?"

"I am sorry that I made you worry. I swear it wasn't my intention at all." She cupped her soft hands, drowning in blue eyes. "I thought it would be better I just—" Warm lips silenced her once again. Eleanor had taken upon herself to shut her up with kisses. Not like Alexandra was against that. Yet, every time she did so, the older woman was always taken by surprise.

"Stay the night..."

The jittering in her stomach was back, intensified tenfold by Eleanor's lips on hers.

"Please," Eleanor murmured, tangling her fingers with the short hairs at the back of Alexandra's head. Slowly, she gave her a hot open mouth kiss, sealing her plea while her hands dipped down Alexandra's neck.

Alexandra's breath was caught in her throat, she could feel her heartbeat inside her ears. She pulled away, stood up, albeit her body screamed to stop and give in. Her mind threw an alarm to run, to hide. Why in the world was she there in the first place, and why was she dipping her head lower? To take in the way her wife looked with lust painted in her once innocent face? "I cannot stay, Lady Stownar."

"Why?" She stood likewise before the blonde, hair undone, lips parted, hands on Alexandra's belt.

Alexandra opened her mouth to answer, but what came out was a frustrated groan. She had so many reasons to leave, but the one reason to stay proved to be stronger than anything she had ever encountered in her entire life.

Eleanor swallowed hard, looked up at Alexandra and took a deep breath. She was tired of waiting...

"Do you not want to finish what we started in the library?"

Silence was her answer. Alexandra stood before her, frozen, masking her eyes with the darkness that the room provided. She could feel that her heart was about to leave her chest.

"Because I do."

She sucked in a breath, closed her eyes, and pressed her forehead to Eleanor's. Her arms came to circle around Eleanor's waist, pulling her close, dangerously close. "You are making me lose my patience and control."

"I do it with the utmost intent."

Alexandra shuddered with want; her hand clutched the soft fabric of Eleanor's robe as their eyes locked. "I—"

"I am done waiting, Alex..." she whispered, pushing the taller frame against her until Alexandra dropped down, sitting on the edge of the bed once again.

Without wasting a second, Alexandra pulled onto the long, white nightgown until it was forgotten on the ground. She looked up, hands gripping the bed sheets, white knuckles, and lips parted in awe. Eleanor saw the person in front of her staring at her as if she was a goddess. As if the mortal before her was adoring. A wave pulsed through and stopped right below her navel.

"You— you are gorgeous, Lady Stownar…" Alexandra murmured.

Strangely, as Eleanor studied Alexandra's face, noticing the delicate features, the long eyelashes, the soft curved lips, the smooth skin, she found herself gripping the hairs on the back of Alexandra's head and coddling herself. She swallowed hard, licked her lips, and dove in for a soft and slow kiss. She had grown addicted to those. There was something about those kisses. Soft, shy then rough and dangerous, hesitant yet indulging.

"So are you, Alex." She gasped, pressing her naked chest to Alexandra's clothed one. "You are beautiful."

Alexandra had trouble breathing as she took in Eleanor's darkened blue eyes. Alexandra inhaled, as if pulling strength from deep inside and rolled over, sprawling Eleanor on the large bed, watching how her chest raised and fell with each hard excited breath she took.

By instinct, Eleanor pulled Alexandra for another soaring kiss. She wanted nothing more than to cover her body with Alexandra's, to fill that warmth upon her and the waves that followed through.

Meanwhile, Alexandra had problems creating coherent thoughts. It was difficult enough to breathe, let alone to talk. Yet, as she watched upon Eleanor's writhing body, words poured out of her chest.

"I want to kiss you everywhere, Lady Stownar." She encased Eleanor in her arms. "You deserve to be worshiped."

The soft, ragged breath that escaped Eleanor drove Alexandra to the edge of insanity. Eleanor's hand came to Alexandra's neck, urgently her fingers undid the knot at the base of the collar, pulling on the piece of cloth used as a tie and freed at least a portion of that skin that she wanted to kiss so badly. Yet, soon enough, and to no surprise, she found her hands pinned up above her head, lust filled green eyes looked down at her, rebuking her actions.

"Please, I just want to touch you," Eleanor whimpered desperately.

"No, not now." Alexandra breathed upon her lips, stopping herself from devouring them again. "This night is about you, not me."

"But—"

"Lady Stownar, trust me." That came out more as a plea than an order.

Eleanor couldn't help but relax under Alexandra's burning gaze and absorb how disheveled and undone Alexandra looked. It was so different compared to the perfectly combed and collected visage carried around at every waking moment. She loved it…

"I do, with my entire existence."

Something inside of Alexandra snapped. She clashed her mouth against

Eleanor's, pouring in all the pent-up tension that she was holding since day one. Her skilled hands played over Eleanor's skin, leaving a trail of goose bumps over her chest, stomach, and thighs.

She became undone by Eleanor's soft mewls that she found herself buried in the junctions of her legs, drowning her thirst.

The old chamber was replete with the sounds of soft moans and whimpers coming from deep down Eleanor's throat.

She had long forgotten that she was in a bed, and instead, her hands flew to clutch blonde strands as she thrashed about the indomitable pleasure that surged through her. Never in her wildest dreams had she thought that what Alexandra was doing was possible, but it was too much too soon for her to even call out and pull away.

She was breathless, and even if she opened her mouth to breathe the only thing that managed to escape her moist lips were sounds that she never thought she could produce.

Time was broken, and before she knew it, Eleanor found herself gasping and wanting nothing more than to breathe.

Alexandra stayed anchored, grabbing onto Eleanor's thighs as she let the younger woman ride the last waves of pleasure against her mouth as Eleanor bucked, gasped, and shook.

Eleanor's breathing was hard, as she came back to her own reality. Alexandra kneeled in front of her, watching, enthralled by the creature that looked up at her with brown strands of hair sticking to her face.

Without even thinking, Alexandra licked her lips savoring Eleanor one last time, engraving the taste deep in her mind. Not long after, she found herself, leaning on the bed, covering Eleanor's body with hers as they shared a deep kiss.

Eleanor sighed in it, tasting herself on Alexandra's lips. She tried to keep their lips sealed if she could, but the other woman had settled next to her, still, completely clothed, except the forgotten tie that had been tossed on the ground moments ago.

Alexandra opened her eyes and turned to look at Eleanor who was taking her sweet time to level her breathing, chest raising and falling.

Their gaze met, distorting everything around them, breaking apart their senses as they both took everything in.

Eleanor was the first one to move. Her hand searched for Alexandra's, and when she found it, she squeezed it hard, scared, excited.

Alexandra closed her eyes tightly and sucked in air. Her skin reacted as Eleanor's hand traveled to her face, pulling it close.

"I am growing fond of that mouth of yours, Alex."

Alexandra's answer was a grunted chuckle before opening her eyes.

"Anything else you might want to show me tonight?"

The look on Eleanor's face is nothing like Alexandra has ever seen directed at her before. It is calm, sweet, inviting, gorgeous, and so full of love...

What have I done?

"I need to go," Alexandra announced, desperate, terrified. She jumped to her feet and stumbled upon the ground with a loud thud. "Fuck!" Alexandra muttered and quickly stood up, trying her best to ignore Eleanor's inquisitor glance.

"Wait, Alex—"

"I cannot stay here. I cannot stay here." Fear poured out of her like a broken faucet.

"But—"

"I do not want to stay here!"

Eleanor pulled her hand back, frightened, yet concerned by the voice that had crawled its way out of Alexandra's throat. It wasn't the usual deep voice; it was something different; as if someone else had spoken.

"I am sorry," Alexandra deepened her voice again, before coughing softly. Without saying anything else, she grabbed her tie and moved to her chamber, not before closing, and locking the door behind her. She heard Eleanor call to her one last time before silence consumed the mansion and the only things heard were the nightly critters.

As if a bucket of water had been thrown at her, Alexandra dawned on what had just happened. She wiped her mouth and was just as surprised as she found tears running down her face. Her chest ached and her hands trembled uncontrollably while her body curved until she sat down on the floor, her back to the door.

She wept, hard and loud, but she was not audible to anyone in the mansion. She covered her mouth and nose with her hands as she closed her eyes tightly as she tried her hardest to stop the burning tears.

They were both in too deep, and there was nothing neither of them could do to back out of this now.

CHAPTER THIRTEEN

It was bad enough that Larkin was up so early, now he had to deal with the carriage's driver, an old man that was hired now and then and whose age was starting to become a problem, at least to Larkin.

But Alexandra thought otherwise since her heart always had a soft spot for older people. The only old person Larkin adored was Nana. That woman sure had a way with words…

Back to the driver, he was placing an excessive number of suitcases and bags on top of the carriage. At the same time, Larkin told him to be careful. If something was broken, Larkin would probably be the one to pay the consequences for not properly supervising. After yelling out a couple of hot-blooded insults which made even the driver blush with fury, Larkin shooed him away and decided to accommodate the luggage.

"Bad night?"

Larkin muttered yet another curse under his breath when he recognized the voice. "It is too early in the morning, Alex. Leave me alone."

Alexandra fixed her coat and buttoned up the end of her sleeve before looking at the top of the carriage. "What is all this?"

"Your wife's crap."

Alexandra tilted her head to the side and opened her hand in disbelief. "What? Where is all my stuff?"

Larkin took out his handkerchief and wiped the sweat off his brow before looking back at Alexandra. "Underneath your wife's crap! Now, will you go and get her so we can get going? Your cousin's house is far from this one, so we better get a move on before it is dark."

"I shouldn't have agreed on staying in that house," Alexandra whined, running a shaky hand through her hair. "I do not think I dare to ask for a second room."

"I do not care. I want to get going," Larkin spat angrily, so unlike him.

Alexandra had to laugh at his words. "You sure are in a bad mood. What bed bug took a chomp out of your balls last night?"

"You!"

"I do not bite balls." She chuckled at the thought of that being the understatement of the year, especially after last night.

Larkin let out a frustrated groan before screaming, "You and your stupid hunting game which ended up in absolutely nothing! Not only that, but also, I think I caught something riding almost half-naked around the damn forest! And in addition to all of that, I know you had a good night! I saw you entering Eleanor's room!"

"Wait." She snickered. "Are you spying on me now?"

"Nana was up and she was giving me some hot tea for my runny nose while you were rolling around in the sheets. When I went back to my room, I saw you. Do not deny it, she knows!"

"I know what?"

Alexandra's eyes grew wide. She stared at Larkin for what seemed an eternity before turning to face Eleanor, who was happily putting on her gloves, looking as perfect as someone could look regarding that they had just woken up extra early for the trip and who also probably had a horrible night thinking why in heaven did her husband leave her chamber after giving her the most satisfying and pleasurable night in her entire existence.

Alexandra chuckled nervously. "What?"

"Exactly. What do I know?"

Larkin started to mutter something, anything to get Alexandra out of trouble, but she was faster.

"We are leaving now."

Eleanor frowned. "What? Did I miss something?"

"No, my lady. Please, get inside." Larkin faked a smile before jumping off the carriage.

Eleanor averted her gaze to Alexandra, whose expression added to the confusion she was having. Something was up with those two, and God as her witness she was going to find what it was one way or another.

"Get a move on with the horse. We better get there before it is dark or we are going to be in trouble," Alexandra said while ignoring Eleanor's inquisitorial gaze. With a sigh, she turned to Eleanor and helped her into the carriage before she jumped in as well.

"Why is it so important to get to your cousin's house before nightfall?"

"The forest is a dangerous place to be during the night. This time the wolves will not be here to serve as our guards," Alexandra answered.

"Do you think Nana will be fine attending the mansion all by herself?"

"She is an old woman, but she has the personality to have all the maids

127

and butlers at her disposal, believe me, I know…"

Eleanor chuckled, yet she bit her lower lip as she studied Alexandra's mood. Alexandra was anxious, uncomfortable, and clearly she wanted to ignore the fact that she was trapped with Eleanor in a small carriage since she was pulling out, what seemed to Eleanor, a small book. Her plan was to focus on reading and to evade whatever questions were thrown her way.

"Do you want to talk?"

Alexandra inhaled loudly, a clear sign that she heard the question, but didn't answer.

"Alexander Dowry III," she probed, annoyingly.

"I had to make sure that the mansion was taken care of."

"Isn't that what the guards are for?" Eleanor was getting tired of the avoidance.

"You were petrified of me getting hurt last night, and now you would've rather have me stay in your chamber and ignore my duties in the mansion."

"I am just saying that it is rather infuriating for me that the master of the house has to take care of so many things when there are other people that can take care of them."

"I am truly dumbfounded, and I cannot understand you at all."

"I guess that makes two of us."

Alexandra took a deep breath and hit her fist, harshly against the roof of the carriage. Within seconds, she heard the driver let out a command to get the horses going.

"You are trying my patience, Lady Stownar…"

"Likewise, Master Dowry."

Silence fell upon them, and once again, Alexandra had put up her walls. Eleanor could already tell, knit together eyebrows, and eyes looking down at the book were the clues that gave it away. She rolled her tongue over her lower lip and sighed before taking off her hat and placing it in the empty space next to her.

"I do not like this."

Eleanor tilted her head upwards. "What?"

"This. There is no reason for us to be angry at each other, on the contrary." Alexandra rubbed her chin nervously before she continued. "I truly enjoyed myself last night, and I want nothing more than to know that you did too."

Eleanor's face was red within seconds. She cleared her throat and nodded. "Well, I— Yes."

"Yes?" Alexandra smiled.

"I… I was taken aback by it, I never thought—"

"I told you that nothing is wrong between a married couple."

"Of course," Eleanor sighed and sat down beside Alexandra. "I wasn't expecting that, though."

"Me neither…"

"So, it wasn't planned?"

"I do not think that you can plan such things…" Alexandra's gaze went from her mother's diary to Eleanor. "You truly have no idea how breathtaking you are and… how annoying and mind-boggling!"

"Annoying?"

"You make it hard to think straight. You make it hard for me to even be around you without touching you. You are different, and the fact that you are here right now, beside me, is throwing me off. I want to protect you, I want to give you all the things you deserve, and I do not mean material things." Alexandra sighed and moved a strand of brown hair away from Eleanor's face. "You deserve better than a crazy…husband."

"It is funny how you always think you know what's best for me. I know that we did not start off like we would have liked. I would have loved to be courted. Go horseback riding, you meeting my mother, having chaperones, writing letters, invitations to parties, having our engagement announced to the gentry, but we went over all that."

"You wanted that?"

"As silly and stupid as it may sound to you, yes. But I do not want you to think that it was because I wanted to fit in. I wanted that for my own selfish reasons. I would have loved to see you, nervous, not sure of what to talk about while we had my maid behind us, watching our every move. I want to enjoy you in every facet, I didn't get the courting one, now I get to have the married one."

"I am not good at courting. I have never—"

"Me neither. I have no idea what to do or say."

"You never had men after you?" Alexandra asked, hopeful that the answer would be no.

Eleanor chuckled. "My father was drowning in debt. I was more of a burden."

Alexandra frowned. "You are not a burden to me. On the contrary, I feel like I am a burden to you."

"Alex, you are amazing, and to be honest, and I am trying to find words to express my most and deepest emotions. Every second that I am with you, I find things that intrigue me and make me adore you even more."

"If you only knew…"

"Knew what?" Eleanor asked, moving her hand to cup the chiseled, smooth jaw.

"How scared I am of actually falling in love with my own wife," Alexandra answered as she slipped her arm around Eleanor's waist and pulled her even closer.

"I think it is too late for that."

"I am scared of hurting you…and then hurting myself."

Eleanor stared at Alexandra's lip before moving closer and claiming a luscious lower lip as hers. She pressed her chest to Alexandra's as she dipped her shy tongue inside Alexandra's warm mouth, images of last night flooding her mind. Eleanor couldn't help but let out a cute giggle. She hid her red face in Alexandra's neck and hugged her tightly.

"I love you…" she whispered to Alexandra's shoulder. "I do not care what you think. I love you, and nothing will change that."

Alexandra looked down at Eleanor for what seemed hours before she wrapped her strong arms around her. She hugged her back tightly and stuck her nose in her hair before smelling her sweet scent.

"Promise?"

"I swear…"

Alexandra took a deep breath. She squeezed Eleanor before pulling her away from her to look at her face. "Lady Stownar…" She licked her lower lip and looked down at her own lap. "There is something you need to know."

Suddenly, the carriage came to an abrupt stop. Alexandra let out an annoyed groan and shook her head. Really? Now?

"Excuse me for a moment." She moved to the door of the carriage and stuck her head out. "What is it now?"

"There is a tree blocking the road." He jerked his head towards the fallen tree. "It must have happened because of the storm we had some days ago."

Alexandra placed the diary inside her pocket and took off her coat. She put it over Eleanor's shoulder and opened the carriage door.

"Where are you going?"

"We need to move the tree before we continue. There is no way around it."

Eleanor's grip on the coat got tighter.

"It is fine. Nothing bad is going to happen. We can start by untying the horses from the carriage and using them to move the trees." Alexandra said as she looked up at the carriage driver. "Get up and help me untie them."

"I got it, I got it," Larkin said as he jumped off his horse.

They grabbed the two horses that were carrying the carriage and tied their long reins to the tree. Larkin did the same with his horse, and all three of them, Alexandra, Larkin, and the carriage driver made the horses pull the tree until they achieved to move it out of the way.

"Is it enough for the carriage to go through?" Alexandra asked as she looked behind her.

"It will be enough, I am sure, Master Alexander," the driver said as he got off the horse and pulled the animal back to the carriage.

"Well, then. Go back to the carriage. I will hurry up and tie the horses."

Alexandra nodded and jumped from the horse. The animal suddenly became agitated, moving around and snorting loudly. The horses backed away from where Alexandra was standing. She, on the other hand, tried to steady the animal, but as soon as she pulled on the reins, the horse got up on his hind legs.

"Whoa! Whoa! What's going on?"

"Stay away from him!" Larkin said as he got closer to the agitated animal. He grabbed hold of the harness near the animal's snout and tugged on it as hard as he could to get the horse under control.

"What is going on?"

Alexandra groaned and looked back to the carriage. Eleanor had literally stuck her head outside the window, looking over at them. "Get back inside. The horse is hysterical."

"Why?"

"Because..."

The air was cut, the words died in everyone's mouth as the sudden blast of a gun echoed through the entire forest.

"Get back in the carriage, now!" Larkin yelled as he and the driver quickly tied the horses back to the carriage. Another shot was heard, but this time it hit something. Larkin fell with his horse, making Alexandra turn around before stepping inside of the carriage.

"Larkin!"

Eleanor shouted, "Alexander, what is going on?"

"Stay in the bloody damned carriage, cover yourself, and stay down!" Alexandra yelled as she ducked and ran over to Larkin. "Larkin! Larkin, did they hit you!"

"They got my horse!" Larkin said as he tried his best to crawl from under the animal.

Alexandra grabbed hold of Larkin's vest and pulled him from under the horse as hard as she could and dragged him over to the carriage. Alexandra opened the door and pushed the man inside before getting in herself.

She began to hit the roof of the carriage while screaming for the driver to go. She didn't have the time to be seated when the carriage started to run over the rural roads of the forest. She fell on the wooden seat and hit the back of her head against the carriage wall.

"Great! Just what we needed, to get shot at." Larkin protested before looking down at his feet. "Lady Stownar!"

Alexandra looked down at herself and cursed under her breath. She kneeled on the carriage floor and helped Eleanor sit down on the seat in front of her. "Are you all right?"

Eleanor was still in a daze, and of course, she was getting motion sickness. The carriage was bumping, and taking every single crater on the road, and not to mention, having two large humans crash in on her was painful.

"I am fine," Eleanor muttered as she sat down.

"Are you sure?" Alexandra asked as she cupped her cheek.

"Yes, Yes, I am sure..." Eleanor then looked around the carriage and tilted her head to the side as she stared at Larkin. "Did the carriage get smaller?"

Alexandra turned around and watched how both she and Larkin took most of the space inside the carriage. She chuckled and sat down beside her best friend. "No," he mumbled.

"What happened?" Eleanor asked as she tried to collect Alexandra's coat and hers. She moved as close as she could to the corner since Alexandra and Larkin had just decided to spread their legs as far as they possibly could.

Larkin gave Alexandra a glare, and for a moment, both had a thirty-minute conversation with their eyes that lasted less than five seconds. Alexandra looked away and scratched her head. "Thieves, probably," she lied.

"Thieves? Then why hide?" Eleanor frowned. "I do not understand."

"Me neither," Alexandra said as she rubbed her face. "Let us all just forget about this. Larkin, I will get you a new horse when we get back to the mansion."

"Thanks." Larkin simply said as he leaned on his knees and rubbed his hands together.

Alexandra sighed and pushed Larkin aside to sit beside Eleanor. The younger woman looked up at her and shook her head tiredly. She wrapped her arms around Alexandra's neck and squeezed her tenderly. "I was scared," Eleanor said before cupping Alexandra's face in her own hands and kissing her lower lip gently.

Larkin stared at both women in awe. She saw how Alexandra closed her eyes and rubbed her nose with Eleanor's and noticed how the younger woman relaxed under the blonde's touch. Larkin frowned. He watched the soft smile spread across Eleanor's lips and felt something inside his chest turning. He groaned and cracked his knuckles.

As soon as Eleanor heard bones cracking, she turned and looked at Larkin. She tilted her head and looked upon his now depressed form. "Larkin?"

Larkin looked at Eleanor, studying her face before answering. "Yes, my lady?"

"Are you hurt?"

Larkin smiled. He shook his head and looked at the floor of the carriage. "Not physically…"

***

"He is here."

A couple of dark green eyes looked up from his paperwork. Tiredly, the young man leaned against his chair and turned his neck to look outside the window of his study. "Is he?"

The older servant nodded and rubbed his hands together. "I am sorry, Master Cassius."

"Never mind, now," he muttered, standing up and cracking his back. "He is here, better treat him like a welcomed guest. The rooms upstairs are clean, am I right?"

"Yes, sir."

"Good work, Silas."

The older man nodded and looked down on the floor before speaking again. "Master Cassius, I am worried about the others."

"Otto and Erik are fine, I assure you," Cassius said. "Now. It is better to let him think that we have nothing to do with that. The party will be held in a couple of days, and after I get more information out of my dear cousin, we can proceed with a better plan."

Silas nodded. "As you wish."

***

"We are here," Larkin announced before opening the door of the carriage and ushering both Alexandra and Eleanor out.

Alexandra had put on her hat and gloves on the way to the mansion, not to mention the coat. She looked at the estate and looked at Larkin. "No wonder he wants another Dowry Mansion… He is pathetic."

Larkin snorted a bit and fixed his hat. "Yes. I know."

Alexandra jumped when she felt Eleanor's soft hand over her arm. Quickly, she moved closer to her wife and smiled at her. "How are you feeling? Are you tired?"

"No, I am perfectly fine, thanks for asking."

"Well, I'll be! I thought you were going to turn down my invitation."

As soon as she heard the voice of that familiar man, Alexandra turned to look at him, taking off her hat and running her glove-covered hand through her hair. "Good day, Cassius."

"How was the ride?"

Larkin threw one of the heaviest suitcases to the carriage driver and let out a loud snort in the process when he heard the question.

"It was…bumpy," Alexandra said as she took off her gloves.

Cassius's dark green eyes went from Alexandra to the gorgeous woman beside her. His back suddenly went stiff, and his smile was wiped away from his face. "I am sorry we haven't been introduced."

Alexandra felt the small hairs on the back of her neck stand. Her arm came to rest in a very possessive manner over Eleanor's narrow waist as she pulled the younger woman closer to her body. "My cousin Cassius, this is Lady Eleanor Stownar. She is my wife."

"Ah, it is a pleasure to finally meet the woman that tamed my cousin," Cassius said, holding Eleanor's hand to his lips. "I hope it wasn't that hard to do."

Eleanor gave him a polite smile and quickly moved her hand away from Cassius's grip to hold on to her Alexandra's strong forearm. "My husband is a good man. He was not in need of being tamed," she said, raising her chin up proudly.

"Oh, really? Is that true now?" He scoffed and turned to look at Larkin and then at the driver. "You can put their stuff inside the mansion. Some butlers will give both of you a room to stay. Meanwhile, Alexander, Lady Stownar, follow me inside the mansion. I just feel like showing it off to my closest family." He chuckled and turned on his heels and walked back to the estate.

"I do not like his attitude."

"Me neither," Alexandra whispered to Eleanor before placing her gloves inside the hat. "Either way, we are only staying for a couple of days. Can you make it through?"

"Just a couple days? Please, Alexander, what do you think of me? I can take a week of this man's annoying attitude. After all, I lived in a city full of people just like him."

Alexandra had to smile at that. "Of course. Forgive me for that silly question," Alexandra mumbled, before giving Eleanor a fast peck on her temple. "Let us go now before he pulls us inside." Alexandra offered her arm once again to Eleanor, and they both walked inside the mansion.

"Silas!" Cassius called out to his butler when he walked into the main entrance of the mansion. He rubbed his hands together and watched as Alexandra and Eleanor walked in. "Welcome! This is my mansion. Of course, it is nothing like yours, Alexander."

"It is fine, Cassius," Alexandra said. Her attention was taken away by the sound of upcoming footsteps. She frowned and turned to look at the middle-aged man that walked towards them.

"Silas! There you are. Please, take those suitcases up to the room set for them and show Alexander's servants their room."

The moment Alexandra's eyes fell upon the butler, she felt a cold shiver run down her spine, paralyzing her. She didn't even notice that she had stopped breathing. Her lip quivered, her hand gripped her hand tighter, and the muscles on her jaw moved under her skin.

Eleanor felt the anxiousness radiating out of Alexandra. She turned to the taller woman and tilted her head in confusion. "Dear?"

Alexandra didn't listen to her. She just stared and studied the man as he picked up some suitcase, spoke to Larkin and the carriage driver, and walked away.

"Alex?"

Alexandra blinked again as if she had just woken up from a daydream. She looked down at her wife and suddenly realized where she was. "I am sorry. I…"

"Is everything all right?" Cassius was a bit nervous by his cousin's sudden reaction to Silas.

"Yes. Everything is fine," Alexandra said.

"Well, then! Please, follow me to the living room."

As soon as Cassius turned his back on them, Eleanor squeezed Alexandra's forearm and turned to her. "What is it?"

"I will explain to you later," Alexandra whispered in her ear.

"But tell me at least something that will calm my raging heart, Alexander. I have never seen you with that look on your face."

Alexandra was about to talk when a young maid came forward and took both Alexandra and Eleanor's coat and hat. She bowed her head to the woman and then slowly pulled Eleanor away. "It is something about my mother's death."

"What?"

Alexandra sighed and rubbed her temples. "We will talk later, Lady Stownar. Not now."

"Are you two joining me or what?" Cassius said from the living room, waving a glass of whiskey.

Eleanor sighed and nodded her head at Alexandra's cousin before walking to the living room, followed by Alexandra.

"Well! This is where the ball will be held. As you can see, the maids and butlers are setting everything up, so forgive me for the mess," Cassius said as he walked to a far corner of the living room where some sofas were put for the guests.

Alexandra looked around the living room and placed one arm behind her. She wiggled her nose and looked around the place before her eyes fell upon her wife. "What do you think?"

"I think our living room is far bigger," Eleanor said out loud.

"Our?" Cassius said, sitting down. He crossed his legs and let out a loud chuckle. "Alexander, cousin, does your wife know that is not her living room?"

Alexandra's neck almost snapped when she turned her eyes to Cassius. She couldn't help it. She frowned deeply and stuck her free hand inside one of her vest pockets. "What are you talking about, Cassius? She is my wife. The moment she said she was willing to spend her life by my side, everything I own belongs to her. So yes," She turned to Eleanor and smiled. "Our living room is far bigger."

Cassius snorted and looked away from Alexandra and decided to stare at Eleanor. "So, tell me. How did you meet my cousin?"

Eleanor gulped down and looked down at the floor. "I…"

"At a ball," Alexandra said, moving to a small table and picking up a crystal glass. She poured in a clear brown liquid inside and walked back over to Cassius. "Please, stand up and allow my wife to sit down. It has been a very tiring trip, and the comfort of that sofa will do well to her tired body."

"Are you telling me what to do at my own mansion, Alexander?"

Alexandra smiled. "You will refer to me as Master Dowry, and yes, I am telling you what to do for I am older than you." She took a fast gulp from the glass and handed it to him. "Stand up."

Cassius took a deep breath and stood up from the sofa. He nodded his head to Eleanor and stared at her closely as she sat down, close to Alexandra. He smiled at that. "It is lovely to see a young couple in love. After all, almost all marriages these days, the groom does not meet the bride until the day of the wedding... practically at the altar. I am sure that wasn't your case now, was it?"

"No. Will you be kind enough to get your dear cousin more whiskey?"

Cassius let out a sarcastic and hypocritical smile. He grabbed the glass and walked away.

"I hate him," Alexandra mumbled and sat right next to Eleanor. "I do."

"Maybe this is a good time for both of you to actually get to know each other and maybe fix whatever feud you have with your cousin."

Alexandra released a loud sigh. She ran her fingers through her hair and leaned back. "Maybe."

"To be quite honest, I think it is enough for today. Cassius seems to be in need to show off his possessions to make himself look superior," Eleanor said, placing her gloved hand on top of Alexandra's knee.

She twitched at the sudden touch, stared at the hand, and then at Eleanor's face. "I know."

"I am tired. Can we retire for the day?"

"So soon?" Alexandra turned her gaze from Eleanor to look at the man who just spoke. Alexandra mumbled something under her breath and stood up. "I mean, the sun has finally disappeared. I thought we could talk some more beside the fire."

"No, that's quite all right. My wife is tired, the ride was rather harsh on her, and I think it is best for us to just go upstairs, unpack some clothes and settle down to sleep."

"As you wish, cousin. Your things have already been brought up to your chamber." Cassius turned away from the couple to make eye contact with one of the young maids in the house. "Please, show my cousin the way."

"Yes, Master Cassius," the maid said, walking to Alexandra and Eleanor and bowing her head to them. "Follow me, if you please."

As soon as Alexandra and Eleanor left the living room, Cassius walked over to the sofa and sat down. He took a long gulp from the glass he had poured for Alexandra and hissed as the liquid burned the inside of his throat.

"Is it hard to maintain a straight face when he is around?"

Cassius closed his eyes in exasperation the moment he heard the gruff voice. "It is harder to smile as if everything is fine. My father was completely and utterly crazy when he continued this stupid game, Silas."

"Your father wanted so many things that he could not have, and I wonder if you are following in his footsteps."

Cassius chuckled and turned to look at the middle-aged man before him. "Explain what you are implying."

Silas shrugged. "She is gorgeous…"

Cassius nodded. "I can see that, but I am not going to do the same thing as my father did. I am not just going to stalk the poor thing?"

"What are you going to do then?"

"Take what I want."

CHAPTER FOURTEEN

"This was a bad idea," Alexandra muttered as she closed the door behind her and turned to face Eleanor. "This is a bad idea."

"Well, I do not like him that much either, but we are already here."

"I am not talking about my cousin. I am talking about being in this place, no guards, no help."

"Larkin is still with us."

"God knows what room. They take the help and place them in the basement."

"I do not think this place even has a basement." Eleanor chuckled.

Alexandra rolled her eyes not in annoyance by what Eleanor had said, but more because she was getting anxious. She sat down on the bed as her hands went straight to her head, tangling her fingers with her hair as she scratched her scalp nervously. "I do not feel safe."

Eleanor bit her lower lip and decided that it would be a good idea to sit down too. Her hands patted at her knees, anxiously, deciding if she should say something, anything to calm the person next to her.

"What happened? I saw you before, you were terrified as if you saw a ghost." She moved away as Alexandra exhaled and got some distance between them. She understood right away. Her husband wasn't comfortable. "If you do not want to talk about it now, I can understand. You must be tired…"

Alexandra's attention was drawn to Eleanor's hands. They had found their way to her tie, and slowly yet steadily, she undid the knot and slipped the piece of cloth from around her neck. Words were lost, so she grabbed the delicate fingers and gave them a firm squeeze, just to remind herself where she was.

"Why do you not change out of those clothes and head to bed?" Eleanor tried to be as casual as she could.

"I cannot sleep. Not now, though." Alexandra put distance between Eleanor and herself. She moved to the window, where she saw a group of what appeared to be butlers, smoking, and laughing.

"I have a hunch."

Eleanor was in the process of untying her hair when she heard Alexandra. "About?"

Alexandra wasn't paying much attention to Eleanor's words. She did hear her completely, but she was more intrigued by the sight outside of the window. Alexandra's eyes inspected the front of the mansion before noticing three men walk out to the front of the gates. She frowned deeply and nibbled on her thumb's fingernail as she scrutinized what the older three butlers were doing or talking about in front of the old gates. "I have this horrible hunch, Lady Eleanor, that the man that Cassius was talking to when we got here has something to do with my mother's death. I've never felt this kind of chill," she said before turning around to face her wife. "I am sorry, I do not think this is the right time to talk about this."

"You never really told me what happened," Eleanor whispered as she moved aside and patted the bed beside her. "I believe that now can be a good time to talk. No one is listening."

Alexandra let out a soft sigh before she made her way to the bed and sat right in the corner. Casually she removed her vest, using the darkness of the room as her aid in concealing her body. She threw the jacket over a chair next to the vanity and turned to look at Eleanor's tired face. "Do you really want to know? I mean, I have not been able to talk about it since the day it happened. Just the other day, when I went back to the town mansion I..." She thought her words over before finishing her sentence. "Exploded..."

Eleanor placed her hand on top of Alexandra's knee. "Just tell me what you feel comfortable saying."

Alexandra looked down to her knee, staring at Eleanor's hand. She placed her callused hand over it and gave it a firm squeeze before pulling it up to her lips. "I can only say much..." she began. "My father used to travel around with his business. I usually stayed with my mother in the town mansion." She sighed and looked back at the window. "When I was just a kid, I was waiting for my father's return. In his last letter to Mother, he said he was coming home that night." She frowned. "He did not..." Alexandra closed her eyes as if trying to avoid bringing back all the painful memories. "Mother had just finished her nightly routine," she whispered, keeping her eyes closed all this time. "She closed one of her large books with her hands and looked down at me. I was on the floor. I was playing. I do not remember what, but I was not that much into it. I mean, I noticed her eyes on me..."

Alexandra exhaled loudly. Remembering every single detail was taking its toll on her, and she squeezed Eleanor's hands tightly.

"She went into the dining room, and that's when I heard it. I heard the gunshot. I heard her screams. I heard her running." Alexandra suddenly opened her eyes and stared at the dead silence in the room as if reliving it all over again. "I ran to the dining room's closed door. I pushed the door open just an inch. And I saw them."

"Who?"

"I do not know who they were. I knew they were there to hurt Mother, and that they were three of them." She squeezed Eleanor's hand tightly. "They took turns. Every time she whimpered; they would silence her with a punch. And I just stood there, paralyzed with fear." Her head almost snapped as she turned to look at her adoring wife. Her pained expression turned into one of realization. She looked at the floor and closed her eyes tightly. "I left her there to die after what they did to her. She called me. I went to her." Alexandra had done all in her power to choke back the tears. "I ran," she whispered. "I listened to her and ran. I did not look back. I left my own mother there to die."

"Alexander."

"No. I pulled Mother up to me. I saw them coming back from the other door. I could have done something! Hit them with something, taken her to safety!"

Seeing her out of control was too much. Alexandra's face was wet with tears and red with rage. Eleanor couldn't take it anymore. She grabbed hold of Alexandra's face and pulled it sharply in front of hers. "How old were you, Alexander?"

"It does not matter how old I was! I was the only one that could help her!"

"How old?"

Alexandra stared at Eleanor's blue eyes. She was pulled back to reality. She acknowledged where she was and she began to relax. "Eight."

"There was nothing you could have done."

"But I ran. I hid in the stables like a coward."

"You were a little boy. You were scared. You need to forgive yourself. I am sure your mother would have wanted you to live."

"Do you have any idea of the images I have in my head? I've had nightmares, night after night after night seeing her bloody face, her hoarse voice begging me to run."

"And you did that. You obeyed your mother's last wishes. You need to let this go," Eleanor said, wiping Alexandra's tears away.

"I cannot," Alexandra mumbled, moving away from Eleanor's hand as it came to wipe the other side of her cheek. "I never heard from those three men again. No one was arrested, no one was held responsible. My father let it go as if it was a mere accident."

"I am sure you will make this all right in its moment," Eleanor said before wiping the rest of Alexandra's tears. "Either that or God will take care of it. I believe in holy justice."

Alexandra let out a snort. "God. Can we change the subject?" Alexandra asked as she stood up and moved away from Eleanor.

"If you wish…" Eleanor said, yet the sudden change of attitude made it loud and clear that the conversation was over.

***

Eleanor heard someone come into the room. She heard giggles from younger girls, and suddenly, the flash of the morning sun hit her blue eyes. Eleanor let out an un-ladylike groan and covered herself with the bedsheets. "No…" she whined and moved to the side only to bump against someone.

"Why…" Alexandra muttered as she sat upon the large bed. "What? What are they doing here?"

Eleanor sighed and sat up too and looked at the three young servants. "Morning."

"Good morning, Lady and Sir Dowry! Breakfast will be served very soon. Would you like to join Sir Cassius?" the youngest servant said as she hid her blushing face with her hands.

"Sure…" Alexandra nodded and waved her hand. "You can go now, thanks."

The maids left in a fit of unprofessional giggles, making Alexandra growl and mutter under her breath.

"Imprudent, little brats," Alexandra said before pulling the covers from her body, revealing that she had slept in the same outfit she had arrived, minus the vest.

Eleanor's brows came together. "Alex, did you—"

"Yes."

"I was going to ask—"

"I fell asleep and was too lazy to change."

"You are a mind reader now?"

"No. I just know what you are going to ask beforehand."

"Alex, that's a mind reader."

"Then I guess I am one." Alexandra gave her a fake smile before standing up from the large bed while searching for her vest. She patted her chest and noticed that the first couple of buttons were open, exposing the wraps.

"What is that under your shirt?"

"Undershirt," she muttered before quickly going over to one of her bags. "I am going to get ready. Do you want me to leave the room?"

"No, that is fine… Why do you wear an undershirt to sleep?"

Alexandra was saved by the knock. She looked at the closed door and pulled up her dark slacks and walked over to open it.

"Morning."

"Morning, Larkin," Alexandra said with a relieved expression on her face.

"Did you both have a good night's sleep?"

"More or less," Eleanor answered as she stayed in bed, covered with the bedsheets.

"Oh well. I need to talk to you," Larkin announced, returning his eyes to Alexandra. "Now."

Alexandra turned to look at Eleanor and bowed her head before disappearing from the room. "What is it?"

"Are you ready for the ball?"

Alexandra frowned. "Of course! Are you ready?"

"Should I be ready?"

"Listen now, Larkin. I want you in that ball. I want you to keep an eye on everything and everyone, especially those three old servants."

Larkin frowned and moved closer to Alexandra's face to hide their conversation from the walls. "Why?"

"I believe those three men had something to do with yesterday's shooting. I need you to be my second pair of eyes."

"I will, Alex. You know I will. You need to worry about keeping Eleanor safe."

"Wait, why?"

"I've heard of Cassius's parties. I have heard about his friends. They tend to get a little wild. They tend to drink a little too much. Keep your wife close."

"Do you have any idea of how many people are coming?"

"I thought maybe you knew."

They heard some footsteps from outside the hall. Larkin's hands flew to Alexandra's shirt and buttoned up the last two remaining buttons and then brushed off her shoulders as if nothing was happening. "Do not trust anyone in this house. Not even the maids."

"I do not," Alexandra said as she grabbed hold of Larkin's hands. "Thank you. I mean it, thank you."

"Do not thank me, Alex. I am doing my job."

"Next time we see each other, we will be at the ball."

Larkin smirked and nodded. "I hope you brought your best dress."

"I hope you did too…"

CHAPTER FIFTEEN

Her green eyes roamed the entire living room, checking each one of the people Cassius had invited. There were a handful of older people, a small portion were people Alexandra and Eleanor's age, and by the looks of it, there were no children allowed at this ball.

"There are a lot of people here," Eleanor whispered to Alexandra as she waited up the stairs. They were waiting to be called down. The last one was the young girl that was going to be introduced to society by her father. Eleanor frowned at that. "I remember my first time… It was horrible."

"Why?" Alexandra asked as she kept looking behind her and over the head of the older couples in front of her.

"I felt like a toy. As soon as you are presented a lot of single males want to get to know you. You are not ready to be wedded. At least, that's how I felt."

"Hmm…" Alexandra grunted and looked down at Eleanor. "I am sure you were a beautiful socialite."

"Thanks." Eleanor giggled and covered her lips with her hands.

"I am serious."

"I know you are, that is why I am laughing. You are always so serious."

"Does that bother you?"

"Not at all."

Alexandra heard her cousin Cassius finally announce the couples. The ball had begun. Little by little, the married couples began to descend the stairs.

"Sir Dowry and Lady Stownar," Cassius announced them both.

They went down the stairs, owning it. The ball was to introduce a young girl into high society. Still, to Alexandra, she was showing off everything that she owned, every power she had over everything in the states. She raised Eleanor's hand over to her chest and pushed her slightly in front of her. All women were supposed to walk behind their Sirs; in this case, Eleanor was the one leading her, the Sir, the master, the husband.

Alexandra raised her chin up, and so did Eleanor. The connection both had was way beyond the understanding of the people inside the mansion. She could see them all whispering to each other's ears, pointing to them, and talking. Alexandra simply smiled at every single one of them and looked at her wife once more. She knew well that they were wondering when the union happened. When did Eleanor Stownar marry the state's arrogant and antisocial Alexander?

She slightly pulled onto Eleanor's hand. The young woman automatically wrapped her arm around Alexandra's and walked away from the multitude of people over to a lonely corner in the large living room.

"We sure made an entrance." Eleanor chuckled as she wrapped her arms around her husband's waist.

"We made a good exit at our wedding..." Alexandra chuckled, rubbing Eleanor's arm tenderly as she looked up at the other couples going down the stairs. "Want to bet on who will fall?"

"Alexander!" Eleanor yelled as she hid her laughter from the people around them by pressing her face on Alexandra's chest.

She smirked and turned to look at her cousin as he made the final announcement. "Stop laughing. Cassius is going to announce the new socialite." Alexandra gave her a light squeeze to silence the younger woman; instead, this earned her a squeal from Eleanor. In return, Alexandra bowed her head and covered her face with her hand as she let out a loud chuckle.

"...And finally, Sir Hall with his lovely daughter, Beatrix Hall." Cassius began to clap his hands together as he looked up to the stairs and saw the tall white-haired man descend with his daughter right behind him.

Alexandra slowly let go of Eleanor to clap her hands also. "Isn't she a bit young to be already presented?"

Eleanor moved closer to Alexandra and waved her hand to her so she could get closer. Alexandra moved her head down and felt Eleanor's warm breath on her ear as she said, "I was around that age when I was presented. She must be at least sixteen, maybe even fifteen."

"Why so young?" Alexandra asked as she crossed her arms over her chest, giving all her attention to her wife.

"So hot catches like you would get to us fast," Eleanor replied as she pulled Alexandra for a soft peck.

She chuckled against Eleanor's soft lips and moved awkwardly away from the people around them. "Stop pulling me like that! Do not make me make a scene here with you."

"Let us dance!"

"There is no music!" Alexandra said, bumping her forehead with Eleanor's.

"I do not care."

"Why are you suddenly so happy?" Alexandra asked as she wrapped her arms steadily against Eleanor's waist. "Settle down, we are going to fall if you keep moving like that."

"Because..."

Alexandra smiled and sweetly kissed the tip of her nose. "I understand."

"You do?"

"Sort of," She chuckled and squeezed Eleanor once again.

"I love you, Alexander." Eleanor placed both hands on top of Alexandra's shoulder. "I really do. This cannot be lust. Not this…" she whispered sweetly before moving her hand to the back of Alexandra's neck and pulling her for another sweet kiss. "You might as well just deal with it."

Alexandra sighed and closed her eyes. "I adore you, Eleanor Stownar." She nodded at her words. It felt right. Maybe it wasn't the most intimate situation, but her words felt just right. Eleanor smiled wildly at Alexandra's words before she felt an interrupting pat on her shoulder.

"Sorry to interrupt," Larkin chuckled as he handed both women a glass. "Here is some— sh…shame pain…"

"Champagne," Alexandra quickly corrected as she took the glass from Larkin's hand. She gave him a fake smile and looked away from him. The least Alexandra wanted was to be interrupted when she had just admitted her feelings to Eleanor. She had only confirmed that her wife was in love with her. She took a long gulp from the glass and hit his chest with it as she handed it back to him. "Seen anything strange?"

Larkin rubbed where the glass had hit him and looked back at Alexandra. "I've seen a young servant around the front yard. Other than that, everything has been pretty normal and calm."

"A servant?"

Larkin nodded and took a sip from his own glass. "Yes, a servant."

"Are you drinking?" Eleanor suddenly asked as she moved to look at Larkin.

"Well, this is a ball, isn't it?"

Alexandra rolled her eyes and shook her head before grabbing Eleanor's hand and walking away from Larkin.

"It is just shamepain!" Larkin yelled.

"Champagne!"

"Whatever. You just pronounce it in a fancy way," Larkin muttered as he grabbed another glass from a passing maid. "That's why I was never an aristocrat." He nodded as he spoke his wise words and drank up the entire glass in one gulp.

Alexandra pulled Eleanor closer to her and started to look around the living room once again. Eleanor noticed this immediately and had to frown. Then she heard it. Finally, the moment she was waiting for. She turned her face to stare at the small orchestra Cassius had hired just for the ball. The violinist was pathetic. Eleanor frowned. Compared to her, he was a first-timer.

"Alexander?"

"Hmm?"

Eleanor scoffed and moved Alexandra's hand to her waist and grabbed hold of the other one. "Alexander! Basic position."

"Basi... what?"

Eleanor looked deep into Alexandra's eyes and raised one eyebrow at her. "One, two, three."

"You want to dance, Lady Stownar?"

"That's why we had our lessons back at our home." Eleanor smiled as she nodded. "Now. Basic position."

Alexandra let out a soft groan and held Eleanor's hand high and placed her other hand behind Eleanor's lower back. She was surprised that she didn't hear any complaints from the younger woman.

"Ready," Alexandra whispered.

Eleanor closed her eyes and began to pray. She just prayed that Alexandra wouldn't step on her feet this time, and to her surprise, she didn't. On the contrary, she took the lead when Eleanor relaxed in her arms.

"Have I mentioned how gorgeous you look tonight?" Alexandra asked as she moved slowly on the dance floor. "You can open your eyes now. You are not going to get hurt," Alexandra said, giving her a dirty look. "I am not that bad now, am I?" She chuckled on Eleanor's face as she squeezed her body tighter to her tall frame.

Eleanor slowly opened her eyes and looked around. "Where are you practicing?

"Probably," Alexandra answered.

Eleanor let out a soft laugh and moved her hand over to Alexandra's broad shoulder. "You are looking pretty handsome yourself. Why, if I were not that innocent, I would say that all the girls…"

"Girls?"

"I mean women."

"Old women…"

"…old women," Eleanor resumed bumping her forehead with Alexandra's chest. "All the old women in the room were eyeing you with a bit of lust?"

"What do you know about lust?" Alexandra teased, letting out her trademark smirk.

"I know a thing or two. A young man taught me something here and there at his house library."

"Lucky bastard," Alexandra scoffed, then smiled wildly at her wife's words.

"Yes, I think he is pretty lucky, indeed," Eleanor said, earning a peck on the lips from her breathtaking husband.

"I have to say that this is kind of nice." Alexandra nodded as her fingers traced Eleanor's lower back. "I might have to take you to more parties…"

"Or, we could just dance at our home…" Eleanor whispered as she rested her head on Alexandra's chest.

"Sounds perfect." Alexandra kissed the top of Eleanor's head tenderly. She relaxed her whole body as she moved around the dance floor with the woman she loved more than anything in her life.

Eleanor was too fixated on Alexandra's warm body that she didn't notice when she stopped moving altogether. She opened her eyes and looked up at Alexandra and saw her looking at one of the doors that lead to the front yard. "What is it?"

Alexandra frowned and squinted her eyes. "I just saw that Beatrix Hall girl and some random man leave," Alexandra replied as she dropped her arms by her side but still held onto Eleanor's hand.

"Let us go." Alexandra pulled on Eleanor's hand and almost dragged her to the front yard.

"Why are we going to the front yard again?" Eleanor asked but was silenced by a tug to her wrist. "Why are we hiding behind the bushes?"

"Because this is fun. You never played around the bushes?"

"… What?"

"I just want to see what they are up to. You do know I have wanted to snoop around the mansion," Alexandra said as she looked around the gates. "There they are."

Alexandra hid behind the bushes with Eleanor while staring at the scene that was unfolding. She could clearly hear everything that was going on and, so she calculated the pros and cons of interfering with both.

Beatrix looked up at the much taller man. She closed her eyes tightly and took a deep breath before answering his question. "I have been avoiding you for obvious reasons, Noah," Beatrix began as she grabbed hold of his hand. "You know how my father is. You better than anyone know him, you are his personal assistant." She sighed.

"What is it? Just hurry up and tell me!" The young man begged as he cupped her face.

"I really do not think we should be looking at them, Alexander. This seems a bit intimate," Eleanor whispered on Alexandra's ear.

"Shh," Alexandra simply answered, bumping her shoulder with Eleanor's. "Let me listen."

Beatrix slowly slid her left hand and placed it in Noah's view. "I am engaged to Thomas Cook. My father made an arrangement. I am to be married in three months."

Noah quickly let go of her face and tightly grabbed hold of her hand. "What! No! No!"

"I tried to make him reconsider, but he wouldn't listen."

"I will talk to him!" Noah yelled as he squeezed her hand tightly. "I will, I will fix this."

"You are a servant, Noah! If you even mention that to him! He will know!" Beatrix half-whispered, half-yelled before throwing her small figure to him. She wrapped her arms tightly to his neck and hung up to dear life. "I am sorry!"

"Let us run away," Noah suggested as he held her in place, not letting go. "I will find a job somewhere else; I do not care! I just want to be with you. I cannot stand seeing you off with that— that boy!"

Alexandra stood up from the bushes, but almost fell back when Eleanor pulled her wrist hard. "What do you think you are doing!?"

"I am just going to help!" Alexandra told her as she wiggled her arm away from Eleanor's grasp. "I mean clearly they love each other. They just need a little help."

"Alexander, if you get your nose in this mess, you might get that man fired, and that poor girl will be forced to marry in a day to this Thomas person!"

"Do you think that I am that dumb? Wait here. Do not move," Alexandra ordered as she stood up once again and made her way to the younger couple. Alexandra slowly walked over to Beatrix and Noah in a collected way. She fixed up her white jacket and coughed, making them know of her presence.

Beatrix gasped when she saw Alexandra beside them. Noah, on the other hand, quickly jumped in front of Beatrix, coming between Alexandra and his lover. Alexandra frowned at them both and licked her lips before speaking.

"My name is Alexander Dowry III," she began. "I couldn't help but hear your conversation with Lady Hall." She fixed her jacket once again and crossed her arms over her chest.

"Please, do not tell my father, Sir Dowry. I beg of you, please! He will have us both killed." Beatrix begged with tears in her eyes as she clung to Noah's arm. "Please, sir, please!"

Alexandra sweetly smiled at the girl, but her eyes went back to Noah. "What's your name?"

"Noah, Lawson!" He quickly answered, raising his chin up, making him look much taller than Alexandra.

"Settle down, Lawson," Alexandra said before turning her gaze to Beatrix. "You should probably go back to the ball. Your father will be looking for you."

"What?"

"I also want to have a private conversation with this young man here." She took out her pocket watch. "It is getting late," she stated before jerking her head. "Get going now."

Beatrix wiped her tears ferociously and ran from both "men." Eleanor was watching from afar. She needed to do something, anything. She could probably start by helping the emotional young girl.

"Lady Beatrix!" Eleanor jumped, stepping in front of her. "You are a mess, are you all right?" Eleanor was trying to be as lovely and sweet as she possibly could. She knew Alexandra was going to help the dark-haired man, she needed to help Beatrix. "Let us go up to the restroom and refresh your face a bit." She smiled at her while raising Beatrix's jaw with her slender fingers.

Beatrix sniffled and wiped her tears once again. She didn't precisely answer

Eleanor, but she did nod. Eleanor smiled and wrapped one arm around her shoulder and made her way inside the living room. She discretely went up the stairs but not discrete enough for Cassius not to notice.

***

"Noah Lawson," Alexandra said as she stuck her hand inside her pockets. "How old are you?"

"What do you want?"

"Do you love her?"

"I am here, am I not?"

"You are pretty mature for your age," Alexandra whispered as she took out what she had in her pocket. She looked at the coins she had in her hands and offered it to Noah. "Here."

"I do not want your money."

"I know you do not want it, but you will need it. That will probably help you for a couple of weeks. Where is her mansion?"

"Eight miles up north from where we are," Noah answered as he looked at the coins.

"Good. So, you are in the northeast villages." Alexandra nodded and rubbed her chin, thinking. "If you decide to elope, do it after the ball; after you are settled back at her home. Then use the night as your friend. If I am not mistaken, there are some small villages to the south of her house."

Noah nodded as his facial expression softened to one of relief. "Yes, yes! That is my home! I come from those villages!" He could already feel the adrenaline and the excitement in his veins.

"Stay there for those weeks. If you do plan everything through, you will have a nice happy ending," Alexandra patted his broad shoulder. "Just go. Do not leave her to marry someone she doesn't love."

"You are really just helping me out because you want to?" Noah asked as he also placed his arm on Alexandra's shoulder.

"There are still some good people on this planet." She gave him a reassuring wink. "Now go on and act like nothing happened at all. If Sir Hall finds out about this…"

"I should know," Noah confessed as he stuck the coins in his pocket.

"Thank you, Sir Dowry."

"Just promise you will let my wife and I know how everything turned out, all right?"

***

Eleanor patted her hands together as she looked down at the young blonde girl. She let out a soft chuckle and playfully raised her shoulders. "Much,

much better!" she announced before fixing Beatrix's hair once again. "This is one heck of a hair-do."

"Thanks for helping me, either way," Beatrix said as she turned to look at Eleanor.

"Just try to smile and go out there and try to have a good time," Eleanor ordered, giving her a reassuring wink.

Beatrix chuckled and patted Eleanor's hand before leading her out from the small study office. "I guess I will do just that. I just hope my father isn't looking for me."

"I am sure he is not," Eleanor said as she waved her hand. "Have a good time now." Saying that, she watched how Beatrix made her way down the stairs. She smiled tenderly at the girl. Eleanor was reminded of the time when she was presented to society. She was so nervous. All she did all night throughout the ball was cling to her father's jacket until she came back home.

"I better head downstairs. I do not want Alexander to go look after me," she said to herself as she walked over to the stairs. She wasn't paying much attention to the people around her to the point that it took her for a surprise the fact that some random stranger was holding her arm, stopping her altogether.

She frowned and looked down at the intruding hand and then at the older man in front of her. He was much about her same stature with a thick beard covering most of his face. She cringed at that but decided to be as polite as possible.

"Can I help you?" she asked, moving her other hand to free herself. Suddenly she felt another hand grab hold of her. She froze and turned her neck quickly.

"Oh, sure, lady. You can help both of us in our little boredom." The other man spoke. He was much taller than the other one and seemed to be a bit younger. Yet, both men's eyes made a shiver run down Eleanor's neck. Without second-guessing, he grabbed hold of her, keeping her steady while the other one covered her mouth with his handkerchief.

Eleanor's eyes flew wide. She looked at the scene around her, and there was no one to help her. She closed her eyes deeply and began to struggle as hard as she could. Great. She was invited to a ball only to get raped by a couple of drunken, bored men. She groaned and raised her leg up and then slammed it with all her force against the man that was dragging her away from the stairs.

"Little bitch!" The bearded man muttered as he let her go. The second man quickly took the lead and opened the door to the room Eleanor was just inside with Beatrix. He pushed her inside and closed the door behind him.

"Lock that damn door!" the older man barked as he bent over to touch his now aching foot. "Wait a moment…"

"What is it now?" the taller man said as he held Eleanor steady by her arms. "Come on and let us get this over with. Cassius said we could have some fun with her."

"This is Sir Dowry's wife…" He chuckled and licked his lips disgustingly.

"Oh, really?" The younger man looked down at her. "She is!"

The bearded man limped his way over to her and looked at her face carefully before letting out a drunken laugh. "I bet that little man hasn't touched the hair of your head!" He laughed again. Eleanor turned her face away from him, disgusted by the smell of alcohol in his breath. "Remind me to thank Cassius after this." The bearded man said as he began to take his jacket off. "You are going to enjoy this…"

Eleanor opened her eyes widely and began to move and thrash about, hoping and praying that someone, anyone would open the door and rescue her.

***

Alexandra's eyes were trailing the entire living room then the dining room, but she didn't find Eleanor. She was beginning to curse under her breath. She walked rapidly back into the living room, bumping into everyone that got in her way.

"Larkin!"

Larkin was sitting on a corner laughing by himself, not having a care in the world. He looked up at Alexandra as she made her way to him. He raised his glass to her. "Hello there! Care to dance?" He teased, opening his arms to her.

"Have you seen Eleanor?" Alexandra asked as she grabbed him by his vest and pulled him up. "Wake up, Larkin!" She gave him a soft slap to get him to pay attention. "Where is she?"

"I saw her with Lady Hall a couple of minutes ago," he muttered as he rubbed his eyes, trying to get the tipsiness to subside.

Alexandra quickly let go and ignored him as he dropped back to his corner. In a matter of seconds, she found Beatrix speaking calmly to her father.

Alexandra's urgent steps subsided for a while as she fixed her hair and her clothes. She looked up at Beatrix's father and let out a polite smile. "Evening."

"Well, hello there!" Sir Hall greeted her as he patted Alexandra's shoulder a little too hard. "What do you think? Isn't she the most beautiful girl?" he asked as he grabbed Beatrix's hand and made her twirl her dress. "She is just like her mother. Gorgeous."

Alexandra quickly nodded. "Without a doubt, sir." She then turned her attention to Beatrix. "Lady Beatrix. Have you seen my wife?" she asked in a soft and worried tone. "I …" She moved closer and whispered into Beatrix's ear, "I just spoke to Noah. I came back, and she was not where I left her. I've been looking everywhere…"

"I was upstairs with her. She was fixing my hair and dress. I did not see her come down, though," Beatrix said, also whispering to Alexandra.

Quickly, she grabbed Beatrix's hand and gave her a firm kiss on her slender fingers. Alexandra walked away and made her way up the stairs, not before eyeing the half-drunk Larkin, signaling him to follow her up the stairs. She jumped three stairs at the time. Alexandra opened the first door and found nothing. She groaned and saw how Larkin opened the second door. He turned and shook his head. Alexandra growled from deep inside her chest and tensed up her jaw. She was in trouble; she could sense it.

Eleanor could hear the doors opening and closing. She could listen to Alexandra muttering and cursing. Eleanor needed to do something, and she needed to do it now. She let out a strained groan and tried to scream as loud as she could.

Larkin walked past another closed door. This time he grabbed hold of the knob and turned it only to find that it was locked. He frowned and began to tug on it forcefully. "Alexander! Alexander! Over here."

Eleanor looked past the bearded man's shoulder. She saw the doorknob moving and knew who was right behind that door. She turned her blue eyes back to the drunk man and moved enough to get his attention.

"Do not worry. They are not going to interrupt us."

A bang came from the door. Alexandra yelled out Eleanor's name repeatedly. Eleanor sighed. She closed her eyes tightly and got herself ready for the impact…

"Lady Stownar!" Larkin yelled as he and Alexandra began to slam the door with their bodies.

Eleanor moved her head back, prayed to God that she wouldn't fall unconscious, and slammed it against the face of the man that was holding her and quickly jerked it forward, hitting the bearded man right on the bridge of the nose. Both men let go of the strained woman, giving Eleanor a chance to take off the disgusting handkerchief from her mouth and run to the door.

"Alexander!" She yelled back, opening the door, and banging it open. "Alexander!" Eleanor let out a relieved sigh before wrapping her arms around her husband's neck.

Alexandra gave her wife a firm squeeze before letting her go. "What in the world is going on here?"

"They came out of nowhere and dragged me up here. They said that Cassius had offered me as a present to them."

"What!" Alexandra shouted, turning to look at Eleanor in disbelief. "Do you gentlemen know that this woman is my wife?"

"No." The young man lied.

"Nu-uh." The bearded man answered as he tried to stop his nosebleed.

"That is a lie! I heard them both! They knew I was your wife!" Eleanor said before rubbing the back of her head, hissing in pain.

Alexandra looked down at both men. She shuddered in rage before shaking her head. "You like raping married women, gentlemen?"

"No."

"Nu-uh"

Alexandra let out a snarl before running up to them. She moved her leg back as far as she could and slammed it against the bearded man's face and then moved to step on the other man's chest continuously. "I am going to kill you both!"

"Alexander, Alexander, no! Let us go. Let us go home," Eleanor said as she pulled Alexandra's arm, dragging her away from both men.

"Yes, Sir. Let us just go home," Larkin mumbled almost incoherently.

"What in heaven's name is going on here?"

Alexandra's neck almost snapped as she looked at her clueless cousin walk in. "You!" She pointed her finger at him before jumping on him.

"Alexander! That is enough!" Larkin said as he grabbed Alexandra by her torso and basically lifted her away from Cassius before she could land her punch. "No! We are going home. This asshole is not worth it. Excuse my French, Lady Eleanor. I am just a bit heated."

"We all are!" Eleanor said as she looked at Cassius. "How dare you play your little jokes on me, Cassius? You messed with the wrong woman," she announced before grabbing Alexandra's jacket and pulling her out of the room. "Let us go home tonight."

"You better stay the hell away from me and my wife, Cassius. I mean it." Alexandra said up to his face enough to make him know who was the strongest and tallest of both.

"Or what?"

"Or else you are the one whose face I am going to kick until you are just a bloody pulp," she hissed into his face before moving away. "Larkin…"

"Yes, Sir?"

"Pack up our things. We are leaving right this instant."

Cassius moved back from Alexandra and watched how she, Eleanor, and Larkin left. He let out a soft growl as he closed the door with the two men inside. "We'll see who the bigger man is…"

CHAPTER SIXTEEN

They had left the mansion in a hurry. They picked up their belongings and left using the main front door. The people at the ball were talking once again, murmuring, and pointing their fingers at the couple and their servant.

Alexandra and Eleanor didn't look back, and neither did Larkin as he carried the bags over his shoulder behind the two women. The carriage was already set for them at the entrance of the mansion. They got in, and off they went in the middle of the night, ignoring any sign of danger that was on their mind.

Larkin moved uncomfortably in the carriage, looking at the couple in front of him. Alexandra was wide awake, looking at the surroundings outside her window. At the same time, Eleanor had found a comfortable nook in the corner of the carriage. Larkin raised his eyebrows as he watched the young woman mutter something about a headache. Eleanor hissed and touched her forehead a couple of times before closing her eyes and groaning.

"Hardheaded man…"

"What's wrong, Lady Stownar?" Larkin asked as he rested his elbows on his knees to take a better look at Eleanor's head.

"Oh, well." She sighed and pressed her hand on her forehead, trying to stop the pain. "Before you and Alexander came inside the room, I bumped my head against both men," she said. "I never thought it would hurt that much."

"Let me take a look," Larkin said, cupping Eleanor's jaw with his large hand. "That's going to leave a mark," Alexandra frowned and pulled Eleanor towards her and away from Larkin before looking at her face.

"You are probably going to look like a unicorn in the morning."

"Thanks for making me feel better, Alexander." Eleanor chuckled before accepting a kiss on the forehead.

Larkin moved back and leaned on the wall of the carriage, frowning deeply. He stared and watched both women interact for a while. His eyes traveled over to Eleanor's smile. He watched how she planted a kiss on Alexandra's lips and quickly moved her hand to wipe away the small smudge it left behind. He looked down at his pants and shifted his boots around uncomfortably before looking out the window too. He bit his lower lip and closed his eyes tightly as he suppressed a sigh.

Was he really giving this situation that much thought? What was he to do about the situation? He turned to look at Eleanor's smile once again. Alexandra was now giving soft kisses to her forehead, saying something about giving her good medicine once they arrived at home. He rolled his eyes and shook his head.

"I've got your medicine right here," he said as he raised his coat and pulled out a sizeable reddish bottle.

"Are you joking?"

"He almost hurt Lady Stownar…" Larkin began as he shrugged and pulled the cork from the bottle. "Me stealing a wine bottle is nothing." He handed Alexandra the bottle.

Alexandra took the bottle in her hands and looked at the label. "1840." She said as she read the year of the wine and nodded in approval. "Very nice."

"You are very, very, welcome." Larkin grinned. "Now, now! Give Lady Stownar some!" He ordered taking the bottle from Alexandra's hand and giving it to Eleanor. "You need it more than both of us."

Eleanor accepted the bottle in her hands. She looked at the bottle, then at Alexandra and then at Larkin.

"Where are the glasses?"

"Oh, please!" Alexandra whined before grabbing the bottle from Eleanor's hands and taking a long gulp from it. "Just drink. We just left a ball, and I only drank one glass of…" she looked at Larkin, a mischievous smile was painted on her lips. "Shame-pain."

"Go to hell, Alexander." Larkin growled before grabbing the bottle and giving it back to Eleanor. "You are among family here. You do not need a glass," Larkin said before giving her a playful wink. "Drink up."

Eleanor looked at Alexandra. She nodded to her, and Eleanor sighed and looked at the bottle's mouth before moving it to her lips and taking soft, short sips.

"Oh, for goodness sake!" Both Alexandra and Larkin yelled at the same time and then tilted the back of the bottle up, causing Eleanor to take massive gulps.

"That's more like it!" Alexandra celebrated before pulling the bottle away from her hands. "See? That wasn't so bad."

"I never drink!" Eleanor coughed. "You almost choked me to death," she muttered while playfully hitting Alexandra on her shoulder.

"Your headache will subside after that, I am sure," Alexandra said, handing the bottle back to Larkin. "Try to go to sleep. It is a long way back to the mansion."

"I couldn't possibly sleep with all this moving around." She leaned over on Alexandra and tried her best to find a comfortable nook on her shoulder.

"Just try," Alexandra said as she also moved around the carriage, snuggling close to Eleanor.

Larkin snorted to himself and tilted the bottle back as he took two big gulps.

"Easy there," Alexandra whispered to Larkin. "You want to get drunk?"

"Sure. Why not?" he asked back, raising his eyebrows. "Nothing wrong with getting drunk once a year." He placed his lips on the battle and drank again.

"You are going to drink the whole bottle?"

He hissed a bit and shook his head as he felt his mind begin to numb. "Go to sleep." Larkin snarled as he turned to look out the window.

"Are you alright? You seem to be angry at something."

"Nope. Never mind, Alex. You go ahead and rest. I will wake you both up when we get to the mansion," the older man said as he gave her a wink.

"Whatever you say, my friend." She lowered her hat and covered her eyes with it. "You should also rest..." Larkin ignored Alexandra's words and took another sip from the bottle of wine in his hands. Slowly he turned to look at the now sleeping women. He drank the entire bottle by himself while gazing at them with a deep frown on his face.

How did it come to this? He was jealous. Overly jealous and with rage. He looked at the empty bottle and grunted before placing it on the floor. He felt a heatwave go up to his face suddenly. His body was reacting awkwardly. Was it the alcohol? Was it the fact that he hasn't slept at all for the past couple of days? Larkin sighed deeply before letting out a ragged sob. "What the hell is wrong with me?" He turned to look at the sleeping couple. "She is married, for goodness sake. What do you plan to do? Kidnap her?" he muttered and turned to look at Eleanor to stare at her peaceful sleeping face.

He moved his trembling hand over to her and pushed a loose strand of brown hair away from the gorgeous face. He could feel the softness of the hair and wanted that feeling to stay. The softness of Eleanor's hair lingered on his hand as he pulled away, cupping his mouth with that same hand.

"I am going insane..."

***

The wolves became agitated... They were running around in circles at the front gate of the mansion, howling and barking and waving their bushy tails to the carriage that had just arrived.

"We are here," a red-eyed Larkin announced as he shook Alexandra awake from her slumber.

"Hmm!" Alexandra opened her eyes and felt her hat fall to her lap. She looked out and saw her two wolves welcoming her.

"We are here, Lady Stownar," Larkin muttered before getting out of the carriage. He turned his attention to the roof as he tried to grab as much luggage as he possibly could.

Alexandra got out of the small carriage and smiled at both of her wolves. "Settle down, you two. I am home." They howled back at her. "I know, I know. I missed you guys," Alexandra confessed as she held out her hand and helped Eleanor out of the carriage. "I think they missed you too," Alexandra said before grabbing an upcoming suitcase from Larkin.

Eleanor smiled at Sticks and Pebbles and quickly opened the gates to greet them. "Aww, I know! You missed Larkin the most, I bet!" Eleanor giggled as she kneeled and scratched the back of their ears.

Larkin snorted and walked past Eleanor and into the mansion.

"What is wrong with him?" Eleanor asked, looking up at Alexandra.

"I have no idea. He has been acting rather weird," Alexandra muttered as she walked inside. She turned to look at Larkin, who was already sitting down in the living room near the table where the liquor was placed.

"Alexander…"

"Yes?"

"I think I am going to head upstairs and rest some more. I am sorry, but being in that bumpy carriage wasn't that comfortable."

Alexandra chuckled sweetly and moved forward to kiss Eleanor's soft lips. "That's fine by me. Go ahead and rest all you want. How is your head?"

"A bit better," she said, touching the small bump on her forehead.

"Good. Then off you go. I will get those suitcases up later."

"See you later then, Alexander."

"Bye, love," Alexandra couldn't help but smile as she watched Eleanor walk up the stairs.

Alexandra let out a loud sigh and closed her eyes. She was going to have that dreaded talk with Eleanor tonight. It seemed that everything was going according to plan. She turned her attention back to Larkin, who appeared to be attacking the alcohol table in the living room. She frowned and called out to him as she made her way over to his side.

As he saw her walk over to him, he backed away into the large window in the living room. He didn't know how it happened, but he felt his control slip slowly with every drop of alcohol he tasted. His eyes were staring at her. Fixed on her face. Her gorgeous face. Her dark green eyes and her kissable lips. Larkin's mouth was suddenly dry, and his hands shook with this uncontrollable sensation that he knew, oh so well. He pulled his shirt and undid his tie. He opened his suit and his vest as he took a deep breath. His body was aching with years of self-control, of denying himself to the touch of someone... Anyone.

"Alex..." he whispered to her and saw how she turned to look at him. She, the woman he watched as she grew up, the woman who he held during nights of frightening nightmares. He had seen her cry. He had held her and whispered sweet nothings in her ear as he tried to drag her out of the world she has been forced into. He always stood beside her, as her protector, as her trustworthy servant, as her best friend, and as her brother. Then why was his body burning like this now? Now of all moments? He had to wait for her to finally say that she was in love with someone else to reconcile his feelings for her.

"What is it? You seem to be drunk out of your mind," Alexandra said as she took off her gloves and placed them on the table. She undid her tie and threw the scarf over the sofa. "You should go to sleep, Larkin."

He shook his head at the thoughts that snaked their way into his mind. He watched like a predator as she took off her suit and placed it on the sofa. He could outline her curves. Of course, he could! He had seen her as what she was. A woman. A beautiful, strong, and powerful woman... She was even probably as strong as him, but he had seen her as a child. He had seen the innocence in those dark green pits. He had seen how she grew up to be a teenager and how her curves showed more and more every day. Then came the training... He was a witness to the molding of her body.

He sighed and covered his eyes with one hand as he grabbed hold of the edge of the large window and fell to his knees. His body was aching, and his chest felt like it was about to explode. He was drunk, and that's why he was letting everything pour out of his heart and soul.

He panted and pulled the neck of his shirt so he could let his heated skin breathe the cold air of the night. "Alexandra..." he called her. Pleaded her to come to his aid, to slap his face, and let him know that he was wrong. He couldn't love her. He just couldn't. "Alexandra."

"Hey! I've never seen you like this!" Alexandra whispered as she placed her hand on his shoulder. "Come on. I will take you to your room."

He felt his heart stop beating. Those words... It was a sick fantasy he had dreamed of ever since he noticed Alexandra's true beauty. He stood up with Alexandra's help and grabbed a handful of her white shirt and vest. He made her face him, and he saw the confusion in her eyes. He smiled.

"It is stupid. If you only knew how much I wanted to ask your hand to your father, but I was... no... I am a mere servant. What could I offer to the great Alexandra Dowry?" He chuckled and pressed his sweating forehead to her dry one.

"What are you babbling about?" she asked as she tightly grabbed hold of his shirt, keeping a steady grip on him as she looked at his dark eyes. "Larkin!"

Larkin felt his words get stuck in his throat. He clenched his teeth and placed his other hand behind her neck. "I was the one that got you, Eleanor. I was the one that pushed you to marry her and look at me now. I am so jealous of her that it is eating me inside!"

Alexandra opened her eyes wide and tried to pull away from him, but somehow, he was able to hold her down. "Larkin, what are you doing?"

"I love you, Alexandra Dowry. Always have, and I always will." He looked at her eyes, tears streaming down his face as his control slipped out of his body. He breathed against her face and let out a sad chuckle. "I love you so much…" His grip behind her neck became tighter. His hand tore her vest when he pulled her harshly against him as he planted his lips on hers. He let go of her shirt and wrapped his arm around her waist, and devoured her with every bit of strength he had in him.

She pulled away from him as hard as she could and watched how he stumbled with the footrest on the floor. She gasped with sudden shock and wiped her mouth with the back of her hand with disgust. "What the hell is wrong with you!? What…" She spat and wiped her mouth again, moving away from him. "You are drunk!"

Larkin struggled to his feet again and panted with the lustful fire that had engulfed him. He licked his lips and shuddered in delight. "You taste as good as I thought you would."

"Shut up!" Alexandra said as she watched him. She looked down at her clothing and saw that her vest had been ruined. She took it off and threw it away before gazing at Larkin angrily.

"You do not understand! I was here first!" he said as he walked over to her again.

"You are going to wake up, Eleanor!" she whispered before ducking his strong arms. "Stop it! I do not want to hurt you, Larkin."

"I am in love with you, and the only reason I've been quiet about it is because of your father. I need to say this."

Alexandra shook her head and walked to grab hold of his clothes. She shook him out of the daze he was in and punched his jaw. Alexandra watched him stumble to the ground again. She wanted to have a serious conversation with him, but clearly, he was drunk, and he wasn't in the condition to talk. "Wake up! You are drunk! It is me! Alexandra! You cannot possibly be in love with me! You are getting it all twisted, Larkin! Come on. I will call a maid so she will take you to your room," she said as she ran her fingers through her hair and turned to leave the living room.

After everything stopped spinning, he saw her strong back as she walked away from him. He groaned and stood up before making his way towards her. He didn't talk. He just acted like any other man would. He wrapped his arms around her torso and tackled her to the ground, pinning her down with his weight. He grabbed her wrists and pinned them over her head as he tried his best to steal another kiss.

"Let go of me! What the hell is wrong with you?" She was able to pull her hands away from his tight grip. She punched him once again, but it didn't get him off her. What was alcohol? A magical liquid that gave superhuman strength to a simple man? "Get off of me, Larkin, I swear I am going to kill you!"

"Kill me! If that will make you happy, then do so, Alexandra! But nothing will change my feelings for you!"

"You do not love me!"

"How can you know?" he said as he pressed his hands on her shoulders. He looked down at her and didn't flinch as she pushed him off her and punched him. Luckily, he had his arms pressed tightly to hers, keeping her still from the waist up. "You should know how it is to be with a man before saying that you love a woman, Alexandra."

"Get off!!"

"No!" He grabbed hold of her shirt, and before moving further, he felt a sharp pain on his head. Something had just broken on his skull, blinding him of everything around him.

Alexandra gasped when she felt Larkin fall on her. She looked over her shoulder and saw Eleanor standing there with a frightened look in her eyes. Alexandra took a glance beside her and noticed a piece of a china vase. She connected it all. Eleanor had broken a vase by smashing it on Larkin's head. She groaned and pushed the man off her, then went back to lay down, arms spread open, eyes closed.

Eleanor gasped, and her eyes grew wide. Larkin had managed to rip Alexandra's shirt open, revealing cleavage for Eleanor to see. She took a step back and covered her mouth in disbelief. "Wh— what is the meaning of this?"

Alexandra opened her eyes as she was finally able to regain control of her breath. She looked at Eleanor with a questioning look before she felt the cold night air touch the skin of her chest. She sat up and looked at her open shirt. The gauze had become loose, unbinding her chest. She looked at Eleanor's eyes and saw how she burned her gaze into her green eyes.

"Lady Stownar... I—"

"You are a woman?" She didn't care that she had just caught Larkin on top of Alexandra. Any other normal wife would flip because of that. She knew Larkin was drunk. She noticed that he was, and from the way Alexandra was yelling for him to get off, Eleanor knew she wasn't playing around. So, Eleanor just reacted. Now, as she stared at Alexandra's chest, she felt like she was about to explode in rage.

Alexandra squinted at the yell. She stood up and covered herself before speaking. "I can explain, just give me a chance to—" She gasped when she felt Eleanor's hand on the junction of her thighs. She felt the small hand cup her crotch, and her trail of thoughts left her in a matter of seconds.

Eleanor quickly pulled her hand away as she got more physical proof of what she had just discovered. She confirmed it all when she touched Alexandra there. Alexandra's body was just like hers. She looked up at Alexandra, angered, incredulous, and on the verge of tears. "You are a woman! My husband is a woman!"

"Lady Stow—" She was silenced by a slap to her face. She took a step back and moved her callused hand to touch the red skin on her cheek.

"What kind of a sick joke is this?" Eleanor trembled with fury. She closed her eyes and covered her ears as she tried to block everything, or at least to wake up from the nightmare.

Alexandra let go of her shirt and placed her hands on Eleanor's shoulders. "Let me explain."

"Do not touch me! Do not put your filthy hands on me! How dare you even speak to me? You lied to me! You lied to me, to the church, to society, and most of all, you lied to God!"

"I did not lie to God! When I swore to protect you and love you for all eternity, I was speaking the truth! I love you, Eleanor Stownar!" she yelled as she looked down at Eleanor. "I do. I was going to tell you everything tonight, but..." She turned to look at the now groaning Larkin. He was waking up and touching his head, noticing the trail of blood that was coming out of it.

"I am leaving," Eleanor announced as she moved to walk past Alexandra.

"You cannot! You cannot leave me!" Alexandra said as she grabbed hold of Eleanor's arms and pulled her so she could face her. "You are married to me. You are my wife. You cannot leave me. Where will you be going?"

"To my mother's! I will ask for an annulment, and I will expose your lie to everyone! You should be put in jail for this!" Eleanor yelled, but her eyes squinted as she tried to hold back her tears. "How could you do this to me? To think that I had married the man of my dreams. To think that I was living a fairy tale and what sickens me the most is that I fell... I fell for you!" She wiped her eyes and pushed Alexandra's hands off her. "I hope they torture you for this! I will make sure you get the punishment you deserve!" She turned around and ran up the stairs.

Alexandra's lower lip trembled. She watched as Eleanor ran away from her. Alexandra looked down at her open shirt and began to breathe hard.

"I'm... bleeding."

Alexandra turned around to look at Larkin. The man was somehow sobering up. Probably because all the alcohol was leaving thanks to that gash on his head. "You son of a—" Alexandra bit down hard, flexing her jaw for Larkin to see. "You stupid son of a whore!" She walked over to him, grabbed him by his shirt and punched him again, knocking him out for the next couple of hours.

She walked to the sofa, grabbed her coat, and put it on, covering her naked chest up. She stared down at the man coughing up blood in front of her before walking out of the mansion. As she ran down the stairs, both her wolves ran up to her playfully, trying to catch her attention. Alexandra just moved her hands away from their snouts as she let out a loud whistle. The dashing white stallion burst out the stables and made his way to his master. Without looking back, Alexandra pulled herself up. She sat on the animal's bareback before hitting it with the back of her boots, making the horse charge outside of the mansion's gate.

Larkin opened his eyes and looked at the floor in front of him. He stared attentively at the drops of blood, concluding that it was his own.

"What is with all the screaming?"

Larkin groaned at Nana's yelling. He pushed himself up enough to sit down on the wooden floor. Larkin held his head as he began to analyze everything that was going on. He moved his mouth to talk but felt the striking pain on his jaw. He groaned and closed his eyes, hissing.

"Larkin! Are you all right, my boy?" Nana asked as she moved to his side and touched his face sweetly. "You are bleeding!"

"Alexandra..." he muttered before holding on to Nana as he stood up. "Eleanor..." He looked up the stairs as he saw Eleanor pull a large suitcase up the stairs. His eyes widened and went to look at Nana's before speaking the words Nana wished she had never heard in her life. "She knows..."

***

She jumped from Snow. The flowers under her feet welcomed her by throwing their petals up in the air as Alexandra's boot contacted the ground. Alexandra let out a loud sigh as she walked away from the horse and sat down a few feet in front of him. Stick surely let her know he was there. He pressed his furry body to Alexandra and then lay by her side, panting contently as Alexandra placed her hand on his soft stomach. Pebbles, on the other hand, was staring at Snow and whatever was behind the gorgeous and breathtaking animal.

"At least one of us is having a good time," Alexandra whispered as she scratched Stick's stomach. The wolf simply looked at her with his tongue hanging from his snout. That's when Alexandra heard something walking behind her. She quickly turned around and saw Pebbles growling at the group of trees that hid the beautiful meadow. "What is it, girl?"

The wolf answered with a soft bark and then showed off her piercing teeth. Alexandra slowly stood up. Stick followed her movements and stood beside his mate, growling, and lowering his body to the ground.

"Who's there?" Alexandra called out as she placed both her hands on her waist. As she asked this, she heard some footsteps heading her way. The wolves became more aggressive.

"Silas," a voice said between the towering trees.

Alexandra closed her eyes to get a better view of the man that approached her. "Who?"

He let out a soft smile as he made himself seen by Alexandra. His arrogant eyes turned into shock as he took a better look at the person in front of him. "Alexander Dowry?"

Alexandra just stood there, defiantly. She held her chest up high without even thinking or caring that the person in front of her knew of her true gender. Eleanor already knew. What was wrong with the entire world knowing? "You. You are my cousin's servant, are you not?"

Silas stared at her, an evil smile creeping his old face as he just watched in disbelief. "Yes... I am." He answered as he raised a small handgun. He ignored the loud growls coming from the two beasts in front of him. "I am also the one that killed your mother." And without a second thought, he pressed his finger on the trigger and shot.

***

Eleanor felt a sharp pang in her chest. She looked at the closed gates of the mansion before finally pulling her suitcase out. Eleanor looked around and didn't see either wolves or Alexandra's horse. She gulped down nervously. Gunshots.

Eleanor turned around and looked at Larkin and Nana behind her. Nana was patting Larkin's head with a wet cloth. When the second shot was heard, she noticed Larkin's worried eyes open.

"Are those..."

She didn't finish her sentence. Larkin rushed out of the mansion and ran over to the stables to get his horse.

"Alex..." Eleanor whispered before dropping everything she was carrying and running her shaking hands through her hair. Nana ran up to her and placed her bony fingers on Eleanor's arm as she tried to calm her down.

Eleanor flinched at the touch. She turned around and stared down at the older woman before frowning deeply. "You knew!"

"Knew what?"

"That Alexander is a woman!"

The chubby maid moved back from the angry woman. "And?"

"And? And! How could you just stand there and watch how Alexander lied to my face every single day since I came here? How could you let this all happen and not even have the decency of letting me know that I was being lied to?"

"Do we not all tell lies, my dear?" Nana said, smiling. "Or are you going to lie to me and say that you do not love Alexandra..."

"Alexandra," she said the name as if coming into her senses. She blinked and shook her head as if realizing the truth once again. "That's her name?"

"Of course."

"She lied to me!"

"And you are lying to yourself! Do not you dare say that you did not fall in love with Alexandra! What does it matter if she is a woman? She is the same person that you desired to kiss every day when she went away on business at the city mansion. She is the person that you dreamed of sleeping beside you every night since you came here! Alexandra is a person, my lady!" Nana frowned. "You fell in love with the person, not the gender."

Eleanor opened her mouth to answer but was interrupted by Larkin dashing out the mansion's gate.

"You are worried sick about her. You want to know if she is all right, and it is killing you to not know."

Eleanor covered her face with both hands and sat on the first stairs at the entrance of the mansion. She felt an earth-shattering sob escape her form.

"There is no shame in love, my dear girl. She needs you more than you would ever need her." Nana said as she sat down on the step next to her. "When she comes back, look at her and answer yourself. Are you in love with Alexandra?"

***

After the hit came a burning sensation. Alexandra felt her abdomen tear itself apart. Alexandra's thoughts were elsewhere, far behind the fact that she had just been shot. Her wide green eyes stared incredulously at the man before her as she touched her now bleeding skin.

The wolves attacked. Stick bit down the hand, holding the gun while Pebbles went for the neck.

Silas couldn't control his movements, so he shot the sky a couple of times before letting go of the gun and making his exit with the two animals still clinging to him. He made it through the trees into a small hidden road in the deep wilderness. As Silas saw his horse, he groaned and kicked the female wolf out of his way.

"Whoa! Whoa! What's with the mutts?"

Silas looked up from his attackers and stared at Otto, and then at Erik. Both men were on their horses, looking at the pathetic picture in front of them.

"Did you get him?" Otto asked as he moved away from the screaming Silas. He watched as the male dog bit down on the back of his knees, making him fall on the floor.

Silas pushed the two ravishing dogs to the side before looking up at the two old men. "Her! Her! Alexander Dowry is a woman! Now, help me, please! These animals will be the death of me!"

Erik's face lit up with excitement. He kicked his horse repeatedly and raced off in the opposite direction from where Silas was laying, wounded from the horrible bites.

"Good luck on getting yourself out of there, Silas," Otto said. "If you die, there will be more money for us. Thanks for the information." He pulled the reins of his horse and stormed after Erik.

Her bloody shaking hand grabbed hold of the forgotten gun. She looked at her horse and pulled onto the reins and climbed. Never in her life was riding a horse this difficult. She let out a strangled groan and smacked her lips, making the horse move. She followed the snarls and the screaming. Soon enough, she was facing the man that had shot her.

"Pebbles!" Alexandra snarled as she jumped off the horse and landed on her weak feet. The wolf moved from biting onto Silas' arm to taking hold of his neck with her teeth. She held him in place and waited for further instructions while Stick ate down one of his wrists enough to draw some more blood out of the beaten body.

Silas' eyes turned to look at Alexandra's green ones. He watched the woman get closer and closer to him, one hand holding his gun, the other holding her bleeding gunshot wound. "Help," he whimpered, before shutting up as he heard the bitch growl.

"Help?" Alexandra chuckled. "My mother pleaded for help. She begged you and... Whoever else was with you to stop."

"Otto and Erik!" Another growl and a tighter grip on his wrist made him shut up again.

Alexandra laughed and closed her eyes as the blood loss made her dizzy. "You sold everyone to save yourself, huh?"

"Cassius."

"I know, you son of a bitch. I know he is behind all of this." Alexandra said, moving inches closer to him. "I hope you burn in hell. I really do..."

Silas looked at the gun barrel that was pointed to his forehead. He traced his eyes to the hand and to Alexandra's face. He let out a sinister smile. "See you then..."

"Goodbye," Alexandra said before pulling the trigger, scaring both wolves away from the now dead man.

She closed her eyes tightly as she walked away from the corpse, as memory after memory of that horrible night came rushing back to her head. She fell, and she felt the energy leave her body. She could sense the wolves walk over to her and then lick her face, reassuring Alexandra that everything was going to be alright. She smiled at the sloppy caresses before falling on her side.

That's when she saw him again. Alexandra let out a sigh and grinned when she saw the pale Larkin rush to her side, screaming her name.

She chuckled. "Boy, I cannot believe I am actually glad to see you." She closed her eyes and fell unconscious.

ABOUT THE AUTHOR

Carmen Cristina Gonzalez Figueroa was born in San Juan, Puerto Rico, on November 22nd, 1988. She grew up in the capital, where she studied at the Central High School of Visual Arts. Later, she began her studies at the University of Puerto Rico, Rio Piedras Campus, where she got her Bachelor's degree in English Literature. Carmen continued her studies and became an ESL teacher; however, her passion has been, and always will be, writing love stories. As of today, she is working as an English teacher in San Juan, Puerto Rico, and is currently working on the second part for Dowry's Meadow.

CPSIA information can be obtained
at www.ICGtesting.com
Printed in the USA
BVHW041457220922
647765BV00003B/96